THE WIFE
AT THE
WINDOW

CARA REINARD

THE WIFE
AT THE
WINDOW

bookouture

Published by Bookouture in 2024

An imprint of Storyfire Ltd.
Carmelite House
50 Victoria Embankment
London EC4Y 0DZ

www.bookouture.com

ISBN: 978-1-83525-251-2
eBook ISBN: 978-1-83525-250-5

CONTENT NOTE

Please note: this novel depicts content that deals with child
death and mental health issues.

NIGHT TERROR—Episodes of screaming, intense fear, and flailing while still asleep, often paired with sleepwalking.

ONE

EMERSON

I'm outside your new place, on a dark street with no sidewalks.

It's taken so much to get here, but all I want is to be on the inside. Wherever you are, Shep.

You loved our old house, a fixer-upper with plenty of green space for our son to run. Before I went away, it was perfect. The wraparound porch refinished and painted, the lattice work revamped—less Victorian, more modern. The playground was right around the corner, a perfect suburb to raise a family.

I understand why you can't live there anymore, but I'm sure our son, Leo, doesn't. He was happy at our old place too.

There are no flowers in the flowerboxes here. Raindrops hang like wishes waiting to fall from black metal tendrils.

Through the window—*no blinds or shutters*—a woman shifts around in the kitchen. She's hacking at something with a large knife. The way she moves her long, spindly arm up and down on the cutting board tells me she's an efficient chopper. The room is backlit with three dangling lights that make me squint—she looks angry.

I can't make out her face, but from a distance I can tell she's pretty, the same way an interesting painting grabs your attention from across the room. Auburn hair falls over a forest green turtleneck, a lovely contrast from my vantage point on the poorly lit street. I know she can't see me hiding beneath my umbrella, crouched outside this cement box my son calls home.

The sight of her turtleneck makes me pull my coat tighter, the chill from the leftover rain sneaking down my spine. The season is turning. I've missed so many already.

I'm sure you're on your way home from the office that demands too much of your time.

This townhouse complex is close to the Stamford train station. You were always looking for a quicker way to flee to the place that bleeds you dry.

Who is this new woman in your life caring for our son?

Your family says anyone is better than me, I'm sure.

I was only trying to protect *her*, Shep. I was just trying to keep Thea safe, but the way your eyes fell on me in the hospital made me feel condemned. Like I did it on purpose.

It's not the first time someone has looked at me like that.

A raindrop plops on my face. My back hurts from craning my neck to peek into the window.

But not as bad as the hollow ache for my daughter in the space where my heart used to be.

Out here, I feel Thea's absence in every waking moment.

The hospital was insular, protective. Reality didn't exist there. Now that I'm back out here, I can't grasp that Thea's really gone.

I find myself still looking for her everywhere.

Walking into different rooms, sure I heard a cry.

Waking up startled in my bed, afraid I've fallen asleep beside her, because she must be somewhere. She can't really be gone, not like they say.

I refused to believe it for what I guess has been months. *Years?* But now I'm back, and you're gone, Shep. You belong to someone else. It's a surreal sort of pain, different from the rest.

You dismissed me so soon.

The only thing I can think about now is my other child, the one who's still here.

And now, it happens...

My sweet boy walks by the window, so much taller than I remember, longer hair—darker? Joy fills my chest like a balloon, so fully, I can hardly breathe. Happiness is an emotion I haven't allowed and it's expanding, taking up space so fast I almost shout out loud, *Leo*. But I can't do that. I've been given strict rules. Breaking them means never seeing Leo again.

Your girlfriend says something to our boy. He makes a sour face. I don't know if she's yelled at him, but it's not a warm exchange.

Her green body and red hair remind me of a dragon. I picture her sharp features contorted into a long snout, flames coming out. I don't have a name for her yet.

She still doesn't notice me, I'm sure, because if she did, she would be scared. I've placed my umbrella on the ground, my face to the pelting sky. I have my arms outstretched—*I'm here... Mommy's here.*

I carried him for nine months, changed every diaper, wiped every runny nose until he was three.

But someone else is taking care of Leo now.

And he does not belong to *her*.

TWO

TALIA

Shep is late. Again.

Talia chops green peppers, red peppers, onions, and mushrooms. Hard and fast, the blade smacks the cutting board.

There's a work project that's been giving them all the runaround, but today he texted her earlier that he had *news*. She tried to pry it out of him while he was eating lunch at his desk, but he told her it had to wait until they got home.

Until they could talk in private.

The combination of peanut oil and soy sauce in the wok rises up to meet her. She's nauseous at the thought of what it could be. It's too early for the announcement of the senior architect promotion. She asked on text message if it was good news or bad news, but Shep never replied.

When Talia's mother used to say she had news, it usually meant she'd gotten a new deadbeat boyfriend or crummy job. It was never good news.

"I'm hungry." Leo pulls on her sleeve. She hates when he does that. She shakes him off.

"Didn't I tell you not to yank on me when I'm cooking. There's hot oil in here. I don't want to burn you."

He ignores her, one-track mind. "I want a fruit snack."

She throws the vegetables on top of the already sizzling chicken in the wok. "Dinner will be ready in fifteen minutes."

"I just want a snack. Can't I just have one?"

When did children become like this? When Talia's mother told her no, the answer was, "not a chance in hell," but Shep caves so often she swears he aims to raise an entitled child.

"No, Leo. You won't eat your dinner then. Please go sit down." It shouldn't take her having to tell him three times, but it works.

He pouts and trudges away, halting at the window, as if he might be able to channel the rain outside into a fruit snack. At least he's not whining. She can barely tolerate him when he does that.

When Talia complained to a mommy friend she met at the daycare's Precious People's Mother's Day breakfast about Leo's craving for crap, the woman made wide eyes at Talia—"After work I give him anything he wants until he goes to bed. It's called survival-mode."

No... it's called bad parenting, Talia wanted to shout.

But she's only stern because she wants so badly to get things right, to step into this family unit with two firm feet, to set a precedent for the brother or sister she intends to give Leo. Although, she feels badly she snapped at him tonight. This *news,* whatever it may be, has her on edge.

Talia shakes soy sauce onto rice noodles and vegetables in the wok and places the lid on top to keep it warm. She can't help doing it with force.

Shep slinks in the door without comment.

He sits silently at the table.

"Do you want me to fix you a plate?" she asks.

"Sure," he says.

Talia makes a bowl for Leo too, picking the vegetables she knows he likes. "Nothing snaily, Talia," he often reminds her.

He means slimy, but he sounds so cute when he says it, she doesn't correct him.

She has a list of items Leo refuses to eat. Only Talia knows them. Not Shep. Everything that goes on in this family is visible to Talia. What's this secret that's too big to tell at work? The last time Shep had a secret of this sort it involved Talia, and she can't help but think it's the same kind of indiscretion.

Why won't you look at me? Are you fucking someone else?

Shep doesn't seem to notice she's anxious as he shovels food into his mouth. Leo eats a few noodles, one chunk of chicken, and a bite of green pepper—"because the texture of mushrooms is disgusting"—before he excuses himself.

He just wants to get to his fruit snack quicker.

She doesn't care. Not one bit. Have the whole box of thirty-six.

The minute Leo is out of earshot she asks the question. "Tell me what's going on? What's this news, Shep? Did something happen with the Wickerham account?"

"It's not work," he says quickly.

Oh no. Holy shit. Is this it? *Talia, thanks for your time in the bedroom, doing my laundry, and running my kid around, but we're done here...*

He sets his utensils down and looks her dead in the eye. Her mouth drops open in horror before he says the words: "Emerson has been released from the hospital."

"*What?*" That can't be. "She was never supposed to get out."

"I was surprised too. After we divorced, I stopped getting medical evaluations on her, but I guess shortly after we separated..." The uncertainty in his voice is gutting. "... she started to turn a corner. I may have..." He stops himself, clamping his lips shut, but she knows what he was going to say.

He may have acted too soon.

"Are you going to say anything to Leo?" she asks, her voice

strained, careful not to release the fear she has of losing her boy. If Shep tells him, Leo will want to see Emerson, but she's dangerous. A lunatic. They can fight to protect Leo together.

"Yes, but I haven't decided when yet." Shep won't make eye contact. Something else is wrong. She can feel the quiet settling between them, a disagreement brewing like an angry storm.

"What's... wrong? She's not allowed to see Leo, right? Restraining order, and all that. Does she have a house arrest ankle bracelet or anything? They can't just let child murderers walk free."

Shep flinches. "Please don't call her that."

She hates hurting him, but it's like he forgets what she did. Talia's certain these discussions remind him too much of his daughter, which makes it impossible for them to have a constructive conversation. He needs counseling, but won't go.

"I'm sorry." Talia gathers herself. She can feel her makeup prickling from where she freshly applied it after the rain had its way with her. *Does he realize how hard she tries to please him?*

"Talia, Emerson would eventually like visitation. He's her son."

"Absolutely not!"

Shep sighs and clears his throat. "If she passes all psych evals and fulfills the other requirements, it may be court-mandated."

"But you can protest the court order for visitation. She's going to endanger Leo. And confuse him. How're you going to explain where she's been? After the last time he saw her... we told him he wouldn't have to go through that again."

"He was younger. Maybe he won't remember," Shep sputters.

"He'll remember, Shep! She was like a zombie." They told Leo that Emme Mommy was sick. That she had to go away to get better.

That's what "they" said.

But little does Shep know that when Talia was alone with Leo, she said that Emme Mommy was sick, and she wasn't coming back. She can't explain herself to Shep now.

"This... is unexpected." He glances up, uncertainty cramping his face. "But the doctors will decide when she's ready," he says more quietly.

"I don't care what the doctors say. We can fight this. You have every right to. We should come up with a plan."

He looks down and chews some more, no response. A tiny piece of noodle clings to his rigid mouth.

This woman nearly destroyed him. Talia won't let her back in to finish him off. He wasn't with Emerson for the right reasons anyway.

Talia's convinced Emerson has a trust fund stashed somewhere from her deceased father, a former finance guru. She wanted to go after it for Leo's sake, but Shep refused. He said, "She's had enough taken from her."

It makes Talia recoil when he says things like that. She's unsettled by his softness, his leniency, terrified he'll let Emerson take her Leo away. Hurt him like she did the other one. No, not hurt—*kill*.

"I'm not sure what to do, but she's his mother and she has legal rights to him, Talia," he goes on. "I'll have to weigh my options." He looks out through the rain-streaked window. "I just can't help but think she's been struggling all this time, thinking about the moment when she might get to see Leo again."

"Or she's just as bad as the last time. Is she even verbal? It terrified Leo when you took him to visit her and she wasn't. We decided it was better that he not see her at all after that. Remember?" It was around the same time that Shep filed for divorce. Leo never saw Emerson again after that, and Talia was led to believe that's the way it would stay.

"She's better now. Her lawyer says she's doing well. Tal—"

"What? What is it?" What's he going to tell her? Her throat closes until all she can release is a squeak of breath.

"If visitation goes well, Emerson would eventually like partial custody of her son. She has to establish residence and a job, but after that... We'll make sure she's all right first, but she's his mother." Shep shrugs.

Talia can't believe her ears. "She's dangerous."

"She made a mistake."

Talia stands up from the dinner table. "Bullshit!"

"You didn't know her!" Shep stands now too, throwing his napkin on the table. "She was perfectly normal ninety-five per cent of the time. What happened to Thea was a freak accident."

He's never raised his voice to her before. She should be alarmed, at the very least, upset, but all she can feel is rage.

"Oh... okay." Talia's on fire. "If someone were to tell you that every time you released your child to a person there was a five per cent chance they could die, would you take that bet?"

Shep's chiseled, tired face falls to pieces, but he doesn't reply.

Talia shoves at his chest with her forefinger, then holds it there. "Because I can tell you that every time you place Leo in my care, he's one hundred percent safe."

THREE

EMERSON

One Year Ago

This old house moans, rousing me awake.

My eyes tap open in the darkness, the blackout shade doing its job, but the sliver of light in the room shows movement. A wave of something in the corner.

My eyes are wide now. My heartbeat races. The taste of something acidic stings the back of my throat. There's a flicker that shouldn't be there, like the projection of a silent movie.

I sit up and squint.

The silk sheet slides down my oversized T-shirt. My body tremors like the leaves beating against the windows.

It's just the wind.

There's a shadow between the dresser on the far right of the room and the back wall.

Not a shadow—a man.

I open my mouth to scream, but nothing comes out.

My arms and legs are lead weights, filled with pins and needles.

I know he sees me now, but he doesn't move. But there's a tension. He can smell my fear, ready to pounce.

The baby monitor plays back fuzz.

Did he get to her first? What about Leo?

"Who are you?" My words stick, my lips numb. He doesn't answer.

The feeling in my arms returns. Fingertips like hot pokers as I tear off the sheets. I beeline off the side of the bed. He's right on my tail. I slam the bedroom door shut behind me.

I run to the nursery. My baby is sleeping. I grab her and pull her to me. Her little eyelids flutter open. My feet leave the plush carpet and hit the hardwood just outside, heading for Leo's room. He sleeps like a rock.

I hear the intruder open the master bedroom door.

I turn for the stairwell.

My heartbeat throbs in my ear. "What do you want?" My voice is a whisper.

He says nothing, only sprints toward me with large, outstretched arms. His hands are covered in gloves.

One reaches out and grabs my arm. Fingers dig into flesh.

I yank away.

I run for the steps.

My foot catches on the hardwood landing, and down we go.

———

When I wake up, he's gone.

She's still here in my arms.

But something is terribly wrong.

FOUR
EMERSON

Now

The halfway house in East Hartford is dirty and crowded. A far cry from our former perfectly curated home in Newtown.

I want to call and tell you about it, and that's the hardest thing about losing you, Shep. The girl who once complained about tenting out in a clean sleeping bag on an inflatable bed is now sitting on a dirty mattress where countless others have slept —her roommate, an ex-con named Georgie who constantly runs to the blinds and sticks her finger in the filthy slat because she swears—"they're watching her."

Every time she does so, I envision her eyeballs popping out of her head through the window.

As an illustrator my brain does that—makes inanimate objects come alive.

Our minds operated in synch, yours and mine. It's part of the reason our marriage worked.

We liked to build things together—decorative shelves and cabinets. Tables and chairs and old treasure chests made to look new again. I told you once, "You and I are hammer and nail, practicality meets art. I'll stain the door after you've measured twice, cut once. It'll swing just right."

"That is our life together. Our life is beautiful," you replied.

You create the outline—black and white—I fill in the color. Together we existed as a whole. One cannot belong without the other, but now we do.

It didn't happen all that much in the hospital, this yearning to contact you, but every other day since I've been out, I think about you all the time.

I've been assigned a journal to write my thoughts, but the only person I want to tell is you.

Joanna, my therapist at Meadowbrook, suggested I start small—"make a list of things to do today. A schedule."

At first, joy didn't come with the completion of the actions, but eventually it did.

Today's journal entry:

Dear Shep,

I wake up remembering the smell of her breath on my skin, the longing for her curled against my breast after she's fed. The nuzzle of her soft nest of dark hair on my shoulder. The gurgle of her toothless smile. The way she lit up when she heard Leo's voice call for her—"Tee-Ah"—how she reached out for him when he shook her favorite toy giraffe that jingled like a rusty old bell.

I want you to know I miss our daughter with every fiber of my being.

Despite what's happened, I feel like she's been robbed from me. You and Leo too.

I went to bed one night a mother of two, and woke up stripped of everything I know.

No one understands the feeling—the inability to remember

something so profound, the death of your child—at your own hand.

It's not what they say, Shep.

It's not dissociative amnesia. I haven't blocked out the traumatic event, and it won't resurface eventually, because just like every night terror I had before this one, I don't recall exactly what happened during it—and I never will.

Remember when you used to laugh about my sleep disturbances? When we first started dating...

The first time we slept together, I talked in my sleep. It was one of the rare occasions that I remembered, because it wasn't a terror. I was just sleeping at a new place and my subconscious mind had something to say about that.

Meekly, I lifted my bed head off the clunky pillow in your studio apartment in the city and said "Who are you? Where am I? Why am I naked?"

The next day, you busted up laughing, recounting the memory, and so did I. Two carefree kids who drank too much the night before at a beautiful Italian bistro in Little Italy. One bottle of wine. And then two. And then... maybe another? Neither one of us was used to drinking wine at that velocity.

"Do you know who I am now?" you asked, your dark hair flopping in your eye, the small space between your teeth practically splitting open at how hard you were laughing at me and my bizarre middle-of-the-night comment.

"I definitely know you now," I said.

A successful artist, you were intrigued by my free spirit, and my wild mind that never stopped, even at rest, you said.

"What the hell are you smiling at?"

I snap my journal shut. "Excuse me?"

"I said, what the hell are you smiling at?" Georgie asks.

"You're staring over here like it's a hot summer's day and my bed is the town's only swimming pool. You aren't planning on doing anything funny to me later, are you?" Georgie looks out the blinds again. "I know where you came from. Meadowbrook."

The label stings even as if it's sewn on. I knew a stigma would be attached to me—a former mental patient—but Georgie's served prison time. And she also apparently suffers from paranoia.

"I was just thinking of something. A happy memory," I admit.

"Mmm... Hmm. Well, you can have those memories when you ain't staring at my bed. And you gonna make yours, or just sit there and write in your little diary like a smiling creep?" she asks.

"Oh, right. Sorry." I get up, place my journal on the desk, and grab the sheets. Out of the corner of my eye Georgie monitors me as I pull at the bedding, so thin I can see the stained paisley mattress through the material. I look over my shoulder until she stops.

Georgie wears a red bandana with braids sticking out of the top. Even though she's irritated with me, she's also lively—active brown eyes, a snarky grin. It makes me think she'd be great to draw—as a character.

I certainly don't tell her that, because then she'll really think I'm weird. But my fingers tingle with anticipation. I'm coming back alive. My desire to create. Illustrate. It gives me the tiniest bit of hope. As I fight to pull the fitted sheet over the last corner (knowing it's too small for the actual bed) I can't help but think —*I want to draw again.*

I'm getting better.

FIVE

TALIA

Talia sits next to Shep on the train as he sips his coffee and reads the news on his phone like every other morning, as if nothing's changed.

But the tension strung between them is like a cold hard rail.

Talia studies Shep's face, the crow's feet that wink at her from the side, the way the gray seeps into his temple like a bad spill.

Does she make him... miserable? Has she aged him?

Was he waiting for this moment? The day Emerson would waltz back in and reclaim him, their family—their old life.

Talia scrolled through old pictures on social media of Emerson and Shep last night.

Ones that lay dormant on Emerson's account from before she got sick. Talia hates to admit it, but Shep's never looked that happy with her in a photograph. All his smiles now are half-baked with sweetness, like he can't fully enjoy the moment.

It's the death of his child, she tells herself. *He's broken now.*

She thought she was the one who could make him whole again, but now she's not sure. Shep somewhat blames himself for what happened to their daughter. Emerson was stressed with work and the new baby leading up to the night her daughter died, and Shep was working late on a project.

"I should've made it home earlier." She's heard him tell the story so many times, she wonders if they've branded him, lodged him in a position that makes it impossible for him to move forward from that space in time.

Does he punish himself so much for his choice to stay late at work that night that he'll forgive Emerson for what she did? It wasn't a question she had before yesterday. Now it's all she can think about.

Is that all I am—a placeholder? For his ex-wife?

Shep had a huge presentation scheduled for the day after the baby died.

Talia remembers. She worked on the project too.

She also remembers his return to work, weeks after the accident. How his face was drained of color the way light disappears when the sun ducks behind the clouds, leaving you cold. He would never be the same. His heart had been vanquished.

She's experienced enough of her own self-contained tragedies over the years to recognize the anguish that comes with smothering grief and regret. Losing her father when she was young, left to deal with her mother in their rural housing that was always falling apart.

Shep's brand of hurt intrigued her.

The way she saw him struggle when he came back to work, a fish left to flap on the dock. No one offered him much help, they just let him flail in agony.

Talia knows what that's like.

When her dad left, she had to work double time as a teenager to help pay the rent. No one stepped in to help. Most used her least favorite dismissive phrase. "Let me know if you need anything."

People who say that don't really mean it.

The ones who show up, the way Talia did for Shep, that's the real deal.

There were afternoons she really couldn't afford two bowls of soup on her assistant's salary, but she sprung for it anyway because she knew he wouldn't eat if she didn't.

And her emotional response to Shep turned into a physical want, all-consuming.

Her mother used to tell Talia to stop falling for men who needed fixing.

"We all need a little fixin', Mother," Talia replied. She just didn't think most men were worthy of the effort.

Shep is different. He's worth it all.

But Talia doesn't believe Emerson can be fixed. And she doesn't belong around Leo.

It's unbelievable that Shep could want to return to her. Not after Talia helped him get this far, stay on course, the only psychologist he's ever known. She'll risk everything to keep what they've built together.

Shep slides his phone into his briefcase. She takes his hand in hers. He looks at her, bags pooling beneath his chocolate eyes. Emerson's resurgence is taking its toll on him as well, and he's not confiding in her because he probably feels like he can't.

"I'm sorry I haven't asked how you feel about all of this. Really, you can talk to me. It was just a bit of a shock yesterday, is all," she says.

"I'm fine, really. Just a lot to figure out." He grins, that space between his teeth showing itself for a moment. She hasn't seen it enough these days.

"Well, I want to figure it out together. I don't want you to think you can't discuss this with me."

Part of that is true. But she also has a strong desire to be aware of every little detail. Anything that could threaten their existence.

Most importantly, she doesn't want Shep to have the opportunity to choose between them again. After their slipup at the company Christmas party a few years ago, he made his stance clear.

Last time... he didn't choose Talia.

"I confirmed the babysitter for our date night. I think we could both really use it."

He stops scrolling on his phone, and she knows he's forgotten. He better not say no.

"Looking forward to it," he says.

Talia's not convinced he wants to be with her at all, but she's determined to make him desire nothing else by the end of the night.

SIX

TALIA

Date night starts with a quiet evening at Trinity Place.

Talia picks at her tuna tartare trying to pretend like she's not disappointed about the crispy trout sushi and sea urchin appetizer she's missing out on. They were supposed to dine on the Upper West Side, Jean-Georges. Shep knew she'd studied the menu for weeks in anticipation of the wagyu beef tenderloin with snow peas entrée.

The reservation was on the books for months, actually, but it was a long day at the office, and Shep said he wasn't up for a three hundred dollar, six plate tasting. Forget the two hundred and fifty dollar uncorking fee for the bottle of wine. He'd have a sandwich and an old fashioned and call it a day, "thank you very much."

They resorted to their favorite haunt near work, a trendy moderately priced venue modeled after a bank, but Talia wonders if Shep chose this one so it wouldn't break *his bank*. They're seated inside of a room fashioned out of a vault, and as hard as they work to make their money, Shep never seems satisfied with their lot in life. She wonders if someone else's expenses are weighing on his mind.

"I bought something special for you later." Talia winks. The boning in her bustier digs into her sides with such ferocity she fears it'll leave marks. The black satin accentuating her cleavage coupled with her comment should be enough to pique Shep's interest.

"Nice," he comments.

She frowns at his response. Even adding extra words to his monosyllabic phrase, like "Can't wait" would go a long way with her.

Talia noticed a few men watching her on the way in, their admiring glances enough to wet the spot between the string of lace fabric that threads the inside of her legs. Just pulling on the new lingerie, imagining what Shep will do to her later, was a turn on.

They are people who want to be wanted—she and Shep.

At the workplace, at home. They both grew up hard knocks —Shep from a working-class family in New Jersey, Talia, the daughter of a single mother in rural Pennsylvania. They moved here to make something of themselves. *To be seen.*

And Talia works extra hard to keep Shep happy—bikini waxes, gym membership, concerted bedroom time, bi-weekly, at least—and one steamy date night away from Leo and the nuisances of childcare, once a month.

Not that she doesn't love Leo dearly, but Talia takes care of her relationship with Shep first.

Shep is usually just as ready for a little alone time as she is, but tonight he seems lost in his sticky toffee pudding. The vanilla ice cream melts to the far edges of the dessert plate. Shep makes an even bigger mess by jabbing at the syrupy mess with his spoon.

"What're you doing? Don't play with your food." She laughs, but she's not kidding.

He glances up at her, annoyed. "I'm not that hungry tonight." He places his fork down.

Loss of appetite is problematic, because Shep is always hungry—hungry for food, hungry for sex, hungry for money.

Talia suspects what's got his goat. "I think the firm has put as much effort as it possibly can into the Wickerham project. If we don't get the bid, it's not our fault. At least you're not the lead on it."

She downs the last of her spritzer, but it isn't enough to take the bite off the double-edged sword she's just thrown at him. The Wickerham planetarium is outside the scope of their firm's typical architectural projects. It was a risky bid, and their department has spent countless man-hours on it in the last year. Shep's competition at work, Augustus "Gus" Romeo, was given the lead on the project because Shep wasn't viewed as mentally strong enough to handle it at the time it was assigned.

He was still healing from his daughter's death.

"Heads will roll if we don't get it." He waves the waitress over for the check.

Talia knows he feels shorted, because he should've been next in line for the project, and she's also aware of whose head he's referring to. Gus will likely get the next promotion for senior architect at Brighton if all goes well, but if it doesn't, the promotion is up for grabs.

She responds, "It was a big gamble. I hope it pays off." Shep is a junior design architect, but the senior managers at Brighton like their designers to take a sidestep into project management so they're "well-rounded" and understand every aspect of the job. As unorthodox as it is compared to other firms, Shep's always willing to do what's best for the company. But what's good for the company isn't the best thing for Shep right now, and the conflict is ever present in board meetings, and now, at dinner.

It doesn't help that Gus is Talia's boss.

Gus, whose curly black top Talia sees more of than his face —head buried in his blueprints, too busy to be bothered with offering her the slightest courtesy of eye contact when he speaks to her.

"You deserve everything that's coming to you and more. I work for Gus, but I root for you. Just know that." She's caught his attention for the first time all night.

"I know you do," he says. She's struck the right chord. "Let's get out of here."

The hotel she reserved for the evening is top-notch. A bottle of champagne waits for them when they arrive. "Celebrate, us, always," she told him the first time she ordered it for a night out. He seemed pleasantly surprised.

Sometimes Talia wonders what his marriage could've been like before it went bad. She can't imagine his ex-wife, a minimalist Plain Jane, took care of him the right way. Talia's careful to tread around the topic of the woman who lost her mind and killed their child. Most women would steer clear of that sort of baggage, but Talia grew up with her fair share. Men who are too straitlaced don't have the bandwidth to understand her strife.

Talia's intrigue with Shephard Kingsley started long before his wife was proclaimed mentally insane though. The very first time she met him, she could tell he was the same kind of amorous creature as her, his sideways glance of her A-line dress as noticeable as it was appreciated.

When she bumped into him at work three years ago, it was like seeing a shooting star streak across the night sky—electric. Talia lost her footing, swore under her breath, blamed it on her high heel snagging the office carpet. She winced, but the pain came from deep within.

Because she knew this man—Shephard Kingsley—was already taken. Married.

She flushed, grasped the area where the top button of her blouse met her breasts—*hot*.

She eventually composed herself, looked up, and fell head-first back into the deep pool of Shep's dark eyes, disappeared into the cute little crinkles at the corners. He was *laughing* at her clumsiness. But there was admiration there too.

Then her eyes slipped to his lips, and she began to wonder what it might be like to kiss them. Talia and he were frozen in their own private study.

It also had a lot to do with Emerson, she realizes. That he belonged to her first. And that Talia couldn't find a single remarkable thing about the woman when she looked her up. A sheltered, spoiled Connecticut brat who was wealthy enough to have both a home in the suburbs and one in the country. Snub-nosed, perfect fair skin, poker straight straw-colored hair.

Talia spent hours studying Emerson after that: a graduate of Vassar, she majored in journalism, probably because her parents wouldn't support her passion for art, but she showed them—going on to become a children's book illustrator where she must've been just successful enough to sucker Shep into financially supporting her for the rest of her life. But Emerson isn't like him. She isn't his kind. Talia is.

It isn't a horrible thing to crave attention.

She hates the word needy. It's not the same thing.

It's not a crime to want to be noticed for a job well done.

For a man to call you beautiful, to find you irresistible.

And when his own spouse wasn't showing interest, it's not her fault if she reciprocated the attentiveness Shep was showing her.

Once inside their hotel room, Talia pushes Shep against the wall and sucks the bourbon off his lips. She unbuttons his shirt and presses her breasts into his middle, taking his hand and placing it in between her legs.

Being upstaged at work has crushed his ego. He needs this.

She slides up her black dress so he can see the garter belt attached to the barely-there lacy garments underneath. "What do you want to play tonight?"

Talia approached him at the hotel bar last time and hit on

him as if they were strangers who'd only just met that night. She understood the turn on, the excitement of meeting someone new. The trick is bottling that excitement and finding ways to keep it fresh.

"Turn around." He removes his hand from beneath her hemline and flips her around so her back is facing him. He pulls up her dress and bends her over.

She gasps, taken aback by his sudden aggression. His hands cover hers. He uses her body to convey the words he cannot say to her. She only wants to give him what he needs.

It's all she's ever wanted.

But something about their exchange feels disconnected, like she's not even there.

Her hair hangs in front of her like a curtain as he groans into her back, and she wonders for the first time in their relationship —whose face is he picturing?

SEVEN

EMERSON

Therapists are the mental flytraps of society. They lure you in with their sweet-nectar smiles, but most are just there to clamp down, pretend to listen to you endlessly flap your gums, and bleed you dry—with or without a prescription.

I don't like Dr. Colin Klinefelter as much as Joanna, the only good therapist I've ever known. Even though Klinefelter says we have patient-client confidentiality, I don't tell him I saw Leo yesterday.

That picture from the window is one I hold inside, a moment I must keep to myself—especially since I'm not supposed to see him yet.

"Tell me how you've slept since you've left Meadow-brook..." He takes a lengthy file folder and pages through it.

"I've slept, but I hate being alone in the dark," I admit. "I pray sometimes until I fall asleep. Concentrate on finding my center."

When I was younger we attended a small Protestant church in Weston. My mother said it was good for the soul. We drifted away from spending our Sundays there as time went on, but after my terrors started up again full force when Thea was born,

I revisited religion. I begged anything or anyone to please make them stop, including God—but the terrors still came.

At Meadowbrook, I met a woman who told me spirituality could be found anywhere—the woods, swimming a lap at the pool—the art studio. Wherever you find peace is your "church."

I think about that all the time. Since I got out, away from the hospital and its meditation garden and supportive staff, I've searched for serenity everywhere I go, only to be met with cold, blank stares.

Klinefelter nods, stone-faced, like most therapists I've met, but he seems put out. I never wondered if Joanna went home and judged me at the end of the day, but I can already see Dr. Klinefelter cracking open a bottle of wine and discussing me later with his partner.

It reminds me I'm back on the outside, in this place where people snap-judge you on a moment's notice, their assessment limited by their own experiences. Inside the hospital walls, I was safe.

Out here, no one is.

"Why do you feel that way, Emerson? Are you worried something is going to happen to you in the dark? At night?" he asks.

"Sometimes... my brain tries to sleep but my body doesn't agree. I lie down, but only partly sleep, the rest of my body in paresthesia."

"Like pins and needles?" he asks.

"Yes... sleep paralysis."

"I see, and what happens while you're... *paralyzed*?"

"Any number of things. Sometimes, it's like I'm falling. I can't wake up. Other times, a shadow lurks, holds me down."

Klinefelter deadpans. "You've been diagnosed with a series of sleep disorders, but the sleep study at the hospital was inconclusive. When did these hallucinations start?"

"There was a fire at my summer home, years ago. We all

escaped with minor injuries, but the terrors started afterward. They come and go. And then they returned full force on those sleepless nights before the baby was born."

"Why do you think the pregnancy brought them on?" Dr. Klinefelter leans forward. I've piqued his interest. I've mentioned *the baby*. My mind scurries away to its safe place as I try to recall—*before*.

"Hormones." I shrug.

Dr. Klinefelter purses his lips. He doesn't get me. Not the way Joanna did.

I want to say more, but I hold back. I don't trust Klinefelter. I don't tell him how I'd lie down, my mental wheels flying—*did you take your prenatal vitamins? Protein? How many servings?*

Caffeine. Caffeine is poison.

Baby gates? Diapers?

Work. Deadlines. Be more creative. You're easily replaceable...

The thoughts would spin and spin and spin...

My eyes would pulse behind their lids, pretending to rest.

The glow of my e-reader would offer distraction.

The moon. The lunar eclipse. Anything to watch at 4 a.m.

I'd lie my head back down, and it was all okay... until they came.

"Tell me about the physical response from the nightmares."

Nightmares sound so juvenile.

I prefer the word terror because that's what they are.

A holy fucking terror.

"They were so inconsistent. Sometimes they'd come after I just dozed off. Other times it was when I was traveling, uncomfortable in an unknown place, under severe stress. But... *always*... there would be a man looming over my bed."

"A man?" Klinefelter perks up again.

He's a sensationalist, I've decided. He became a therapist because he gets off on hearing about other people's tragedies.

Perhaps it makes him feel better about his own problems. I'll give Klinefelter the bare minimum until I can get Leo back.

"Yes, a man. As real to me as a predator."

"And what was the predator there to do?"

I look away. It seems unfair of him to ask this already. We barely know each other. In a flash I can see Dr. Klinefelter and his pretty wife or husband, drinking Merlot beneath stringed lights on his bricked-in patio, talking about his new headcase who sees shadows chasing her in the dark. I want to walk out, but this therapy is necessary if I ever want custody of my son—a must-do.

"Kill me," I rasp. My throat aches from talking. My vocal cords are still not adjusted to speaking at this length.

"Pardon?" he asks. His sweater has a matching argyle diamond pattern on each side. I can't work with someone this orderly, but I don't want to put in for a new doctor yet either. It will only delay the process.

"You asked what the predator was there to do. He was there to murder me," I clarify.

Dr. Klinefelter shrinks back into his leather chair, barely noticeable. But I see it. "How do you mean?"

"I don't know, exactly. It's more a feeling, a knowing. Most of the time, I feel trapped, my arms and legs glued to the mattress like they're being held down."

"By him?"

"A different force. Like gravity. The shadow never touches me." *Except for the night Thea died.* But I don't feel comfortable enough telling Klinefelter that.

"It's as if fear traps me from the inside out," I explain.

"Did anything happen to you when you were younger, Emerson? Anything to do with a man holding you down, trying to hurt you?"

This is what people often assume when I tell them about the terrors, but it's just not true. It's hard on everyone, not having an explanation for this phenomenon. *For me.* "No. My childhood was pretty normal. A little boring. I'm an only child."

"I see." Dr. Klinefelter seems disappointed by this information. "Do you call for help? When the nightmares come?" he asks.

Terrors.

"Sometimes I can't scream even if I want to, but often there's bloodcurdling shrieks."

"That sounds... very disruptive."

"It is. But I have no one to interrupt anymore," I say sadly.

Shep would shake me awake until I came to, and then collapse back into his pillow.

He was already back under by the time I realized what happened.

Every.

Single.

Time.

I don't remember the in-between, only the cold sweats, the heart palpitations, the thought that I died and came back to life. I sank into the sheets afterward, embarrassed.

And we got through it because it didn't happen often and— "it's just a nightmare." We decided to try for another baby, because everyone told me to give Leo a sibling. I grew up with none, and the waking hours were so good with Leo I didn't argue the point.

But the second time I became a mother, my sleeping patterns were worse than the first.

A barely audible timer clicks.

"Time's up for today," Klinefelter says.

I nod, and I think we're both happy about that.

EIGHT

EMERSON

The bus station does nothing to quell the anxiety from Klinefelter's session.

Joanna made it clear I wasn't supposed to contact her upon release, but I could really use a small dose of her kindness right now. I dial Meadowbrook and the switchboard picks up. I'll have to lie or they won't patch me through.

"Hi, yes, this is Bridget, Joanna's sister-in-law... No, it's not an emergency, but I do need to talk to her."

Joanna spoke fondly of Bridget, her brother's wife, who Joanna described as the closest thing she had to a mother. I never pried about what was wrong with her real mother, although I wondered.

"Just a minute..." the receptionist chimes.

"Yes, Bridget, is Kurt okay?" Joanna asks, and I hate that I've worried her.

"Joanna, it's Emerson... Wilder."

"Emerson," she whispers. "Why're you calling here? And why are you pretending to be my sister-in-law? You could get in big trouble."

"I know. I'm sorry." The bus pulls up and I wait for everyone else to board first. "I just needed to hear your voice."

"Are you okay? What's that noise?"

"The bus. Therapy is not... going well." I step onto the city bus and take a seat up front, by myself.

"I'm sorry to hear that." Joanna's voice wavers. "Is it... your sleep... are you—"

"No, they're not back. My therapist is this man who doesn't understand me at all. He's dismissive about my sleep disorder, wants it to connect to something in my past, enthralled when I bring up my child's death." My voice wavers. "It's like he wants to place me on a shelf, but he can't figure out which one and it irritates him."

"I know his type. Therapists who aren't satisfied if they can't diagnose. It's like dating a man who's only interested in your problem if he can solve it."

I choke on my laugh, the bumps in the road rattling out a stray tear here and there. Joanna's words are exactly what I needed to hear. "That's it. He looks at me like I'm a puzzle he'll never be able to solve. I'm afraid if he doesn't, I won't get the checkmark I need to see Leo."

"No, don't think that. Listen, just get through the mandated therapy sessions. If you're completing your basic tasks—steady room and board, no episodes, no legal issues—then he'll pass you. He's court-mandated and he doesn't get paid as much for you from the state as he collects from his private clientele. Trust me, he's just as motivated to check your boxes as you are to have them checked."

"Thank you so much for saying that. Sometimes... I wish I could still talk to you."

The sound of the hospital intercom blares in the background. I'm ashamed to admit I miss the sound.

"There's a lot happening here right now. We had a sudden

death here recently, and I'm getting called away by the authorities. I'm sorry," she says.

"Oh my god. No, I'm sorry."

"Emerson, let me give you my cell phone number. I can't have you calling in here again, but... if you need to talk to me, I don't want to cut you off if it's going to hinder your recovery. Do not tell anyone I gave this to you. I could lose my job."

"You have my word."

I jot down the number hurriedly in the Notes section of my phone. "Okay, I got it. Thanks, I'll let you go."

The leers from the other passengers aren't making this ride any easier. I lose myself in my cell phone for a bit—the way normal people do.

We weren't allowed social media at the hospital.

And I can see why now.

It's hard not to look at who's stepped into my family, the woman who replaced me. She looks so put together, in every photograph.

Younger than me by at least five years, but her education and history are unlisted. Tall, athletic, thick reddish-brown hair that swoops up at the end, a smile that curls into something devilish. She has that little bit of spite in her eyes that makes her the dragon. I'm sure she's controlling too. And... I bet Shep hates it. He once said that one of the best things about me being a messy artist was that I wasn't fussy about other things.

That he felt at peace in my presence.

Enough of this. It's bad for my brain. I shut it down.

I tortured myself enough last night on social media, scrutinizing a photo of her and Leo watching a Broadway show together this past spring. I zoomed in to see if he looked truly happy. And he did.

I waited too long to come out of my mental fog. I lost time. And there's no way to get it back.

Maybe their little family wouldn't be so far along if I'd *woken up* sooner. I don't remember much about the past few months. I was only able to recover some of my thoughts when they finally weened me off my meds to rehabilitate me.

And now this woman has taken my place. She's become comfortable walking around in my shoes, preparing meals for my son and—sleeping with my husband.

As long as she exists, I'll never have my life back.

NINE
TALIA

"He's in a mood today. Just warning you." Neve flips her dark hair out of her eyes as Talia hurries into her boss's office. Neve thinks she's extra bougie with her lopsided hairdo and her designer pumps she buys from invitation-only trunk sales in Soho. These are the sort of personal details Neve went on about over happy-hour apps when Talia thought they might actually become friends.

"Why this time?" Talia asks.

Neve cups her hand to whisper. "Heard the competitor undercut the Wickerham bid by ten percent. Gus is trying to prepare a counteroffer, but I don't think they're biting. Surprised you didn't know that already."

Ever since Neve beat Talia out on the last promotion, spirited jests have turned into snotty banter. It's fine. Talia can play this game too.

"That's not good news for *any* of us," Talia reminds her since she also worked on the bid. "How can I help?"

Neve shrugs her slight shoulders and saunters off leaving Talia in an emotional lurch.

This won't bode well for Talia, forever an administrative

assistant, tucked nicely in Neve's junior project management shadow.

Once Neve's boss, Terrence, finally retires, Gus will likely be promoted to senior architect. Even though Shep's been there longer, Gus has been sniffing Terrence's coattails so hard Talia's afraid he might disappear into Terrence's ass.

Somedays Talia would rather drink molten lead than the coffee Gus makes in his office, and there's even more days she'd like to drown his condescending face in his own sludgy brew, but starting over somewhere else is career suicide—and she can't abandon Shep.

Talia lightly raps on Gus's door. "Here you go. I collated the printouts and organized them into color-coded sleeves."

"Thanks. Just set them down."

Talia places the files in his receiving bin, not surprised Gus doesn't look up to acknowledge her presence. She has witnessed him regard his stay-at-home wife at social events the same way. There's being absorbed in your work, and being self-absorbed, and Gus is the latter. At least Talia shows up at all the events. She's put in the time, yet constant last-minute skippers like Neve get the promotions.

"How're Connie and the kids, Gus?" Talia asks.

Gus glances up—surprised. "Fine. Fourth, sixth, and eighth grade. Basketball, lacrosse, and cheer," he says, as if it's his practiced response.

"Wow, you even assign your children a number. Time to take a break from crunching them. Where does Connie rank here?" Talia's baiting him to see if he'll reveal any troubles with the account by mentioning numbers, but he only offers a tight smile.

"Looking forward to some downtime around the holidays. And Connie is my number one. Always and forever."

Talia places her hand over her heart. It's the nicest, and possibly only thing Gus has ever said about his wife. His phone rings and he waves at Talia—*bye now*. Talia walks back to her flimsy cubicle outside of Gus's office.

Neve passes her for the second time.

"Did he snip at you?" Neve asks.

"Not really. He just seems... busy."

Neve twists her glossy lips. "You didn't say a word about it, did you?"

"No, I didn't."

Neve shakes her head. "How do you expect him to confide in you enough to consult on projects if you can't talk about the tough stuff? Terrence said he promoted me because I'm a natural problem solver."

Ouch. Talia's ears are burning. *This woman has no idea how many problems I had to solve when I was younger.*

Just because Talia avoids confrontation now doesn't mean she doesn't know how to deal with it. She just prefers not to these days.

"I don't want to overstep. I know you have no issue doing that," Talia jabs.

Neve smiles as if she's just been complimented. "Right. Speaking of overstepping, how's Shep doing, Tal?"

Double ouch. "He's well. Thanks for asking." Talia looks away. Neve's not the only one who's made Talia feel guilty for swooping in and taking another woman's husband. But someone had to look after him. He was a total mess after his daughter died.

"Nice to hear. Have a good day." Neve struts away.

Talia watches her wiggle to the nicer side of the floor, with the offices that have glass walls and doors, before Talia sits down at her open cubicle.

In the early days, Neve revealed over a company cocktail hour that one of her ex-boyfriends claimed she had a personality that belonged on the dark triad pyramid. Talia knows which arm of that triad applies now—Machiavellianism. Neve's beyond motivated to secure her position as top woman at the firm.

"She's such a bitch," Priya peeps. "I don't know how you do it."

Talia peers over the partition she shares with Priya, the girl hired to replace Neve a year ago.

"Ya, she's really extra today, isn't she?"

Priya smiles at Talia. She might consider Priya a work friend if she didn't resent her so much. Only twenty-three, Priya scored her position at Brighton right out of school because her dad sits on the board of the company.

And here Talia is, sitting pretty, right next to her at nearly thirty. If Shep hadn't completely fallen apart after Thea died, he could've taken Talia with him to the top. She'd have Neve's position. Priya's great fun, though, and they have a common work frenemy in Neve, so Talia tries to be pleasant to her.

"I remember you suggested they not go after that Wickerham bid. Now, they're almost a year in and it doesn't look good for Neve. She supported the project," Priya says.

"No, no, it doesn't," Talia says.

Something about Priya's comment hits her sideways.

Sure, I said it didn't look good, but Neve made me sign off on all of Gus's designs because I was his admin and he was always —too busy—to be interrupted.

Neve may have supported the idea in the conference room, but the deal has Talia's signature all over it.

Talia stands up, exasperated, feeling like she's been had. *I have to fix this.*

It's hard to be good here.

It's hard to be good anywhere lately.

TEN

EMERSON

It's my second time traveling anywhere all by myself in a little over a year. On the bus, the brick buildings, the city sidewalks, the blinking signs, the people—they whiz by in a montage of overstimulation.

The passersby leap off the pavement and onto my bus, on the seat right beside me.

I'm strangely curious about all of their stories.

It's the place I've been trying to get to for so long—Normal Life.

Today is all about recovery. And positive affirmations. I chanted the phrases to myself in the meditation gardens at Meadowbrook. First, as part of my therapy. Then, voluntarily.

> I am listening and open to the messages the universe has
> to offer today.
> I am more than my circumstances.
> I belong here, and I deserve to take up space.

Even so, physically speaking to people is hard. There's learning how to use my voice again, and remembering that I don't particularly like to. My happiest days were with my kids and Shep, living a simple life at home, engrossed in my work. My literary agent did the selling part.

She dropped me after the accident, of course—like the rest of the world.

I walk down the ancient steps in the church on Farmington Avenue. The survivors' group meeting is in the basement. Dusty folding chairs are positioned in a circle. The leader's chair is the only one that's padded. It's to distinguish it from the others, but as I fill my Styrofoam cup with stale coffee, I can't help but think it's sending the message that the group leader's chair is the only one meant for comfort. The rest of us are here to suffer.

My thoughts are entrapment.

Shep always said I think too much.

I drift, remembering now the first time he told me that. Anything to distract myself from *this*.

"Whatcha got there?"

You're peering over my shoulder, the first morning you caught me sketching a character. I had my degree in journalism and worked for a New York City magazine, but my true passion was drawing.

"Oh, it's nothing." I shut my sketchbook. I had loads of them I kept in a chest at the foot of my bed under lock and key.

"Why won't you let me see?" you ask. Your hair falls in your face.

"I was just doodling." I push the hair away so I can see your eyes.

"If you don't let me see it, I'm going to assume you're sending love letters to another man." You sit down next to me at my tiny apartment table. Your elbow bumps my coffee, and the

*mesh shorts you wear as PJs brush against my knee as you wait
for me to open the book.*

*I never showed anyone my drawings before. I didn't have a
diary, but this was the next closest thing.*

*"Come on, Emme." You sound offended, and a small part of
me thinks you might really believe I'm writing elicit love letters
to someone else if I don't let you see my paper. Which is crazy
because I'm no flirt. You and I only met after I was assigned an
article on the top architectural design firms in the city, and your
company ranked first.*

*I open the sketchbook and sigh at my stupid little insect
graphic.*

*"Oh my god. Is that a lightning bug? What does it say on his
tag? Around his neck?" You inspect it with such interest, I can
hardly keep myself from indulging you.*

*"It's Freddie the Firefly," I peep. "I used to chase fireflies at
my summer home. He's a friend from my past. I imagined their
lights were magic and that they talked to each other in Morse
code using their flashes to avoid humans."*

*You stare at me, bemused. "Emme... this is so freaking good. I
think that's a cute storyline too. I know you like to write, but
maybe you can do both—"*

*I shake my head. "I don't like to write that much. It's just
something I can do. Does that make sense? It's what people
expect me to do. This doesn't fit. And it probably doesn't pay
either."*

*You turn your head sideways at this revelation. "You think
too much." Then you squint at me, trying to figure me out. "If
you love to draw, then you should."*

And, after that, I did. I started drawing more. It was Shep's
validation that pushed me to follow my dreams and submit my

illustrations to publishers. Freddie the Firefly never made it into print, but other characters did.

I wish I could tell him where I'm at now.

The work that I'm doing to get better.

I wonder if he's in therapy too. I don't think that we had a single real conversation after Thea died. He couldn't even look at me.

We both cried.

He didn't yell much.

I remember wanting him to.

"Hello, my name is Dr. Maggie Blake," a woman says, interrupting my thoughts. Maggie wears a bright, grass green blazer and jeans and sits down in the padded chair. "When I was thirty-five years old, I attended a neighborhood pool party where there was alcohol. I had too much to drink and didn't notice when my four-year-old son, Robbie, climbed into the pool without his water wings on. By the time we realized, it was too late."

The other "survivors" sip at the black tar that passes as coffee. I glance around, but try not to make eye contact as Maggie says these painful words without stumbling. I don't know how she does it.

"My husband left me. I didn't fight for my marriage because I didn't feel like I deserved his love. I moved from the small community where I lived because I couldn't take the gossip. I went back to college, received my PhD, and now I help others like me. It's my job to bring you to the other side of your tragedies, no matter how long it takes. Help me, help you. I shared my story and I hope you'll share yours. It's the first step to moving forward."

I don't realize that anyone is talking to me at first, his

whisper like a breeze of air nipping my cheek. I turn my head slightly at the sound, frazzled to find a man with a dark beard finishing a sentence right by my ear. "...every time."

"What?" I whisper back.

He leans in so close the stubble of his beard brushes my cheek. His skin smells like Old Spice and soap, his breath, fresh mint. "She tells the same story every time."

I nod. Maybe Maggie does it for the benefit of the newbies, like me.

This man has obviously been to group before.

"Who'd like to go first?" Maggie asks.

This is a club no parent wants to be a part of.

I listen to the most horrible stories I've ever heard in my life —an impoverished mother with a faulty car passenger seatbelt who waited too long to get it fixed, resulting in the death of her middle schooler who went through the windshield during an accident. A rich mother with a pill-popping problem whose teenage daughter got into her stash, OD'd, and died. A familiar looking mother of a toddler who choked on a grape she failed to cut up. "First time mother, and last time mother," she says sadly.

My body chills. *I have another child. I'm not a last-time mother.*

The bearded man, Jacob, goes next, and his story is the worst for me. Probably because I resonate with it most.

"I was working double shifts as a nurse at the hospital. My wife and I were trying to buy this house, so I was working over-time. She usually took Linc to daycare, but she had a work conflict that morning, so she asked me to. Linc fell asleep in the car in the backseat, and I-I forgot he was in there."

I shut my eyes because I know how this story ends. I remember hearing about it on the news.

"It was a hot summer day. I parked at the hospital and hopped out of the car like every morning. I remember thinking it was beautiful outside. It was the worst day of my life. By the time someone reported Linc in my backseat, it was too late. When they pulled his little, limp body from the car... I'll never strike the image from my mind..."

Before I realize it, my hand is on Jacob's shoulder. The word —limp—it buries me.

Therapy in the hospital helped me recall the events I blocked out. Like a rubbery doll being lifted from my chest, but she wasn't a doll. She was gone.

He looks up with heavy eyes. Jacob stares at my hand like it's making him uncomfortable. I remove it.

I understand how haunted he is. The memories, the guilt, the feelings they bring with them—they don't go away.

They *never* go away.

You can't wish them gone. All you can do is live through them like pushing against a wave that's constantly trying to take you down, throw you under. The pressure is so great somedays, you relent, let it conquer, engulf you fully until you swell in your own misery, fighting just to take a breath.

I choose not to share today, because I can't yet. But for the first time ever, maybe... I want to. It's a tiny victory—if that's what you call it.

———————

After the session concludes, I want to call Joanna and tell her about it.

I check the time and see that it's after working hours.

Joanna picks up on the second ring. "Emerson, I've been thinking about you."

"You have?"

"Yes, sorry I was so brief before. I'm on my way home so I can talk a little more freely now. How's therapy going?"

"Really good. That's what I was calling to tell you. Today, I went to the survivors' group. I hated every minute of it, but by the end, I understood why I was there."

"That's the case with healing. The hard parts are the most rewarding."

"Today was the first day I found myself wanting to talk about what happened. I couldn't yet. Some of the other stories were even worse than mine, but I think I might try soon."

"Great! One of the benefits of a support group is surrounding yourself with people who've been through a similar experience. There's a sense of community that you're not alone on your journey... I hope you take the time to make a friend or two."

I think about Jacob's vulnerability and ability to share even though he's hurting inside. I feel cold as ice most days. Maybe he can teach me how to warm up. "I may have found one today."

"Happy to hear. Listen, there's a question I wanted to ask you. I was going through your discharge paperwork and saw a visitor log for Brooks Stauffer. I don't remember you telling me about him. Who is he?"

"Oh..." *Why does she want to know?* It's an extremely hard question to answer. Brooks is many people—all at once—and no one at all—a ghost when he wants to be. "He's an old friend from prep school. When the other kids made fun of me for the sleep disorder stuff, he had my back. We... looked out for each other."

"I see," she says curiously.

"Why, is there something wrong?" I ask. *With Brooks, there usually is.*

"It's nothing. You get home. I'm glad today went well, Emerson. You'll have good days and bad days. Just keep going. Don't quit until you get your son back. You can do this."

For the first time, I believe her.

On the bus, I skip through my emails and there are several

from Kent Bessler, a man who lives in the same country town where I used to vacation as a child. He's been bugging me for years to sell the land where my parents' abandoned farmhouse sits. He's included a link with a proposal this time.

He says that he knows I'm out of the hospital—*a little creepy* —and to *please,* click on the link to his website, which features my family's summer house and its history—but that's not the home I'm concerned with right now.

It's the last piece of my old life I can barter with, if I'm desperate for money. But the property is in such bad shape, I know I won't get much for it.

And, my parents loved it.

They wanted me to have it. They wanted it to be the summer home I used for my own family. I wanted that too.

Shep and I had full intention of restoring it, but between the birth of our two children, and our exploding careers, we could never make the time.

Someday... It was always someday...

Someday has come and gone.

ELEVEN
TALIA

She shouldn't be on the street corner spying on Shep's ex, but what other choice is there?

Talia heard Shep mumbling in his office to his lawyer about the state of Emerson's health. He sounded happy, almost giddy, that the reports on her well-being were favorable.

"That's so good to hear," he said.

How good? Talia wanted to know.

Good enough for Emerson to tie her own shoes without assistance... or... well enough to hold a job, drive a car, care for another human being?

The thin tip of her stiletto digs into the slit in the uneven concrete in the alleyway like she's attempting to pick a lock with her heel. She steadies herself but tries not to touch her surroundings. The red brick beside Emerson's building stinks of urine and spilt beer. This stretch of Connecticut was never on Talia's list of places to visit, and she'll be fine with never returning once she gets a read on just how much of a threat Emerson is going to be to her family.

And what she can do to stymie her progress.

A few bad moves and Emerson will be back in lockup.

A completely sane woman can't smother her child and be fit to raise another one a year later. The rest of the world will agree. Talia's the more appropriate role model for Leo.

She digs her heel in further at the thought of someone hurting Leo.

He told Talia yesterday not to pack yogurt in his lunch anymore, because it's too *snaily*. Yet another item to add to Leo's do-not-eat list, and Talia loves that she's the one to keep track of things Leo likes and dislikes. He's her little boy. Not Emerson's.

The poor environment he'll be subjected to if Emerson brings him back *here* is reason enough to keep her away. Leo attends one of the best Montessori pre-schools in the area, and she and Shep already decided on a private kindergarten for next year. They're on a waiting list, but still... visitation in Hartford wasn't part of the plan.

Emerson will not mess up Leo's life. *Or mine.*

A man holding a brown paper bag, glass bottle sticking out of the top, ogles Talia up and down as he walks by. She searches for her pepper spray keychain in her pocket, ready to fire, but the man keeps staggering past. Talia abhors drunks. She's a one or two glasses of wine, max, kind of gal. Defense mechanism since adolescence.

Although, she's not as hesitant as she should be on this street corner, all alone. She had to scrap for her safety in her rundown rural town when she was helping her mother try to pay her bills.

She knows her strength. She remembers when she fought before—and won.

———

She'd had a friend she used to play basketball with at the playground, Cass Laurent, who'd drunk too much with a bunch of boys and ended up doing things with them that she regretted.

Cass wasn't right afterward. Talia asked Cass if she wanted her to get back at the boys—hurt them.

Even then, Talia knew she could cause harm.

Cass told Talia she just wanted to forget about it, and please, don't tell anyone.

She did as her friend asked, even though it killed her inside because none of it was Cass's fault. The cloud of silence and shame that surrounded her friend because of whom she wrongly trusted was a constant reminder to Talia not to do the same.

So she was ready when her mother's boyfriend, Glen, had been brought into her life...

"Well, aren't you pretty."

Glen strokes her cheek, his breath a warm waft of whiskey and lust on her bare shoulder.

Talia recoils at the touch. It takes everything she has to move away instead of raking out his glassy eyes.

In the bathroom, Talia finds her mother dotting her face with cheap powder. She glosses her cracked lips with bright pink lipstick.

"I don't like Glen," Talia says.

Her mother scowls and continues to paint her face.

"It's you and me against the world," she had told Talia after her father left. But her next words rock Talia to the core.

"Glen's helping me pay the rent this month, so just cool it. Don't be trouble."

...She should have said no.

She should've listened to her gut the day Glen asked if he could come in and wait for her mother to get home from the diner.

Her reaction was total instinct when Glen backed her up against the long coat closet that housed the hunting rifle. Her daddy had taken her deer hunting a few times. No room for a gun safe in that house. Talia used her fingernails to scratch Glen's face, then pushed him away and reached for the gun. When he raised his hand to strike her back, she took the butt of the gun and bashed it into his forehead.

He stumbled backward.

When she turned that gun around and pointed the barrel right between his eyes, he put his hands up and begged for mercy, but it was too late. She stepped back, pulled the trigger, and his body rocked something fierce when the bullet hit his forehead, his brains splattering all over the wall behind him.

She remembers shaking—and smiling because she'd won.

She'd gotten the bad guy.

It was for her, and it was for girls like Cass, and it was for her mom, even if she didn't realize it yet. Glen wouldn't hurt anyone again, and there was victory in that.

It wasn't her mother Talia called for help afterward, though. It was her dad.

He was—just passing through—and surprisingly came right away even though they hadn't talked in six years.

He grabbed a tarp and rolled Glen's body inside and then lifted him in the back of his semi like he was picking up a load for work. Talia watched, unaffected, still simmering with adrenaline and hate as her father grabbed the bleach and bucket and cleaned up the rest of the mess.

"I was hoping you would get your mother's genes, not mine, but here we are..." He said the words quietly as he mopped up the man's remains, as if she'd inherited his bad eyesight, something of insignificance.

"What do you mean?" Talia asked, unable to assist him, but too scared to leave the room. Her father was tall with russet hair and a full beard. His facial hair was coarse, like a Brillo pad. He looked intimidating from afar, but he had kind blue eyes—when he wasn't drinking.

"My father called it the curse of the red. Red hair. But I think it's something else. We get angry. We can't control it. We do *things like this."* He points at the blood on the wall as he uses his muscles to scrub it off. *"I didn't want to leave you, but I was too afraid with all the fighting that I'd accidentally harm you or your mother."*

Talia cried then.

She'd never understood why he left her. How he could. She was so angry at him before and promised herself she'd never forgive him. But she called him anyway because, somehow, she knew he'd know what to do. She also couldn't call her mother and tell her she'd just shot her boyfriend dead. *"What happens now?"* Talia asked.

"I'm going to take care of this guy for you, and no one will find him, I promise you that. I'm so sorry if he hurt you." He looks at her then to gauge just how badly she'd been assaulted.

"He didn't... he didn't..." she stammered.

"Good. I'm so grateful to hear that." He let out a huge sigh. *"Don't you go and feel guilty about what happened, neither. It's one of the reasons I left the gun. For you. I'm sorry I wasn't here to protect you."* His voice wavered. *"You've grown into a beautiful young lady..."*

"It's okay. I understand now why you had to leave," she said.

"Try not to let it happen again, okay, sweetheart. The more of these that pile up the harder it is to keep them buried." He bared his teeth then, and in that moment she knew her father was a murderer. And he was right—in that case, it was best if he wasn't around. *"It'll be our little secret. Try to be good, though, you hear?"*

She hugged him then, bleach-soaked flannel and all, and then he walked out, and that was it. Afterward, Talia decided to open his letters and cards. She wouldn't see him again for years—until she needed him again.

Talia's heart is in her throat, a half hour later, when finally someone exits the halfway house where Emerson's staying.

Talia lied to Shep and asked him to pick up Leo so she could attend a late spin class with Priya in the city. Shep and Priya never talk at work, so it shouldn't be a problem.

The woman exiting the building has a cluster of braids that spring out of the top of a handkerchief. Emerson chases after her shouting something. Talia whips out her phone, zooms in, and takes a picture of the two. She hopes to capture an altercation, but Emerson is trying to catch her... new friend?

Talia trails behind them as they make their way down the street.

She realizes she should've changed if she was going for incognito. Talia pulls her trench coat closer, also remembering she doesn't have exercise clothes with her to back up her spin class story. It would be odd for her to return home dressed in her work clothes. If Shep goes into their tiny townhouse basement where they keep their Peloton, he'll see her spin shoes sitting there on the floor; but she can always lie and say she rented a pair, as gross and unusual as that is for her.

She wonders if Shep would even question it. Does he even know her? The real her? Has she been the girl of convenience, the one to do his bidding, a warm body to satisfy his needs when he still has feelings for his shaggy-haired, frail-looking ex-wife? Tonight, she wears men's overalls and a thermal T-shirt.

Does he dig the simplicity of Emerson?

Talia doesn't care. She just needs to prove Emerson's still crazy.

But Talia notices that the two women ahead of her aren't arguing.

They're having a fiery conversation, yes, but the other woman looks intrigued by what Emerson has to say. Emerson's housemate couldn't be more different looking than she is, urban and gritty meets artsy-suburban Connecticut. A knot congeals in Talia's stomach, because not only is Emerson able to tie her shoes, but she's also apparently capable of blending in with all of society too.

This is bad for Talia. *Very bad.* She can't lose to Emerson *again*.

Not after all the hard work she's put in to make Shep hers.

TWELVE

EMERSON

It's better if I don't spend any more time than necessary with Brooks. He asked me to meet him for coffee, but it's never just about sitting and having a drink with him.

He'll confuse me and charm me and I'll get lost in his deep blue eyes, a mix of sapphire and onyx. I'll trip over his fast talk, just like I did back in prep school, unable to remember what exactly he said to convince me to do the things I did; a perfect person to work in politics.

"It's nice to see you," I say.

"I would've come sooner, but I had to wait until you could talk back to me. It's not any fun to tease you if you can't reciprocate." Brooks manages to jostle a grin from me.

"I bet..."

"How're you feeling?" Brooks is either a deeply loyal friend or an emotional vampire, I can't decide which. But it means a lot to me that he's still by my side, so much so that I overlook my misgivings about him.

"I'm okay. I'll never be one hundred percent without..." I can't say Thea's name out loud without crying, so I stop myself. "My halfway house is disgusting, but my roommate is interesting. I applied to a posting for an illustrator position for a new children's book series, already purchased by the publisher. The original illustrator had to back out due to health reasons. And I have an interview next week. The editor loved my portfolio."

"That's wonderful, Emme! But you know you can always come stay with me." He raises his sandy eyebrows.

"And you know that won't work. Are you still in Chelsea?" I can't make the same mistakes of my youth. Brooks doesn't believe in monogamy and my heart is too sensitive to share it with anyone else.

He smirks. "You know I'll never leave New York. My candidate had his rally here today."

"How did it go?"

"Great. We're pushing for leniency on females with mental health issues, and parental custody for that population." His teeth gleam white, and I know in an instant that he forced this agenda for me. He told me as much in Meadowbrook.

I grip my coffee mug. "And?"

"And... if my candidate gets elected, I have judges who owe me some favors. You'll have at least partial custody of Leo before you know it."

"How soon?" I ask.

"Election is in November."

I suck in the cool October air, a relief that strings may be pulled in my favor very soon. I hate to use Brooks's connections. I know they are dirty, but I need all the help I can get.

Especially as I don't trust Shep's girlfriend with my child.

Something about the way she spoke to Leo the other night made me uneasy. And the rate at which she's taken up space in my old life makes me wonder about her intentions with my family. Shep doesn't realize when he's being taken advantage of. The woman he dated before me ran up his credit cards and bolted.

"How can I repay you?" I ask.

"We've done things for each other over the years. I haven't forgotten." The answer to that question is always the same.

I look away. We have secrets, Brooks and me. There's something about the bonds you make before adulthood that stick like glue. My connection with Brooks is more like part of my foundation rather than just a window I see myself through.

Sometimes I think Brooks pops in every few years, sprinkles in a gift, to keep me quiet for all our past transgressions. For my wedding present, he bought us a Baccarat Louxor vase valued at a thousand dollars, saying it represented both Shep and me, as if built in the image of one of Shep's buildings, glimmering with the originality of my art.

Even though Shep enjoys high-end decor, he was still a little uncomfortable with the value of the present; but I saw it as more than that. It was hush money in the form of crystal.

"There hasn't been an exchange of services in a long time. I'm all take and no give," I joke, but it's true.

"Oh, you've given." Brooks glances away, his Cheshire cat grin spreading across his face. "You just don't know how you've contributed yet."

"What did you do, Brooks?" I whisper.

"Emerson, our opponent is a bad person. He wants to prevent mothers who've made mistakes from regaining custody of their children. Mothers like you. No chance for full redemption."

When he gets something in his head, he's dangerous. He always has been...

My mother thought if she sent me away to a place like Culver they could discipline the sleep sickness out of me the way people down south nearly drown their church members in baptismal rivers to cleanse them of their sins; but that's just not the way it worked. There was no serenity at Culver Military School.

It only made my symptoms worse. I couldn't hide it from the girls in my dorm.

And the stress and anxiety brought more terrors.

After a couple of weeks of torment—girls in the dorm walking like sleep-deprived mummies, bumping into me, and then the ding-dong-ditching on my dorm room door at late hours of the night—I had enough. Scarlet was the ringleader. I'd answer the knock on my door with no one on the other side, just a hallway full of hushed laughter.

The whispers. The stares. The shoves in the hallway. The awful nickname—Zombie Girl—that stuck until senior year.

The taunting would've never stopped if it wasn't for Brooks.

He swiped a key from the biology teacher's desk, and snuck in and grabbed "Mr. T"—the tarantula. When Scarlet was in the shower, Brooks let the spider out in her room. It took about a half an hour before the shrill screams ricocheted through the dorm.

The pleasure I felt from this was unparalleled to the pure glee that emanated from my coconspirator.

Over the years at Culver, his pranks evolved way beyond a misplaced spider.

He rattled off to me that he found pleasure in seeking revenge on people who wronged others.

I tried to turn a blind eye to all of Brooks's shenanigans. I couldn't defame my only supporter.

My skin grows hot and itchy. This is what Brooks always does, makes the argument that justice was served—and that is the cement that binds us.

But it's more than just conviction for what he believes is right. He finds reasons to rationalize the wrongdoing he performs to get what he wants. The diagnosis didn't exist back then, but Vindictive Narcissism Disorder fits him too well...

I'm worried this time if it will also be our undoing.

"Well, thanks for helping me." I swallow the lump in my throat when I realize it's been too long since I spoke.

What did you do this time, Brooks?

THIRTEEN
TALIA

Shep can see her leaning on the doorframe as he speaks to Emerson on the phone. He holds up his finger at her to *wait*. She'd like to chop it off.

But she retreats. Talia is a skilled eavesdropper.

Emerson's chipping away at their relationship, bit by bit. Whether she knows she's doing it or not makes no difference. The result is the same: Shep is growing closer to Emerson and pulling farther away from her. Talia's being silenced so he can better listen to Emerson, and this is not okay.

"That's wonderful." He speaks into the phone, a smile on his face. "If Quigley is a children's cohort of their parent company, Quigley Tree, it's on Avenue of Americas... Yes."

Oh, good, we're giving directions now, how chummy.

If Talia doesn't figure out how to get Shep back on her side, the side he can't live without—"his savior"—he even once said, she'll lose him. He'll realize she's just a backward country girl, notice the dirt hidden beneath her fingernails she's never completely been able to wash away when she let that swinging screen door slam behind her, and ditch her—just another office romance gone wrong.

But, they're so much more than that. Their connection started before Emerson had her accident.

Talia waited for things to fall apart. She was the one who respected their relationship. Now it's Talia's turn and Emerson needs to do the same. This won't end well unless Shep realizes Talia's not only worth keeping around, but also better than the fractured woman he left behind.

He hangs up the phone, that stupid grin still on his face, wide enough that his eyes crinkle at the corners. She hates that Emerson can bring him such joy. If they weren't legally divorced, Talia would be positively fuming. The office door would need to be shut for the conversation they're about to have, but she'll let it remain open. What kind of man gets back together with a woman he divorced? Surely, he's too proud for that.

"Who was that?" Talia asks, even though she knows.

He doesn't look up. "Emerson has a job interview. At a publisher."

Talia has her arms crossed at her chest, and what does he expect her to say? Does he want her to be happy about this? Surely, he can't expect that. "Shep, do you really think these fast moves toward a visitation with Leo are best? He hasn't seen Emerson in over a year. We haven't even talked about it with him yet. He barely even remembers her."

Shep leans back, the smile dripping off his face like a melted ice cream cone. "Yes, I do think it's good news, Talia. She's his mother."

Talia steps back. Each time he grants Emerson that title, it wounds her more. Strips her of everything she's done for their family. "I don't trust her with him. How can you?"

"Visitation will be monitored." Shep stares out of the skyscraper window into the bustling city below that once made Talia feel like her possibilities here were endless. As long as she was in this place of infinite opportunity, she'd never run out of chances to have everything she's always wanted. But all she desires at the moment is a real life with Shep and Leo. "So you want to depend on the social services system and some court-mandated quack?" Talia asks.

Shep looks at her like she's the one lacking mental clarity, but knows better than to challenge her.

She wonders if Shep really even cares about Leo's safety. *Really cares*, like she does. Her mother told her once in regard to her father, "If he left with no reason, he can't come back with an excuse." It wasn't until Talia was older that she really understood what her mother meant by that. In actuality, her father left for their own good, but she could never tell her mother why. Emerson's leaving was for their own safety too, and she cannot come back.

There is no excuse.

Shep's office phone rings and he picks it up. All Talia can think: *First Emerson came before me, and now work.*

"Yes, Mr. Prescott." He shoots Talia a stern look to scoot, and she leaves in a huff, feeling as though she's losing more ground by the minute. She tears off once out of sight of his office, rounds the corner. And crashes right into Neve.

The hot coffee Neve holds splashes all over her blouse.

"Oh my god!" Neve stumbles to the ground, clenching her chest. The mug drops, overturns and spills all over the carpet. "You idiot!" she screams.

Talia hurries to the breakroom and grabs a fistful of napkins. When she returns, Neve is on the ground as if guarding her mess, clearly upset. Her hair hangs over her face like a sullen child.

"Did I burn you?" Talia asks.

"What did you say to me?" Neve glances up, livid. Talia offers Neve a napkin. Neve dabs at her chest, her hands shaking. Talia's never seen her so upset.

A crowd has gathered, and Talia hears a faint chuckle.

"Come on." She grabs Neve by the elbow and ushers her into the breakroom. "I'm so sorry, Neve. I was completely distracted. Are you okay?"

Neve takes a few deep breaths, and Talia can see the red marks. There are burns on Neve's chest ebbing into the shoulder of her cream blouse, which is stained with wet brown liquid.

"You were leaving Shep's office, no? What's he got you so upset about that you didn't even see me?" Neve asks, her eyes red-rimmed.

Oh my god. Did I hurt her so badly, she's crying?

Talia needs a good reason to cause injury. She hopes Neve doesn't sue. Lord knows she doesn't have much to her name.

"It's his ex. She's out of the mental ward and she has a big job interview at Quigley Press, some children's book publisher. A stable job is necessary for future custody; I just can't—"

"Well, what did you think, Talia? That she was going to get out and not try to see her own son? Why're you debating this?" Neve walks to the freezer, snags an icepack and applies it to her tender skin. She pulls a business card out of her purse.

"I think she's dangerous," Talia says.

Neve shakes her head. "Courts always give kids back to their parents. Your word that she's dangerous means nothing. If you want this woman gone, you have to prove it." She holds out the card. "This investigator is helping me out with a private matter. I won't divulge the details. But they can get you the proof you need, help you save your relationship." She says this so genuinely, Talia's taken aback.

"What would you know about relationships? Yours last five minutes." Talia shoves the card in her pocket.

"I have someone who would do *anything* for me. You don't know love like that. But right now I'm focused on my work. Which is going to shit if you'd open your eyes. Gus just left in a hurry, with his hard hat."

Talia has many questions about what Neve's just revealed but... "What? Why?" Talia asks.

"He's going to the Wickerham site. He got the court to file an injunction because the company we're losing the bid to isn't building to code. I guess the permits weren't filed right on top of everything else. Five Star is a new builder so eager to get the job they didn't get their legal straight."

"That's insane."

"He's going to try to underbid their offer. Gus can't stand that he lost it in the first place. His wife put an offer in on a new house which was contingent on the bonus he'd receive from this job."

"Why do you know all this? He's my boss."

"Everyone knows! You would too if you were paying attention."

Neve places the icepack back in the freezer and brushes past her through the exit. This is all very bad. Gus is sullying the company's name, and she hasn't been around to advise him otherwise. It's not like he listens to her, but she could have at least been present today, tried to tell him that he lost the bid, they'd get another and to cool his jets.

Shep enters the breakroom next. "Talia, what in the hell happened? Someone said you threw hot coffee on Neve."

Great. "That is not what happened. Not even close."

"I don't know what's gotten into you. First you lie about going to spin class with Priya. You've been awful about Emerson getting out." Her chest caves at being outed. "And now this..."

Talia glances up at him, a doe in headlights. "What about spin class?"

What does he know? Hopefully, not all of it. Did Emerson see Talia taking photographs of her?

"Oh, come on. You hate working out in public places. That's why we got the Peloton. And the studio in the city you said you were going to has no showers. Priya lives in Midtown. You weren't going all the way there to shower. And you came home smelling like a rose... so..."

Damn it. "How do you know where Priya lives?"

"Because it was my first question, right before I asked her how she enjoyed the exercise class with my girlfriend the other night."

Oh no. "It's not what you think, Shep."

"Just like you didn't throw hot coffee on Neve?"

"I didn't. Let me explain."

"You know what, Talia. I don't think I care to hear your excuses anymore." He storms out of the breakroom.

This is the absolute worst. He's caught her in a lie and no longer trusts her judgment. Anything she says about keeping Leo away from Emerson will be brushed away.

She has to get him back on the right side—team Talia.

FOURTEEN
EMERSON

I hang up my borrowed suit in the closet, zip up the suit bag, and thank Georgie again for asking her cousin to lend it to me.

"It's nothing. You probably don't even have to dry clean it. You only wore it for a couple of hours." Georgie smiles.

"Oh, I'll get it cleaned. My way of thanking her for the good luck suit!"

I haven't quite come down from the high that came with hearing the editor at the publisher tell me they loved my portfolio. "You should see a contract in a few weeks," she said.

Publishing deals without literary agents happen, but I never had the courage to try for one before. Selling my work is my least favorite part of being a creator, and the legal aspects of contracts were always better left up to the contract people. I still haven't recovered from Caryn, my last agent, ditching me in my weakest moment, so this opportunity was just what I needed.

How would I even search for new representation? What would my query letter look like after all I've been through?

Dear XX, I've parted ways with my agent after a long hospital stint in the mental institute...

"I can't believe they gave you the job. Just like that. I've been looking for months," Georgie says.

"They didn't do a background check yet." It's no secret employers rarely extend offers to someone with a criminal record.

"Your crime was an accident. They'll let you slide," Georgie assures me.

"I'm sure you'll find something soon. I have the luxury of using a pen name—E.B. Wilder. All of the news reports with my accident use my married name, Emerson Kingsley. Hopefully, they use Wilder when they run my background report." *And, I slip right through the cracks...*

Note to self: Contact Brooks to make sure I slip through seamlessly.

Using him has always been a last resort, but when it comes to getting Leo back, I need all the help I can get. Or, at least the opportunity to explain myself if I'm found out.

Georgie scowls, probably jealous, and I don't blame her. Being paid to do what I love and the ability to do it from the privacy of my own home is a blessing I don't take for granted.

"Thanks, we'll see. I appreciate you, Georgie." Someday I'll be able to tell her how meeting her is part of the reason I was able to manifest this illustrator position in the first place. The graphic novel series is based in an urban, futuristic setting where teenagers have to take the world back from a villain called Hypocrisy. I enjoyed the satire in the book, and the editor said my sketch of Georgie was almost a spitting image of the way the author described Birdie, the protagonist in the story.

I tuck my portfolio beneath my bed, the one with character sketches of Georgie that are better left concealed for now.

"Gotta run, but happy for you, Em." Georgie walks out of our crappy apartment, and I can't wait to leave too—for good.

I am so buoyed by the thought, that even my journal entry is filled with optimism.

In my mind, I return to my sage green fixer-upper with the white fence I helped paint. In this alternate universe, you're waiting with our two babies, like this has all been a bad dream.

In that dream, I've still chosen a pen name, and I tell you, "There was E.B. White and now... there's E.B. Wilder."

You smile at me, and say, "How appropriate. Maybe you should dust off Freddie the Firefly and do a collaboration. He can get stuck in Charlotte's web, and all the farm animals can aspire to set him free."

"I'm sure there would be copyright issues with that..."

You wrap me in your arms. Thea pulls on my finger until I stop kissing you and look at her instead. Leo whines because he wants to play on the swing with me.

I leave the baby with you, and Leo and me walk over to the swing set, two full-sized red swings. There's one blue baby swing for Thea too. The sunshine hits my face, the smell of fresh cut grass and new paint heavy in the summer air.

I smile at the thought, and then stop. Like all temporary moments of grace, mine is stolen by reality.

I shut the journal I'm writing in and think about all the other people in the world who've written letters they haven't sent, and what a different world it would be if they had.

I can imagine Shep all I want—how he used to feel with his arms around me, his body inside of me, his voice in my head, cracking jokes—but he's not here.

I wonder, though, if *she* wasn't, would there be a place in his life for me now?

The way he spoke to me on the phone earlier made me believe that he doesn't hate me. Dr. Klinefelter was the one who encouraged me to reach out to Shep. "Be assertive, show you're taking control so he feels comfortable with the idea of eventually allowing partial custody."

Shep sounded like he wanted good things for me.

But, does he still *love* me? And is that love strong enough to endure what we've been through?

Something about the relationship he has with the new woman doesn't seem real.

For as many online pictures as I've seen of her living in Shep's place, tending to my child, there's something about how staged they all are that makes me feel like she doesn't actually exist. No candid photographs. Maybe it's because I haven't met her yet, but her place in my family's life seems about as unauthentic as she is. What kind of a woman just swoops in after the recent death of a child and assumes that life? How can she even understand what we've been through?

Shep's not good alone. I was the primary caretaker of the children. In my mind, she's a temp.

Once I'm hired for this job and a publisher gives me a new shot, maybe Shep will see that I'm getting better—and give me one too. At least to be his friend. It felt like we were getting there today... It was nice to hear his voice. Heartbreaking too.

I miss you, I wanted to tell him.

It's almost time for my survivors' group meeting. I don't want to go back there again, but it's part of my assigned therapy. So far, I've almost checked every box. And the election is soon.

I keep telling myself I just have to wait a couple more weeks, and I'll have a job and my therapy goals complete, and then... finally...

I'll get to see my son.

FIFTEEN
EMERSON

A man with burns over half of his body tells a horrific story at the session about how he tried to pull his son from an electrical housefire and failed.

I'm reminded of the fire at our summer home.

Some nights I can still hear the screams of the girls who attended my sleepover, and feel the fear that I was going to die as I ran out of the basement door—and then, the relief of seeing my parents—alive—in their pajamas, scrambling around the corner to find us all.

After the fire, I moved back to the city permanently. My parents rebuilt the summer home, but I couldn't return. After the fire, there were inklings, verbal slips, that made me believe Mother thought I was somehow responsible for the blaze. My mother eventually stopped vacationing there too after the townspeople expressed displeasure with the more modernistic, hardy board exterior rebuild—actual complaint letters sent, as far as our Westport home. The summer home became a place of hassle, eventually abandoned altogether.

It's too bad this man has to live with his horrible memories forever. Every time he looks in the mirror, his son's tragedy is his reflection.

My back involuntarily shudders at the thought.

Jacob places his hand on my shoulder. He seems equally shaken by the story. I arrived late and gravitated to the spot right next to him without a greeting.

"Emerson... we haven't heard from you yet," Maggie says.

Oh no, they're calling on me.

Jacob offers me an encouraging nod, but she's caught me in the wrath of all the fires—past and present.

"I'm sorry. I can't today." I stare at my Vans tennis shoes, wishing I was braver. Once I tell my story, that report goes back to Klinefelter, but I'm still not ready.

"That's okay. Next time, maybe," Maggie says with a bright smile.

My phone buzzes in my pocket and I retrieve it to see a missed call from the publisher, with a voicemail. My eyes light up with glee. Jacob catches me and smiles back, so happy for whatever I'm happy about because a minute ago we were both so fucking sad.

I motion to my phone and dart out the church doors. Maybe Quigley Tree needs me to fill out a generic application online or my social security number, or one of those trivial pieces of personal information to start the hiring process.

I listen to the voicemail.

"Hi Emerson, this is Gracen Pierce from Quigley Tree. Thank you so much for coming in and displaying your exceptional work. I wanted to call you personally because I know I was preemptive in saying you should receive a contract soon, and I wanted to apologize for that. We've decided to go forward with another candidate. The author you were partnering with was anonymously made aware of your... history... and unfortunately doesn't want the negative press to affect the children's series. Quigley Tree agrees. Best of luck, Emer-

son, I'm sure you'll find something with your brilliant artwork..."

The line clicks, indicating the message is over, and I can't believe it.

Group ends, and people are rushing around me as I stand pummeled in failure.

Jacob appears beside me. "What's wrong?"

"I didn't get a job because of my personal history. A job I really wanted. A job I was very qualified for. I need it to eventually get custody of my son."

Jacob places his hand on my shoulder again. Human touch feels foreign, but good at the same time. "I haven't been able to find work as a nurse. At least not the kind of nurse I used to be. I don't think anyone feels as though they can entrust me in their hands," he says.

I stare back at the longingness in his dark eyes, and we're both so hollow it's amazing we're still living, breathing creatures.

He tries again, realizing his words, albeit true, do little to comfort me. "You'll find something else. It may not be the perfect gig, but that's okay. It's not about going for the big job right now, ya know? Small steps."

We take our own slight steps down the stairs to the sidewalk. Jacob's holding my hand. Ever since I met him, his unintentional gestures become intentional long after I've noticed. It's strange and natural at the same time.

"Do you want to spend the day with me?" He opens his mouth and then clamps it shut, as though the thought just dropped from above, landed in his head, and fell out of his mouth. *A... mistake?*

Even so, I reply, "Yes," because the idea of spending the day with someone I don't have to explain myself to sounds like a great invitation.

"Okay. Good. I have food at my place. I've actually taken on cooking as a healthy stress reliever. I just usually cook too much for myself."

"You want to cook for me?"

"Ya, I mean you could help if you want. Or not."

I look at him, puzzled. What an odd yet intriguing proposition.

He says, "It's stupid. We can just grab—"

"No, no! I would love to cook with you, Jacob Martin."

Jacob drives us to his place in Asylum Hill. I don't mention the reference as we pull up to his condo. He lets us inside and the ease of Jacob, from the very first day I met him, infuses all around me—his neat space, clean lines, tall, open windows, the smell of cotton and linen. "Is that an air freshener?"

"It's a diffuser. I turned it off before I left. Does the smell bother you?" he asks.

"No, I like it. Your place has a very nice vibe."

"Thanks. I need a relaxing spot after dealing with cranky patients all day. What did you say you did for a living? Before..."

"Oh, I'm a children's book illustrator. The job I lost was for a new series I was really excited about." The cheery space grows gray, as does everything when I try to find a spot of sunshine. I wonder if there's a place in the future where the past won't cloud my present.

"Your job sounds amazing. I got the seal of approval from an artist. Yay, Me!"

I smile. "Don't come to my place, you wouldn't think much of my approval then. Not until I get one of my own anyway." My smile slips. "Securing this job was a big part of that endeavor."

"There'll be other opportunities. Come here, help me cut these vegetables. I find keeping busy makes me feel better."

I slide behind a galley counter, a bearded man and a plate of carrots and celery awaiting me.

"That's for the stock. We're going to make chicken and rice soup. I heard it was good for the soul."

"I thought it was chicken noodle."

"The comfort comes from the chicken. That's why they call it Chicken Soup for the Soul, and not chicken noodle soup for the soul."

I giggle. "*Oh... okay.* Are you sure you're not the one in the storytelling business?" Jacob's kindness and quick wit reminds me of Shep. And I don't want to be reminded of Shep right now, in this sleek condo with this handsome stranger. The first one who's looked at me as something other than a science experiment in over a year.

I finely chop the carrots and celery. Jacob handles the onion. I can't help but think it's so I won't have to endure the tears that come along with it. I've cried enough.

As the knife slices into the vegetables, Talia and her efficient chopping comes to mind.

And, her proficient stealing of my husband.

I don't want to think of either of them right now—Shep or Talia—but there my old life looms like a buoy of hope I can't quite grasp.

My chopping is complete. "Do you mind if I use the restroom?" I need to rein in my thoughts before they corner me and ruin my day. I can't let that happen. I want to have a good day. I want to call Joanna later and tell her about what a great day I had—with Jacob.

"Sure, around the corner."

He points to a hallway and continues to prep the food. I walk down the long, dark hallway, seeing only one door, straight ahead. I try to turn the knob, but it's locked. I twist it again—nothing.

"Jacob? Is the bathroom locked from the inside for some reason?"

Jacob hurries from the kitchen. "No, no, not that one! I'm sorry. I keep that one locked. I thought you'd see the one already open." He motions to the clearly open bathroom door I missed right off the entrance of the hallway on the left.

"Right, sorry. Hiding buried treasure in there?" I point at the locked door.

Jacob's mouth hangs open, and he can't tell me what he's storing in there, but it is something. For the first time a lurch of danger settles like a rock in my abdomen. "Yes, that's it," he says.

I slip past him, into the bathroom, breathing hard.

And this is why I don't want to date men now or in the future.

The same reason I didn't want to in my twenties.

The fear of becoming locked in their basement or closet somewhere, and the fear of what they might have... locked in theirs.

SIXTEEN

TALIA

The timing of this man's phone call couldn't be more wrong... or right. "I'm at work. I can't talk right now," Talia whispers.

"Well, I thought you'd be interested to know your target is at a man's apartment. They're getting cozy in his kitchen. Cooking together. More to come..."

He hangs up before she can reply.

"*Shit.*"

"Who was that?" Priya asks.

Why should I tell you, little backstabber?

Priya's the reason Shep is so pissed at her.

A real friend would've been quick enough to get that Talia was trying to cover her tracks where Shep was concerned. Instead, Priya threw her under the Brighton gossip bus. It wouldn't be long before the whole office heard the news, Talia's reputation ground up beneath the corporate wheels.

Talia's silence speaks volumes.

"I'm sorry about Shep. If... you wanted me to be a part of your evening plans, you should've told me. He caught me off guard."

"It's fine, Priya. I'm worried about the Wickerham project

right now," she lies. She couldn't give a fuck about that project. What's lost is lost.

But she's fiercely protective of the things that are hers—Shep, Leo, the life they've built together—at the very top of her list. And she'll pull out all of the stops before she lets it all just slip away.

Priya says, "I heard Gus is going down there, trying to do some... unorthodox bidding. I don't think my father—"

"You didn't tell him, did you?" Talia pops her head above the paper-thin office partition.

Priya glares back at her in alarm. And for a minute Talia sees her for who she really is—a recent college graduate, more intrigued by office gossip and starting trouble than their consequences to other people, no worries in the world with her daddy's money to fall back on. But then, Priya peeps, "No, I didn't."

"Please don't say anything to your dad. Gus will figure it out." That's all Talia needs, the board breathing down her neck because her boss lost his shit and single-handedly tried to pirate a multimillion dollar deal.

"You heard about his house, right? And Contessa?" Priya asks.

"Neve said something about him bidding on a new house. He'll just have to pull out of the deal."

"I don't think that's an option... If he wants to remain married."

"What? Connie doesn't seem like that type of wife."

"Quiet doesn't always mean kind," Priya says.

You would know all about it, wouldn't you, Priya!

"So, she really said she'd divorce him if he didn't buy her that house? Maybe he's better off."

"I don't think she sees it that way. It's more to do with the fact that he promised her a different life once he got this deal which sealed his future for the next promotion. More time with the family."

"Okay. That makes a little more sense." Gus worked horrible hours, but Talia always assumed it was because he'd rather be at the office than at home. But maybe he was grinding now so he could jump to upper management quicker—a more relaxed spot at Brighton. The grunt work fell on middle management and its subjugates, like her.

"How do you know all of this?" Talia asks. Priya has been here a total of one year!

"Everyone knows."

"That's what Neve said. How do I not know?"

"You've been preoccupied..."

That one stings. It's clear her personal life has interfered with her professional life. "For the record, I did not throw coffee on Neve. She ran into me. Or maybe, I ran into her, but in any case, it was an accident."

"I never heard otherwise. You know they let her go home early. She complained to Terrence that she was in pain and that she needed to tend to her burns."

Talia fights an eyeroll. "I better not get in trouble for this. Did she contact HR?"

"I don't know. I just saw her on her way out. She had this kind of—*Eat shit in this glass box, I'm outta here*—look on her face," Priya chants.

"Perfect. Maybe she'll thank me for her day off tomorrow."

The new proposal on Talia's screen brings her hope. She was contacted by a city art director for a bid to transform an industrial warehouse on Brooklyn's Waterfront in Navy Yard into a new art gallery. Talia's tongue slides over her lips, the proposition so tasty she can't wait to share it with Gus. Maybe it will take his mind off the lost planetarium—*the lost planet*.

She's almost forgotten Priya is there, when she says, "Talia, who were you on the phone with? Just now?"

Why, Priya? So you can tell your dad that the desperate almost thirty-year-old you share a desk with is so paranoid she's going to lose her boyfriend that she hired a private detective to tail his ex?

Well, Talia's not going to subject herself to that type of scrutiny. Someone of privilege would never understand what it means to have experienced as much loss as Talia has. "It's nothing. I just have someone checking on something for me."

"Uh huh... When I was at Princeton..." Priya starts. Talia no longer fights the eyerolls. "...there was this married couple who worked on campus. He had a reputation for flirting with the female students. The woman, an English teacher, hired a private detective to follow him. The PI caught questionable photos of the husband and a student in his office, but everyone seemed to blame the wife, and they eventually divorced."

Talia stops typing. She hates that Priya is so perceptive. She's more angry about the fact that her intentions were so damn obvious. "Why in the world would they blame her?"

"Because she chose to go behind his back and have him investigated instead of confronting him. He blew up at her, right on campus. I'll never forget it. He said—the philosophy teacher that he was—that all people act differently when they're not being watched, including her, and it wasn't fair to capture him in those private moments without his permission. As if she'd stolen a piece of him, a bigger crime than his obvious flirtation."

"That's... gross." Talia pounds on the computer keys, pissed at the male-dominated world and its glaring contradictions.

"My point is, I believe in the phrase, honesty is the best policy. Even if honesty sucks. Even if it hurts. Just some food for thought before you try to drag me into your next false alibi."

Yep... she deserved that.

"Well, thanks for your terrible story to add to my awful day."

"The day is young. There's still time to turn it around."

The moments before Talia scoops up Leo from Precious People daycare have a way of forcing her to be her best self. She pushes aside whatever crap day she's had and turns it into a smile for him. Leo has only her and Shep.

There's a responsibility to being this little boy's whole world that she's never taken for granted. She's longed to give him a brother or sister. She and Shep talked about trying after Leo entered kindergarten, but Emerson's return has derailed all her plans.

"Tell me something good that happened today," she says to Leo as she grabs his backpack. She started asking him this question instead of—How was your day?—after she received so many—goods. "My day was good..."

"I made a friend named Aron who told me he lives with his mommy every other week."

Talia tightens her hand around Leo's. "Oh, well his mommy and daddy probably don't live together. So they split their time between two houses."

"They're divorced," Leo says. The word sounds so harsh coming out of his little mouth.

They walk to the car park near the train station. "Do you know what that word means?"

"Ya, my mom and dad got divorced because she got sick. I told Aron that."

Talia kneels down in front of Leo, stopping him in his tracks. "Who told you that? That is not what happened." But as Talia fumbles for words, she can't seem to rearrange them in a different way.

That isn't what really happened, is it?

Her wheels spin with a lack of clarity. For the longest time,

Emerson wasn't coming back so these questions didn't matter, and somehow now they do, and the logic behind them doesn't sound fair to anyone involved. "It wasn't just because she was sick. It was because it didn't look like she was ever getting better, and you needed someone healthy to take care of you."

"But, she's back now. Isn't she?" Leo asks.

"Why do you say that, honey?" Surely, Shep couldn't have told Leo about Emerson already without her... grounds for war.

"I saw her. Emme Mommy." Leo looks around at the surrounding cars as if Emerson might leap out from behind one of them.

"What do you mean, Leo? Where did you see her?" A watchful eeriness drapes over Talia. She twists her head, left to right.

"Outside of the window. The other night."

No, no, no. "And you remember what she looks like? Emme Mommy? Could you tell it was her? Did she wave at you?" Stepping on their property per the court order is not allowed. But more than that, Talia never wanted Leo to see her. At least not so soon. It will confuse him.

"Yes, I remember her. She used to sing to me." Sadness cramps his delicate features. "I only saw her through the window. I couldn't hear her."

"It wasn't her. You're mistaken." It's easier for him if she tells him that. Why would Emerson walk around their home and not stop in to see Leo? That's hurtful to him. When did this happen? How has it affected him?

"Oh, okay." Leo climbs into her car without saying another word.

She finally has some ammunition against Emerson. She's proving to be the unreliable threat that Talia knew she was, sneaking around their property, messing with Leo before he's ready to meet her.

Talia has eyes outside of the city, but she has cameras

around their place too, and a Ring doorbell app. And if Emerson shows up on it, Talia's going to nail her to the wall with that footage.

This is Emerson's first slipup, but it won't be her last, and Talia's going to catch her. She phones her friend in Hartford. She won't dare tell anyone what she's doing. There's no lengths she won't go in order to protect Leo.

"What do you got for me?" she asks into the phone.

SEVENTEEN
EMERSON

Inside the bathroom, I search for a window.

Five floors from the ground, a jump would hurt, but maybe there's an outside ledge. At Culver, I excelled at climbing. My slight upper body is a detriment, but I know how to use my bottom half to my advantage, my sense of balance, spot-on.

Maybe I can reach a neighbor's window.

But, I quickly discover the window in the bathroom is too small to climb through, more a skylight, narrow and sleek, like everything else in Jacob's apartment.

You're overreacting.

I hope so, but my breath is ragged, the nerves in my body building into something eruptive.

Jacob was adamant about not wanting me to go in that room. *Something is in there.*

My imagination is a panacea of bad scenarios of what it is—dead bodies—a live body being held prisoner—a weird pet. Weapons of mass destruction...

I envision them all. *Why am I like this?*

"Emerson, everything okay in there?" Jacob asks. His voice

sounds frantic. Like he's not in the kitchen, cooking, as he should be. Chicken soup stock wafts from beneath the door.

Maybe he's going to cook *Me*.

"I'm fine," I shout through the door.

I am not fine. I open Jacob's medicine cabinet and look for drugs. *Clues*. It's awful, and who am I to judge? But I'm also afraid. I'd call someone but my purse with my phone inside is on Jacob's kitchen counter.

Inside his cabinet, I see a prescription for Lexapro. And one for Xanax.

That's it? One med for depression and anxiety and a little Xanax for an occasional panic attack? No melatonin to help him sleep? No Ambien to keep him asleep?

Not everyone has trouble sleeping, Emerson. Not everyone has memories that are so hard to forget they have to medicate themselves so they don't reemerge.

"Soup is done. I turned it off," Jacob says.

I stare at the four almond walls, no escape. It's time to leave the bathroom.

I take a deep breath and steady myself. When I exit... Jacob's right there. "Hey," I say.

I turn away from him. His dark eyes are too intense for me, ultra-focused. Too much of something, but I can't put my finger on what. My pulse ticks in my neck.

"Listen," he tells me, sighing. "I don't want you to be frightened. I'll open the spare bedroom door." That's why he looks like that. He's homed in on my fears like some sort of practiced telepath.

"Oh, I'm not," I lie.

I don't know what I expect to leap out of that door. The hallway is narrow, and the smell from the soup singes my eyes and nose.

Why did I decide to come here? Dr. Klinefelter told me to

watch myself with strangers because I'm still healing and my judgment may be off.

Jacob slides around me like an alley cat, slick and determined to open the door.

I can see my purse on the kitchen counter.

Just beyond it is the apartment door. If I sprint, I can snag my bag and possibly reach the outside world. Jacob stretches his arm to the top of the doorframe. I notice a ripple of taut muscle from beneath his T-shirt as he reaches for the key.

I want to run, but I'm frozen—intrigued, maybe.

He unlocks the door and inside I can see... baby toys.

I'm drawn to the primary colors on the wallpaper, the red Fisher Price brand name poking at my eyes, the shelved Little People vehicles—planes and trains and ambulances—on carefully displayed wooden shelves.

The heartbeat that relocated to my neck lightens up as I walk to the entryway. The room is none of the threatening things I imagined.

It's a shrine to Jacob's dead son, Linc.

"I know it's weird, but I recreated part of his old room. Took some of his things when I moved out of the house... Sometimes I come in here and talk to him." Jacob shrugs. "I haven't shown it to anyone. They'd probably think I'm mental, like I can't move on, but I thought you might understand."

"I do," I choke out. I crave Thea's things, actually.

I've thought about her favorite blanket and her squishy giraffe. Did Shep keep them? It's one of the questions I want to ask him, but our conversations haven't reached the subject of our dead daughter yet. I'd give anything to wrap myself in my baby's scent one more time.

"It brings me peace. Like a part of him is still here with me." Jacob looks at his feet, as if shamed, and I don't want him to be.

"It's actually a form of spirituality if this room brings you peace," I whisper, thinking of the woman from Meadowbrook who told me so.

It's bright and cheery in here, yet filled with so much sadness and loss. There's a picture of the three of them—Jacob and his beautiful, smiling blonde wife, both in their nursing scrubs. She holds Linc in her arms tightly, like the three of them are laughing and she's afraid he'll squirm away. What a curse, to have a job where you specialize in caring for others, but can't save your own.

This was a happy family; anyone can see that. Just like mine.

The fragility of how one wrong move can destroy something so beautiful slaughters me. One bad day, and your life is—gone.

I stare into Jacob's heavy eyes, and in that moment I know he's having these same feelings too. Not only that, but I know *him*. Better than I know myself. I can feel everything he holds inside of him. The agony left behind by those who are no longer here. Some dead. Some still alive. Either way Jacob and I have both been left behind—the unforgiven.

He pulls me out of the room and shuts the door.

His hand is on my arm, but I want it to be closer. I want him to reach inside my chest and put the pieces of my shattered heart back together. Maybe I can do the same for him.

His lips are inches from mine, and my hands are in his hair before I can stop myself. They travel to either side of his cheeks, his beard thick beneath my fingertips. His lips meet mine, and they're not gentle, they're hungry—needy.

He's unbuttoning my clothes, and when I nip at his neck, he pulls my hair so hard, I almost cry.

I know it's not right, and way too soon, but we need each other—two empty people looking for something or someone to fill us.

He picks me up, my legs wrapped around his waist. We stumble a bit and I feel my body press against the glass window that has no blinds. A thrill courses through me as he carries me to his bedroom, and lays me down on his unmade bed. He didn't expect to have someone in his room today and I certainly didn't intend to end up here, but his body is warm next to my bare skin and I haven't been this close to another human being in so long, I crave his touch.

And nothing about our union is gentle as he lays me down, but I don't stop him, just glad he's there—making me feel something again.

Afterward I can't say a thing, and neither does he. We doze for a bit, tired from the dance that's led us here, but there's beauty in our silence. Solace too.

By the time Jacob brings me soup in bed on a little tray table, I've dressed and I'm not sure what just happened here. I slurp at the soup and everything on my body feels sore—my scalp from where the roots of my hair were yanked, the muscles in my arms and legs from how they tensed when they were wrapped around Jacob's waist, the space in between my legs I let him intrude. Everything that felt so right minutes ago seems somehow wrong now.

I fall away into the past when the world was a better place. Nothing about this reminds me of the way it was with *You*.

"I'm trapped," I say. We're rolling around in bed and you've cocooned me in my sheets You kiss my nose, and I can't move my arms or legs. I'm laughing hysterically.

"Does it really matter? Is there anywhere you need to be right now?" you ask.

We've just made love three times. The kind where you kissed me slow, teased me, made me beg you for more.

"I suppose not," I say, kissing you.

I could've stayed in that bed with you all day. I think I did, actually...

But that's *not* the way I feel with Jacob now. Everything that happened today is a replacement for *You*.

But Jacob is not *You*, and I need to leave now.

Jacob is sitting on the edge of the bed, no headboard. "So, being an artist, are you a fan of musicals, I could—"

"Thank you for the soup, Jacob. Today was nice, but I need to get home..." I wave at him, still in his boxer shorts. His stomach is nice and muscled. He seems like a caring person, but he's not mine. He cannot be mine.

I place the tray down.

"Okay. Well, see you at group then," he says, disappointed.

"Thank you." I walk toward the door.

"Wait." He grabs my arm and forces me to look at him one more time. I wish he knew how strong he was and how threatening it feels to be in his grasp.

"What is it?" I rip my arm away. This was such a mistake. It's great to be wanted, but it's also too much for me right now. I need to stabilize my own center before I can be the focus of someone else's.

"Promise me, you'll call me when you're ready. And if you need anything..." He whips out a business card with his number on it.

He hands it to me. I snag it from his fingers. "I promise. I will." I grab my purse off the counter. "Bye, Jacob."

As I leave his place and order an Uber, I notice a man with a camera strung around his neck taking pictures. Filled with regret and anxiety, I can't help wondering if they are of me. Relief rips through me when the driver speeds me away.

EIGHTEEN

TALIA

The story Emerson tried to sell Shep versus the reality of the situation is so glaring and contradictory, Talia might need a pair of shades when she tells him everything she's just learned about his darling ex-wife.

Ninety-five percent *fine* most of the time. Ha!

Emerson wasn't fine the day she woke up on top of her daughter, and she's not fine now.

And Talia will lie down in front of oncoming traffic before she lets that erratic woman take Leo in her possession for even a moment.

Shep admitted that Emerson could get lost in her own brilliant mind for hours, and that she had said at one time that she wasn't sure she wanted children.

But Talia's focus was sharp when she was with Leo. She and Shep only had maybe four hours a day with Leo during the work week. The least they could do was pay attention to him when he was right in front of them.

Weekends, Leo was center stage. Talia couldn't imagine how adding another child could drain the battery so much that a mother could become completely unengaged.

Unless parenting wasn't something the mother was really inclined to do in the first place.

Or something she even enjoyed.

"Give it some more time," Shep had said, when Talia had voiced some of these thoughts after she had moved into Shep's townhouse. After he could no longer stay in the home where his infant daughter had died and his wife had been carted away in handcuffs.

After Talia already assumed responsibility of Leo.

She'd spent plenty of *time* with him.

Shep's comment was insulting—as if she didn't know about childcare, even though she'd been spending countless hours taking care of his child.

She can hear the garage shut and Shep approach before the door opens, his footsteps enough to make her hands knock a glass into the side of the sink. She carefully lowers it. She'll have to handle him like fine china for this to work. Shep enters the kitchen and stares at her wearily. He doesn't look like he's in the mood for an argument.

"You're home late." She looks at the clock on the microwave as she boxes up the rest of dinner, one plated dish wrapped and left out for Shep. "It's nearly ten o'clock."

"Sorry. I was at my spin class. It ran over," he says.

Talia flinches. She deserved that. "Hungry?" She points at the plate she made for him.

"I already ate," he says. "Is Leo in bed?"

"Yes. He tried to call you to tell you goodnight, but you wouldn't answer." She takes the plate for herself, unravels it and begins to pick at it.

Shep leans on the kitchen island, his body stiff, his expression hard, a smudge of black city smut on his cheek, a scuffed tube with the Wickerham blueprints in his hand. "I had business to attend to. I also received the oddest call from my lawyer that the position Emerson was offered has been rescinded. Do you know anything about that?"

Talia lets the piece of meat disintegrate on her tongue as she takes in this information. "No, that's too bad. Did they say why?" She takes a sip of ice water.

Shep cackles, but it turns into a cough. "Something about her mental health history coming out and her public image not being good for a children's book. But she was using a pen name."

"Companies have a very thorough background check these days." Talia fights to keep down her inner joy. This is great news for her and will pair well with the information she's about to tell him.

"You didn't have anything to do with it?" He looks at her with such disgust, she knows if she answers yes, it's over between them.

"Of course not. Why would you ask such a thing?" Talia places the covering back over the plate to keep her hands from shaking. This type of tension is the exact kind she never wanted in a relationship. It makes her think of what her mother had to put up with to support them. It reminds her of Glen. Anything she keeps to herself is for her own protection.

"Seems an anonymous caller contacted the publisher to let them know about Emerson," Shep says.

Well now... this information adds another layer to the story. "It wasn't me."

"You knew she was going for the interview. You knew where. And you weren't happy about it." There's such a bite to the end of his words, she's fearful.

"Shep, I didn't make a phone call to this publisher." She pauses, thinking about the best way to deliver the ax that will cut the tie between Emerson and them for good. "But, I did meet with someone who lives in Emerson's neighborhood yesterday. That's where I was. I didn't feel comfortable handing over Leo to her, and you weren't going to do anything about it. This person told me that Emerson is sleeping with a man. One she just met. From her survivors' group."

"What? That's ridiculous. She's only just been released from a mental institute."

As expected, Shep isn't asking the particulars about Talia's contact, or requesting a name, both things Talia can't offer him. He's getting tangled in the weeds of betrayal just as she predicted. Even though Emerson is no longer his, she's still the mother of his children, and—*He*—must remain the source of her desire.

He'll never admit to it, but he's appalled she let another man lie her down and claim her as his own. She's been sullied in his mind, and he'll never be able to look at her the same.

Talia slides the photographs across the table. "He took these of his own free will. The man she's been with lives in Asylum Hill. His name is Jacob. He's a nurse. Maybe he can take care of her now so you don't feel like you have to anymore."

Shep shuts his eyes and then reopens them as if she's flashed a big light in his face. *That's right... wake up!*

Talia watches as Shep mentally devours the photographs in a way that sickens him. She suspects he's been having regrets about divorcing Emerson. She needed to put his doubts to rest—for him—for all three of them.

Shep drops a particularly steamy photograph of Jacob's muscled arms wrapped around Emerson as she straddles this stranger, her bare ass pressed up against the windowpane that faces the street. Shep flips the photo over so he doesn't have to look at it anymore and grasps Talia's hands across the table. "I'm sorry I made you worry about Leo. I was convinced you were fed up with all of this drama and had found someone else. That's why I thought you lied to me."

She exhales in astonishment and relief, his words breathing life back into theirs. The irony is not lost on her—she was so distraught she was stalking Shep's ex and all the while Shep was upset because he thought Talia was cheating on him. "I would never betray you." Her eyes linger on the photograph.

She knows the photos shred him. They're everything she needed to pull him back on her side.

He makes eye contact with her then, sweet and sincere, very much the same man she fell in love with. "I know you wouldn't."

"Shep, I don't want you speaking to her anymore. Please. She's not good for our family, and she's not telling you everything. What if she brought Leo around this man? We don't even know who he is. You're way too cordial with her and it's disrespectful to me. I say only go through the lawyer to contact her. No more courtesy calls."

He nods. "I think you're right. I've had a long night. Let's go to bed."

She shoves the plate in the fridge and follows him to the master. She doesn't have a foot in the door before he's pulling at her pajama bottoms, rubbing his calloused hands that used to be soft over her breasts. She knows in that moment that he's all hers again.

Bye, bye, Emerson.

NINETEEN
EMERSON

When my eyes open, a shadow moves in the distance, closer to the dresser, near the door.

Groggy. "Who's there? Georgie?"

No... she's on a date and won't be home until later...

I try to move, to scream, but my tongue sticks to the back of my mouth.

I can't breathe.

The shadow edges closer. Slowly.

It creeps... long branch-like fingers reach out.

Like that woman's chopping knife from Shep's townhouse.

Wake up!

I am. My eyes. Are open.

The shadow moves to my bedside.

There is a space in between my chest, beneath the bones that make up my ribs, that pumps with vigor. I can't control it. The beating is incessant, moving so fast, to make up for all the other parts of my body that cannot.

My heart screams beneath the surface.

My lungs won't accept air.

I see the outline of him—a hooded sweatshirt, jeans, six feet tall.

Looming. His hood is pulled around his face, but I can see an angry outline.

Everything in my body pulses faster. I try to yell for help, but nothing comes out.

My breath whistles. I can taste the fright in the back of my throat—bitter and swollen and toxic. Choke on my vomit. Suffocate from fear.

He lunges.

My heart explodes in my chest. I scream now.

My tongue is no longer stuck. My arms and legs were paralyzed, shot with anesthetic, but now that I can move them—I can't. He has me pinned.

He places his hands over the top of my mouth. Sound stops.

I still can't see his face.

"You killed her!" I choke out from beneath his fingers. It has to be the same man who killed Thea. He's come back for me. Tears fill my mouth.

My windpipe touches the back of my throat. Crushing.

This is real. This is real! I gasp. My consciousness fades. Dying...

I hear someone coming up the stairwell.

A window opens.

Georgie turns on the lights. "What in the hell?"

I struggle for air. There's a man dressed in cargo pants there too—Georgie's date?

I roll off the bed, a sweaty mess, coughing, begging for help.

"I'm calling the police," Cargo Pants says.

I lie on a heap of papers on the floor. It's only then I notice there're pages everywhere. Torn pieces of my journal, my sketchpad, and my artwork, litter the floor.

Georgie picks up a sketch of Birdie. "What's going on here?

Is this... me?" My character has on a red and paisley headwrap that resembles one Georgie often wears.

I catch my breath, but I'm still coughing. "No... It's one of my characters. My sketches. For the project—"

"Bullshit. That's me! You've been drawing me. And having weird fantasies about me and now you're screaming and looking for my picture. I knew you were one messed-up girl!"

"That's not true." I still can't pass air through my lungs correctly. My oxygen level is depleted. "That man was real. Did you see him? Go out the window? You had to have seen him."

The window is open, the blue and white threadbare curtain flapping in the night air.

"No, we did not, Emerson. There was no man. And you cannot be my roommate anymore. I'm calling this in."

The police arrive, a report is filed, and I am displaced, once more.

The paramedics have me on a stretcher.

"It's not psychosomatic, it's anatomic. She has windpipe obstruction. We have to take her in," the medic says.

I don't disagree with them. Breathing is so hard. Arguing is harder. There's a cop there with a five o'clock shadow and hooded eyes who looks like he belongs on Daytime TV. "I'm Detective Ramsey," he introduces himself. "I'll be looking into your case."

"Thank you," I say, and then I'm wheeled away—back to the hospital.

The heartrate monitor beeps as my mind rolls around in the world of—*what ifs*. I could stay in this place all day, but no one has made an exact diagnosis or found a cure for what I've got going on upstairs. At first, when I woke up in the hospital I checked my arm to make sure it wasn't fastened with a handcuff —like last time.

I could almost see Shep's eyes burning into me from across the room beneath the fluorescent lighting like I was the monster.

Joanna was the only one who showed me kindness that day...

"Emerson, do you remember what happened?"

"I'm sorry. I don't."

"It will be more favorable for your release if you can recall the events leading up to the incident."

It all started with her. Genetics.

"My mother had insomnia," I blurted out. "And so do I."

"Did your mother ever do anything to you in her sleep-deprived state?" Joanna asked.

"No, and neither have I. I wasn't awake when my baby died."

Joanna flips through a formal report. "It says here that you were."

I haven't trusted myself a day since.

Before the decision was made to send me away to boarding school to temper my wildly creative imagination, my parents used to have heated discussions about me.

"The guidance counselor said that maybe we should have her evaluated for neurodiversity so we can put her on an IEP. Get more help," my mother said.

Over twenty years ago, the word—neurodiversity—was just starting to make it into mainstream academia. My father wasn't a fan of buzzwords or spending his precious nickels on validating them.

"Are you kidding me? Don't buy into the crap. Just another way for the healthcare system to capitalize on the misbehavior of children. If it were my parents and all I wanted to do was paint and color, they'd give me a swift kick in the ass and tell me to spend my time doing something more constructive."

"She likes to write too."

"And thank goodness for that. At least it's a skill she can get paid... a little... for."

"What about the terrors?"

"I don't know. Give her some whiskey in her tea or something before she goes to bed to settle her mind. It's like she has a live wire up there that won't shut off when she does."

It hurt to hear how he spoke of my struggles, although to this day, it's the closest thing anyone's said that makes any sense to me in regard to my condition.

But, I'm convinced that the loose wire is the same one that makes vivid images leap from my mind onto the page. If someone gave me the option to perform a surgery to fix it, I'm not sure I would. My life would be an empty void without my art.

But maybe my daughter might still be alive...

Those with RBD—REM Sleep Behavior Disorder, which I likely have—are much more likely to develop a neurological disease later, namely Parkinson's disease, or an early form of dementia.

So, there's that to look forward to...

I've always had the inclination that I'd die young. When I mentioned this to Brooks at Culver he replied, "All bright stars burn out more quickly."

He had a way with words. He always knew what I needed to hear. Every other person told me I was crazy for saying that, not to wish an early death upon myself, but not him. "Sometimes we know what we're to become long before anyone else does," he also said.

I'm going to have to contact him.

I already called Shep several times. It went to voicemail. He's probably with his new family, sound asleep.

I have nowhere else to go.

I wish I had my parents' old house in Westport to return to. The one I had to sell, half of the proceeds going to charity, the other to me. And now Shep has the money all rolled up in his townhouse.

I invested everything I had in our life together.

Now he's the one person turning me away.

TWENTY

TALIA

There's a strange buzz in the office, and Priya isn't at her desk. Talia saw Priya's father, Mr. Agrawal, in the conference room; and the only time he shows up on their floor is for a scheduled board meeting.

Talia cranes her neck around the partition to see who else is in there, but they've closed the blinds. *Damn it.*

Even though they're supposed to stay off their cell phones during work hours, Talia texts Shep.

What's going on? The board is here...

I don't know. But something is definitely up.

Do you think they're doing layoffs because of Wickerham?

There's bubbles on the other side, but no reply.
And where the hell is Gus?
No Priya. No Gus. Neither one of them is ever late. Gus is too devoted to Brighton and Priya is too anal to not be on time

for anything. She keeps tide pens, baby wipes, Ibuprofen, and a lint roller in her top desk drawer. She's *that* girl.

When Talia shows up late—because who can possibly be on time *every day* with constant mass transit delays—Priya says things like, "Oh ya, there's an app for that. I saw the train was delayed so I took an Uber."

Who has time to check apps every day before work? Or the money to just—take an Uber?

Priya does!

Was Gus able to persuade the project back into Brighton's hands? If so, why wasn't Talia alerted?

She taps her foot under her desk.

Shep won't text her back.

Talia doesn't like not being in the know. Especially when major shifts are happening all around her.

It's like when she finally learned what her father was capable of and why he wasn't around anymore.

This feels *big*—like *that*. But she can't put her finger on why.

"Hey."

Talia jumps. She finds Neve hovering above her like a nervous bumble bee dressed in autumn gold.

"Sorry, didn't mean to startle you." Neve appears pale and uncertain, her hair hanging over her eye. "Do you think something is wrong? Everyone is in that board room."

"Who's everyone?" Talia asks.

"Mr. Agrawal, Prince, Sauder, and Kimpton." She gulps.

"Kimpton?" Kimpton is the president of Brighton. They only see Windell Kimpton when he's presenting the annual earnings report, and he rarely sticks around for questions.

"Yes, he's in there," Neve says.

"*Shit.*"

Neve's number one strength is her absolute dedication to

her work. Neve's weakness is also her absolute dedication to her work. It's all she has. If this ship is sinking, it will destroy her. "Can you..." Neve hems and haws, "ask Shep if he knows anything?"

She shakes her head. "I already did. He said he doesn't know why they're here, but that something is definitely up."

Neve glances around. "I think Priya is in there," she whispers, pointing to the boardroom.

"Did you see her this morning?" Talia asks.

"No," Neve says. "But she's never late."

"Neither is Gus, and I haven't seen him either."

Neve shoots Talia a wild-eyed glance. "What is this, Talia?"

"I think it's either a celebration because we landed Wickerham and Gus is in there being patted on the back and preemptively promoted. Or... we didn't land Wickerham and some of us are being laid off."

"No... You think they'd..." Neve says.

"Maybe they already let Gus go, and that's why he's not here."

Neve places her hand on her lower abdomen as if she might be sick.

As if on cue, the boardroom door opens.

A weary Terrence, senior architect, and pretty much floor captain, pokes his turtle-like head out from the door. "If I can have everyone's attention, we'd like you all to come in the boardroom for an emergency meeting."

"*Emergency meeting*," Neve whisper-screams.

Neve places her hand on Talia's desk, and Talia almost thinks Neve wants her to hold her hand, but then Neve withdraws it, and they walk together reluctantly into the conference room. Maybe to their doom?

Glum faces loom at them from around the long rectangular table. Priya sits among the heads of the company, next to her daddy.

But, something is horribly wrong. She's been crying. Her eyes dart all around the room, except at them—Shep, Neve, and Talia.

Shep gapes at Talia for a brief moment, worriedly. This is most certainly a layoff, and Gus, who's missing from the room, is already gone.

Talia feels like it is her fault. She's his assistant and she wasn't around to offer advice that going to the actual site to reclaim his lost bid was a mistake. He couldn't be stopped. He was a man on a mission. Talia gets it. She's been in that same mode lately.

"Thank you all for joining us..." Mr. Tyron Prince begins. He's the head of HR, and Talia guesses the most suitable one to lob out pink slips.

"There's been an unfortunate incident in the wake of losing a project I know everyone in this room worked very hard on. As I'm sure most of you are aware, we did not secure the Wickerham bid and it's gone to newcomer architectural firm Five Star."

There are grumbles and whispers, but none from Talia. Old news.

"Before we deliver the next part, which may be difficult to hear, we want to let you know how much we appreciate all of you."

Butter the ax so it goes down easier over our necks, go on...

Shep looks at Talia with desperate eyes, and she knows why. If he gets shit-canned as a project manager, a sidestep from his true calling of senior architect, he'll have to start all over again. It will be years before he reaches his full potential. Kiss private school for Leo goodbye.

"We know you put countless hours into every project you take on, and I'll couple that by saying the board must approve all of them. They have great responsibility in choosing which projects are worth our time and resources, so we never want you to feel like these decisions rest solely on your shoulders."

The board goes rigid at this part of the speech, but doesn't comment.

Wait... what? It's going to be hard to fire us if the board takes partial responsibility for our actions.

"I know everyone thought fondly of Augustus Romeo..."

Thought is past tense. Gus has been fired.

"As did we. We welcomed him and his wife, Connie, and their three children into the Brighton Family over five years ago, and he's made great strides to rise up through the ranks here. His efforts were vast—including the recreational sports plex in Manhattan, the outdoor outlet mall in Rosyln, the secondary school in Westchester. The beautiful buildings he designed and helped build here at Brighton will forever shine on in the eyes of the patrons who occupy the buildings he brought to life."

A little heavy of a sendoff, bosses... Can they just tell me if I have a job? If my boyfriend has a job? If we're both going to be unemployed and bitter for wasting our time here?

Prince goes on, "Unfortunately, this particular project, the Wickerham bid, drove Gus to break our company policy. Gus visited the Wickerham project site, one which we weren't contracted for, after hours."

Ah... So they're going to make his firing about breaking company policy. Not losing the bid. Classic Brighton.

"And, it's with a heavy heart, I must let you know that Gus Romeo is..."

Fired.

"Dead." Prince's word come out in a hard rut. Gasps fill the room.

"What?" Talia screams out loud, the only one to do so, but—
what the what?

Huh. No. Oh, no...

TWENTY-ONE

EMERSON

My throat still aches from the attack, but the medical staff told me I was lucky my windpipe wasn't broken.

I've come to hate the word—lucky.

Everyone who's used it lately has made me feel the opposite of the actual meaning. "You're lucky you're getting a second chance."

"You're so lucky your trachea wasn't broken."

Some days I wonder if everyone would be better off if I would've just stayed in Meadowbrook. Myself included. But there's no going back now.

Detective Ramsey had a difficult time digesting the idea that I somehow injured myself, despite my history of a sleep disorder.

I have a hard time with it too.

Brooks will make it better if only for a little while. I'll take it though.

His apartment has always reminded me more of a spec model than a place where an actual human being lives. In the heart of Midtown—Chelsea—long slender windows reach from floor to ceiling like a lithe woman performing a ballerina stretch. They are mirrored by equally tall bookcases with ornate sculpture pieces and framed photos.

Brooks is an art collector. It's one of the reasons we bonded so early.

He washes my hair in his clubfoot tub.

I didn't feel stable standing in Brooks's shower, and he wouldn't let me go another day with my sweat-head, as he called it. So he insisted he make me a bubble bath, and that I let him wash my hair.

I don't have to look at the shampoo products to know they're from a high-end salon. Brooks's fingers feel good as they massage my scalp. I must let out a little moan because he says, "There's my girl."

"Thank you for taking care of me," I say.

"You bet."

To anyone else, our relationship would seem completely bizarre, but it's right on par for us. There's intimacy in touching someone without sexualizing them. We crossed that line once at Culver, and then never again.

Brooks said he valued my friendship too much, and that he was incapable of loving me the right way, so we left it at that. All I ever told Shep was that my relationship with Brooks was completely platonic, but I suspected he thought something happened in our past.

He admitted to me once that when it came to sexual partners, for him, if a woman had too many, it was a major turn off. He said in relation to his ex and her high school beau, "Every time I saw the two of them together all I could imagine was him fucking her."

It was a crass statement, but I also wondered if he was just being incredibly honest. If maybe all men thought that way too and Shep was the only one brave enough to admit it. In any case, I didn't divulge my slipup with Brooks and ruin Shep's impression of him forever. It wasn't worth it over one careless night in my teens.

"So, tell me again what happened last night? Now that you're relaxed. The words might come easier now."

His voice soothes me as he rinses the soap from my hair. The shower head in the halfway house was so weak it barely trickled, whereas this one has so much water pressure it's bliss on my follicles.

"I-I woke up to someone in my room. A man. He tried to strangle me," my voice is quiet and strained.

"Sounds like a rough evening," he snarks. "Any idea how he would've gotten in?"

"The window was open."

"Can you tell me where the window is in proximity to your bed?"

"Pretty high up. Above my dresser. It's usually locked. There's a ledge on the other side of it, and a fire escape."

Brooks lathers in the conditioner. I can practically hear his attorney wheels spinning as his fingers make circular patterns on my head. I'm shocked he's this good at washing hair, as if he's been working as a shampoo girl on the side for years.

Although I shouldn't be so surprised at Brooks's adaptive skills. In prep school Brooks somehow mastered the use of a forklift to plant a handcrafted bees nest in one of the school parking lots. He said he swore he didn't know the boy who was stung had an allergy, and that he'd only wanted to give him a good scare after their argument. The boy tried to drive himself to the hospital after being stung, but crashed on the way, causing irreputable damage. The boy never returned to Culver.

And then there was the incident with the boy and the crew boat. Culver was special in that it had its own manmade lake. Good thing they were all great swimmers. Brooks and his pranks...

"And you said you landed on the ground. They found you there. On top of scattered papers."

"Yes."

"And you couldn't breathe?"

"That's right."

"It doesn't make sense that you would take the time to reach up on top of the dresser to open the window during your attack. Unless... you were trying to escape."

"I never opened that window. I was trapped."

"Have you ever destroyed your own work before? During an attack or otherwise? Are you... one of those extremist artists who tear up projects that aren't perfect?"

I laugh at the absurdity of his statement. "I'm just a children's book illustrator. I'm not to be likened with Michelangelo taking a hammer to Christ's leg in *The Deposition*." Brooks giggles. "And, no. Those pages were one of a kind. Part of my portfolio. I have screenshots of them, but it's not the same as showing someone the actual sketches."

"Of course." He rinses the conditioner out. "And, who had your address in Hartford?"

"Shep. The hospital. The publisher where I applied and got rejected. I had a date yesterday. I think I told him where I live."

Brooks stops massaging my head. "A date. With whom, Emerson?"

"A guy I met at my grief counseling group."

"How did it go?" Brooks turns off the sprayer. The water drips down my face.

"Not that well."

"Sit up," Brooks tells me.

I breach the water, the suds clinging to my breasts. I gather more suds and make myself a better bubble bra even though I know Brooks isn't looking. He begins to pull a comb through my matted mess, and it feels so strangely good to have another human being brush my hair, I want to cry.

"Do you think he could've done it? Your failed date?"

I sigh. "It's possible. He was a little rough."

Brooks stops brushing. "Did you sleep with him, you little minx?"

"I did. Then I regretted it."

"Sounds like me every Friday night. I don't blame you. A year in solitude and I'd be looking for love in all the wrong places too. Give me his address. I'll find out if it was him."

"No, *no*. I can't remember my attacker's face, but I don't think it was Jacob. My date. I'm surprised you believe the bad guy was a real person. No one else does."

"It doesn't add up. The window. Your drawings. I've known you a long time. I just can't see you destroying your own work. If you were trying to defend yourself, why would you do that?"

"Exactly." I exhale, a bubble tinkling up and into the air vent. "So, tell me about your newest love interest?" I ask him.

With Brooks, there have been so many. When I used to catch up with him, my favorite thing to do was ask this question.

"A no bullshit business executive. Brunette. Great style. Bad temper."

"Oh. Will she be pissed I'm here if she's no bullshit?"

"It'll probably be our downfall, but it's about that time..."

"You're so bad."

He laughs. "Stand up."

I shiver as I hoist myself up using the lip of the tub, aware of how vulnerable and exposed I am with the water dripping off my naked body. Brooks wraps a white, plush, terrycloth robe around me. I sink into it like a warm hug and step out of the bathtub. "Why're you so good to me?"

"Because I have to be good to someone, or else I'll be all bad." He grins and leads me to his dining room. Somehow there is dinner already prepared and waiting—beef medallions in a brown sauce and rice.

"And, if your ex-husband stood by his wife like he was

supposed to, he'd be the one doing these things for you. Does—
in sickness and in health—mean nothing to that bastard? I've
thought about paying him a visit." Brooks's eyes are hard and
dark.

"Please don't do that. Leo still needs him," I say to Brooks. I
like to believe his good outweighs his bad, but sometimes I'm
just not sure.

"Of course," he says.

"This smells delicious," I say.

"Let's stop jabbering then and eat it."

I savor the food, the first good meal I've had in weeks—
maybe years—and take in the one and only person who's stood
by me through it all. I don't understand Brooks or why he helps
me, but with so few people by my side, I don't stop to question it
either.

"My therapist at Meadowbrook, Joanna, asked me why your
name was on the visitor log."

Brooks stops chewing. "Why're you still talking to her? I
thought you weren't allowed to once you left."

"I'm not. But I called her anyway."

He smiles. "Rulebreaker."

"Total rebel. But why, Brooks?"

"I'm just some guy who bought my best friend some art
supplies." He's on his last medallion. I'm so tired I've only
muscled through two.

"That's what I told her." I shrug.

"Good, then, don't worry about it."

Famous last words from Brooks.

I stare out at the city lights, the bustling traffic, sitting across
from a brilliant man who's cooked me dinner and paired it with
a great cabernet my mother used to drink, Stag's Leap.

He plays classical music—Chopin or Tchaikovsky—my ears
were never as good as his. The piano keys pacify me in a way I

haven't allowed in ages. I've found my meditative garden on the outside, my center, if only for a moment.

I wonder how long it can all last.

My stay with Brooks.

This feeling of absolute calm.

Peace.

TWENTY-TWO
TALIA

Dead...

As in she won't be able to hand in the report on zoning to Gus that they just discussed yesterday on the Navy Yard art gallery space...

Dead.

As in she can't confirm Gus's flight scheduled for later this month.

Dead!

As in the surprise party for Gus's birthday in three weeks that Connie emailed her about will never happen, because Gus won't be having anymore birthdays *dead.*

It's only when Shep takes Talia by the shoulders and steers her toward the exit that she realizes she's standing in the empty conference room all by herself.

"Oh..." She blinks and looks around at the long, waxy wooden table and empty chairs. "I'm sorry, I think I zoned out. It's all... shocking."

"Yes, it is." Shep looks like he's going to be sick, withdrawn, and a tinge on the green side. "I'm going to need you to pull it together, though, Talia."

"What do you mean?" *Doesn't she deserve a moment of silence?*

Gus was her boss. She may have not exactly liked him, but they did have a working relationship for a number of years, and this is *a lot*. Not only did this happen at a job site, but Gus's motivation to go down there stemmed from pressure to get the account or lose a promotion. The whole thing drips with corporate scandal.

"Didn't you hear the new assignments? Kimpton put me in charge of the Freedom Trail walkway project. You were the one booking Gus's transport to Boston in a couple of weeks, right? I know Gus preferred the train. I'll fly. Whatever gets me there the fastest." He looks away, uncomfortable, almost overeager to fill a dead man's shoes.

"We can talk about it at home, Shep," Talia says in a hushed tone.

"Right," he says, all hyped up. "I've got to go." He kisses her on the cheek and then shirks back. "I'm so sorry I did that." His eyes are wild and bloodshot. Did he not sleep last night?

She's sure everyone is just wigged out from this entire situation, but she and Shep never show public displays of affection at work. Everyone knows they're together, but it's just not something they do.

"It's okay. It's been a morning." Talia takes a quick sweep of the office and whispers, "I don't think anyone saw us. As you were." Talia curtsies as if that doesn't make their entire interaction even more awkward. Shep scuttles away like a boy at the middle school dance returning to his side of the room.

When Talia reaches her desk there are security guards clearing out Gus's office. Neve is waiting for her, a grim expression on her face.

"Already? Is his body even cold?" Talia asks, pointing to the guards.

"Probably, they said he was lying there all night. The morning construction crew found him."

"Jesus, I didn't mean literally. Never mind. Did you... need something?" Talia asks, because she could really use a minute to reset. She rubs her temples, trying to ignore the work murmurs all around her. How can everyone just go back to business as usual?

"Is this how you always talk to your superiors?" she asks.

Talia tilts her head sideways, not getting the joke. "I'm sorry, what?"

Priya pops her head above the desk divider. "Talia, Neve is your new boss. Did you not hear Kimpton roll out the assignments?"

Talia's face spreads with a slow warmth. The ground feels as though it's shifting beneath her. She didn't hear anything, it appears.

Neve and she started at the same time and now Neve is her... *boss*.

"I went into a state in there. I'm sorry, I didn't catch it," Talia says.

Neve's dark eyes widen in surprise. "Didn't think you'd miss the memo. Anyway, it's been a rough one. What do you ladies say we go to lunch? My treat. I want to make sure we get off on the right foot. This position is a huge lift for me and I'm going to need your help."

"Lunch sounds good to me," Priya says.

"I need a minute..." Talia says. Of course, Gus, senior project manager, would need a replacement. And even though Talia had worked directly beneath him and knew more about the projects he was working on, they chose Neve over her because you can't go from administrative assistant to senior project manager. Talia holds her hand over her stomach, still processing this.

She realizes everyone else is about fifteen minutes ahead of her, which in Brighton minutes is like lightyears.

"I'll let you think on it," Neve says to Talia as she walks away, her wide-leg trousers swishing in a way that makes Talia hope she trips.

"How could you not have known Neve was your new boss?" Priya speaks in a low, irritating voice.

"I went into shock, I think. I can't remember much after they said Gus was dead. I thought they were going to tell us he'd been fired. I just... can't..."

"It's awful, but he shouldn't have been at that project site. Afterhours, especially. And all alone. He made really unsafe choices."

"You're not blaming him, are you?"

Priya's face is a cold slate. "That would be awful. Blaming the victim and all, but I'm not *not* blaming him either." She sinks back into her desk chair. "The board is going to have a lot to deal with on this one."

Talia cringes. Priya is thinking of her father. What about Connie and her three children? Talia imagines Connie probably blames herself for wanting that expensive house, the catalyst to Gus's actions. He was just trying to make her happy—*always number one in his book, his one and only*. It's such an intangible state of being—*happy*—and—we're all just trying to get there.

"How do you know he was alone?" Talia asks through the thin wall that separates them. She has neither the strength nor the tolerance to invade Priya's space.

"What do you mean? They found him on the ground after he'd fallen from the scaffolding," Priya says.

What would Priya know about the harsh realities of life and the fact that just because someone ended up dead, didn't mean it was by accident? Years later, if they ever found Glen's body, they might decide that was an accident too. Although her father promised her they never would. "How do you know he fell?" Talia asks.

"What's the alternative, Talia?" she asks.

Does Talia really need to spell it out? "I'm not sure."

"You've been watching too much late-night TV. Your mind becomes what you feed it."

Talia presses her mouth into a tired line. Such a statement of privilege. We don't all have content control of what we're fed when we're younger.

"Have you read the police report?" Talia asks.

"No," Priya says.

"Well, then I wouldn't be so sure you know all the details until you do."

"Talia... I would be very careful about the types of accusations you're potentially making at the moment."

Talia seals her lips shut. Priya's right. If Gus's death is marked suspicious the police will determine that. There's no sense speculating criminal scenarios and having it circulate around the office.

Talia met the crew at Five Star from Jersey only once, at a vendor convention, and they were definitely more blue-collar than corporate. A couple of the executives had square necks better suited for lifting lumber than wearing ties. She'd never say it out loud, but she can see a scenario in which Gus went down to the project site, raised hell about the building codes, and paid the ultimate price for it.

Talia starts to type an email to Ingrid Svensson. Ingrid was supposed to meet with Gus this week to discuss the Navy Yard project.

Dear Ingrid Svensson, I'm sorry to inform...

Talia stops typing. What's she supposed to say to clients?

Was that also covered in the boardroom meeting and she missed it? She'll have to ask Neve for direction—*the worst.*

Talia's architectural lust for the art gallery bid is real. She developed an online crush on Ms. Svensson, whose website was an ode to creating a peaceful existence and all things hygge—the Danish way of life that places an emphasis on a cozy, comfortable living.

Will Ingrid pull out of the deal if she learns her project manager died on the job? That type of catastrophe certainly doesn't fit in with her life-is-Zen, bring-the-peace lifestyle. "*Shit.*"

Talia finally understands how Shep could be thinking about flights and train schedules.

And why Neve was quick to get back on Talia's good side.

Gus's death could really mar their business and all their hard work.

Kimpton is probably quick to close on the Boston project before the buyers hear about what happened here, and the Navy Yard gallery is in flux until someone—not the original project manager assigned to the project—can meet with Ingrid.

The clatter of fingernails on her desk distracts her.

She glances up to find Neve again in her neat plaid pants and matching vest, silk blouse, red lipstick. It's like she dressed up for the occasion of being promoted without knowing it. "Come to lunch or you're fired."

"What?" Talia says it so loud, other heads poke from outside of their cubicles.

"I'm kidding, Talia, my god."

"Oh..." She feels so stupid. She still doesn't like the superiority jokes. Coming from Neve, they're not funny. "Okay, fine. I have some questions for you anyway. I don't know how to address Gus's clients."

"We'll discuss it. It will be a good conversation. I want us to work together," she says, enthusiastically, like she genuinely means it, but only because she's finally on two ladder rungs above Talia—first project manager, now senior project manager—*dread*. She needs Talia to cooperate. Neve's success depends on it.

"Got it. Where to?" Talia asks.

"Felice 15 Gold so we can have a drink," Neve says.

"Should we be drinking on the job?" *Is this a test? To see if I'll booze and boardroom, as they politely call it here. But it's more like, Don't booze and boardroom.*

"Have you seen how frantic this place is?"

Talia looks up from her computer screen and notices the actual NYPD there in addition to Brighton's security. They're occupying the conference room, and everyone else in the office seems to be pretending to work while taking sideways glances every which way. "Right. Let's get out of here."

"And, besides. I'm your boss. If I say you're allowed to drink, you're allowed to drink. Priya, did you hear where we're planning on going?"

She stops mid-keystroke. "I've been listening to your entire conversation."

Talia shakes her head. "I really need my own office... boss."

Talia chokes on those words as they circulate in her ears—*boss*.

For as many times as she says it, she'll never get used to it...

TWENTY-THREE

EMERSON

All morning, I float through Chelsea market like a leaf in the wind, my senses on overdrive at the sheer amount of life around me that I'm so unused to.

Fresh pastries, rows of twisted breads and donuts, and bagels, overpower my line of sight and smell. Upscale clothing I can't afford entices and taunts me from storefront windows. I stop in a bookstore and skim through pages of poetry in collections I have no intention of buying.

Canopies of white string lights transport me through one urban escape to another. Metal on three sides of the tunneled shopping center make me feel like I'm inside of a spaceship made for flying far away from here.

Forget spaceship—time machine.

Take me back.

I'd do it all differently—like schedule appointments with medical specialists to figure out what's wrong with me instead of hiding in the dark, in embarrassment, until I do something terrible in the space between awake and asleep that I cannot take back.

I find the tail end of the High Line, one of Shep's favorite variations of a park built on a historic rail line, elevated above the city. I walk the northbound trail toward the other end at 34th Street and revel in all the new art displayed; a harp made of twine and rope, for one. I have the urge to strum it even though I'm not supposed to.

This is what living feels like.

The buzzing inside of me is too good for everything that's gone wrong. Hot coffee hits the back of my throat reminding me of my pain.

Making me recall I was attacked. By a shadow. Or a man. Or myself...

I left Brooks's apartment with a to-go cup. He asked me how I felt this morning and I said, *good*. Not sure about that, but today, I long for the city and its energy.

I miss going for walks for hours with no destination, all by myself, for no reason—taking in sculptures and eavesdropping on strangers' conversations.

Shep used to call me a *watcher*.

I sit on the wide staggered steps of the High Line—art in themselves—thinking of Shep and what he would say, as if he's still mine.

It's impossible to explain to other people that I feel like I've stepped out of a time capsule, woken up from amnesia, been unthawed from one of those pods in a Sci-Fi movie, only to discover everything I knew before the freeze is gone.

My mind was shattered, and in putting it back together the pieces aren't sitting right.

It's hard to believe Shep isn't mine. That Thea is gone. It becomes a little more real every day, but it's all still so raw.

People filter all around me—a mother with a baby in a city stroller who's more blessed than she can possibly fathom. A man speaking Portuguese, another Mandarin. *This* is what I miss about the outside world. The various cultures. The differences that make us all uniquely part of the human race. *Where do I belong now?*

Not with Brooks. I explained I couldn't continue to live with him, and he didn't fight me. He just said he was working on a job lead for me as he left this morning.

A city job won't suit me, I told him. I need something close to Leo for our visitations. We'll see what he can drum up. Brooks rarely disappoints.

The trouble is wondering what he'll ask for in return.

When I had a short stint on the crime beat in my journalism days, Brooks once asked me for a press badge during a heated criminal trial. I let him borrow it, and I never did find out what he used it for. I also didn't ask. I was afraid to, and even more fearful when the defense attorney in the case turned up missing. Brooks was still in law school at the time, but who knows what he could've been cooking up. The attorney was never discovered and his client was found guilty.

My phone rings, and I'm not surprised to see who's on the other end.

"Hey, Joanna." The wind whips over the steps, and I imagine I'm the leaf swirling above the city.

"*Emerson.* I had a detective stop by my office. He told me what happened and asked a lot of questions. Are you okay?"

I glance at the beautiful autumn sky, the trees topped with a mottled mix of burgundies and citrus colors fit for a Bob Ross painting. I borrowed Brooks's Patagonia puffer jacket and hold it close to my body as I try to sip my coffee without scalding my larynx. "Right now, I am. But I'm afraid my brief hospitalization will be a setback. I have my weekly session coming up with my therapist. I have to plead not to let what happened interfere with my visitation scheduled for the end of the month, following the court hearing."

"I have some things I can advise on what to say to him. But listen, there's more. Can I meet you for lunch today?"

"I'm in the city, staying with a friend. In Chelsea."

"That's okay. It's probably better if we meet there, actually. Less of a chance anyone will see us together. I'll take the train in."

"Okay." I exhale, wishing not to have my good day ruined, but excited to see her.

"Do you know where The Commons is? Casual joint. Sandwiches and burgers?" she asks.

"Sure, I know it. What time should I expect you?" I'll probably still have time to do the mile and a half walk and circle back. The exercise is good for my soul—my temporary serenity.

"Let's shoot for noon."

"Okay, see ya then." I hang up and watch as an ombre-colored leaf falls and settles in the crook of a quilted jacket that I don't own, in the backdrop of a life I no longer recognize, in a reality I wish I could rewind—and start again.

I see Joanna before she sees me, her coif of blonde hair styled and sitting on top of her head in a springy mane, her fall tweed coat flapping behind her. She's dressed up for me.

"Emerson!" She waves.

I stand and embrace her. "Hi! Sorry for dragging you all the way out here."

She waves me off. "I love reasons to come to the city. Gives me a chance to leave my hole. I haven't made much of an effort since Eddie passed," she says of her late husband.

I get it now. Joanna didn't dress up for me. She dressed up for her. We all need a reason to feel good about ourselves. "Okay, then. You look great."

"You look amazing! Your hair has grown."

I yank on it, hardly noticing, and realize it's probably Brooks's special products that've given my cut an extra touch of pizzazz today. "I think I'll let it grow. I'm just grateful I'm not gray yet. Although I don't know how that's possible with all I've been through." I let out a half-hearted laugh, and Joanna grimaces back.

We sit and order hot drinks. The air has turned crisp, and now that I'm inside I can feel my nose prickle from the heat.

"Emerson, why didn't you call me when you were in the hospital?" she asks.

I think on this. "At the time... all my energy went into finding a new place I could stay. My roommate kicked me out. And afterward, I just didn't want you to know I relapsed." I shake my head, because I know she'll see this as a personal failure.

"I don't want you to worry about that. I wish you would've called me."

"I hope it doesn't happen again, but if it does, I will. Now what insider tips do you have for what to say to my therapist?" I bite my lip, because Klinefelter doesn't seem like the type that'll let this go. Thirty days, episode free, was part of the arrangement before I saw Leo.

"Oh yes. Tell him, you were triggered by the grief counseling session mandated by him. You were asked to share that day before you were ready. Tell him it's the last time you'll do that, an isolated incident. Keep rounding back to the fact that it was on his agenda for clearing you. His fault..."

"Ohh, good. Won't he assume I'm a 'danger' to Leo though?"

"If he tries that, explain the visits are supervised in the daytime. Your terrors only happen at night. You pose absolutely no risk. It's ridiculous to think you'd be a threat during a supervised, daytime visit given your history."

I smile. "You're good. Thank you. I'm using all of that."

Our waitress delivers Joanna a coffee, and hot tea with

honey for me. The earlier coffee was too harsh and I had to throw it out.

"Why do you think the terror occurred? Was there added stress? Besides the job loss at the publisher? What else happened that day?"

We both place an order for soup and a sandwich as I try to detract from the question.

I'm outside of Meadowbrook. I can tell Joanna as little or as much as I want to. And I'm not sure I should mention Jacob. But I do see Joanna as a friend. And she did just give me helpful advice.

"I went on a date," I say, simply.

"Oh... really? Where did you meet this person?"

"At group. He just asked me to spend the day together after the meeting. We didn't do much. We just cooked together."

Joanna raises her frosty eyebrows at me. She's one of those women whose hair is so blonde it's practically white. "Sounds romantic."

"It was no big deal," I say.

"Did anything romantic happen?" she asks, and now it feels like she's prying. In the setting of the hospital, a question like this might've sounded like therapy, but between two women having lunch at a café, it leans toward intrusive. Dr. Klinefelter mentioned part of living in my new world is developing boundaries.

"No, he just pecked me on the cheek and I told him I didn't want to go out on a second date," I lie.

Telling Brooks I slept with Jacob made me feel a little dirty, but not judged. Joanna will make me feel both.

"If the date went well, then why no second date?" Joanna asks.

"I just... don't like him that much. He made me miss Shep. I kept comparing the two. I know you're not supposed to do that, but I couldn't help myself. I think I should try and make sure things are over between Shep and me before I can move forward."

"He's moved on, Emerson," Joanna says.

"He's not married," I say. "It's hard to just let him go, give my old family up. Maybe there's a chance before she's sunk her claws into him for good."

Joanna eyes me with surprise. "I have to admit, it's shocking hearing you talk like this, but it shows me your thought process is operating fully. It's just that you have to remember how Shep left you. While you were sick. When you couldn't fend for yourself. Is that someone you want back in your life?"

I cough up the honey and some of the tea, dabbing the napkin over my mouth. "I'm sorry. My throat is tender from where..."

"You were choked," she says.

"Yes... And, I know Shep did all those things, but it was because he couldn't deal with Thea's death or the fact that it was my fault. But maybe, after all this time..."

"These are dangerous thoughts, Emerson. You're making excuses for him. I wouldn't advise pursuing a relationship with Shep. You do deserve closure though."

I nod. Our soup and sandwiches arrive. The soup goes down easy. I pick at the cheese at the corner of my sandwich and muscle it down.

"Now, what else did you want to talk to me about?" I ask.

Joanna grows serious. "You said that your prep school friend, Brooks, visited you and gifted you art supplies."

"That's right."

"Were the supplies inventoried through the intake nurse?"

I'm surprised by the question. "No."

"Why not, Emerson?"

I don't look at her, because I don't know why. Brooks just slid them to me slyly in a plastic bookstore bag, and I was so excited when I saw what was inside, I didn't give them to

Gemma, the new nurse on the floor. I was afraid she wouldn't
allow them. "It was a gift and I was getting out in a few days. I
guess I didn't think it mattered. Why do you ask?"

"Where are those art supplies now?"

"My colored pencils were under my bed in the metal tin
they came in. Georgie, my roommate, might've disposed of them
by now," I say sadly. I need to get all my stuff. I've been negli-
gent, playing tourist today instead.

"Was there a palette knife among the tools?" she asks.

I nod. "There was. I don't think Brooks understood what I
use to create my art. He's a lawyer. There was paint in the kit
too, even though I mostly just draw."

"Do you know where the knife is now?"

Why does she keep asking me this?

"No, I haven't seen it. I might've thrown it away because I
wasn't going to use it. Why, Joanna?" I dip toasted bread in my
broth, hoping to soften it up.

"Do you remember that sudden death I told you about at
Meadowbrook? The reason I had to get off the phone the first
time you called me?"

"Yes." I place my sandwich down, a hot rush of something
slithery sliding down my back.

"A patient found your palette knife. It was left behind in
your room. And she killed herself with it."

I close my eyes and shake my head.

Rewind... rewind... the clock.

How can so many decisions I make result in horror and
death?

But, Brooks gave me those tools...

"I don't want to upset you more," Joanna says.

"Am I a suspect?" I ask, exasperated.

"You weren't. I mean you're not. But Gemma has been
fired."

"No. She's a single mom. She just got that job. She was so

excited." I hear my voice turn into a sad wisp. I was having such a good day...

Joanna places her hands on top of mine. "I know. It was very upsetting, but it was the right thing to do. She should've checked what was coming into the facility."

"Did they say where I left it? The knife?"

I try to make my brain recall where I placed that palette knife, but I can't remember. Once I start creating with my pencils, I fall into a zone and everything else fades away.

"No, it was found... inside the patient."

I slap my hand over my mouth. "I'm so sorry." I think back to the first day I called Joanna, distraught over my therapy session, and what patience she expressed toward me after all this had just happened. Or maybe they just hadn't pieced together where the tool came from at that stage.

"It's not your fault, of course, but my job is under review because I was supervisor on the floor. I should've been watching Gemma."

"Oh no." I cannot have Joanna lose her job because of my carelessness.

"I've given you enough for today. If you remember where you put the knife, it will be helpful."

My mind is a smattering of broken paintbrushes and palette knives transformed into deadly weapons, sharp edges.

My eyes drift away from Joanna like the leaf. I'm blowing away from the restaurant, over the buildings, to the tippy top of the sky where no one can reach me.

TWENTY-FOUR
TALIA

Lunch is an awkward thing with Priya and Neve. Two people who've never so much as asked her to split a croissant with them before. And now they're crammed at a four-top, dining together.

Brighton breeds such competitiveness that no one feels like a friend. And Neve's suddenly all—*let's go out to eat and work as a team!*

Talia's not really having it. It's part of Neve's Machiavellianism. This lunch is a manipulation to get them on Neve's side so she can use them. She's going to step right on their backs to get to the top.

Priya's smiling as she holds her menu. Befriending those who can benefit her is a part of Priya's social strategy, whereas Talia finds it abominable. She detests disingenuous people, which has made it almost impossible to find true female friends in this city.

"This whole situation... I just can't believe it." Neve blows out hot air, her overpronounced curtain bang flipping off her face. That chunk of hair is so bolus, Talia wonders if she stores nuts under there for the winter.

Priya places the menu down, sympathy threaded on her

thin face. "I just can't imagine what his family must be going through. Three kids..." Priya makes praying hands, and Talia can't stop thinking about Connie and the kids either.

"I know. I didn't even get a chance to say anything to him the day he ran off. As his assistant—" Talia's voice catches. She doesn't know why she's revealing so much, and then she realizes what's wrong. She feels guilty.

"You can't think what happened to Gus is your fault. He was being so erratic that day. Too hotheaded. He ran out of Brighton without speaking to any of us," Neve says.

Talia offers a half-hearted smile, relieved no one holds her accountable, although logically she doesn't know why they would. Her emotions probably stem from her culpability in the death of a different man.

Talia says, "I'm just not sure how to move forward. With Gus's projects. With our clients. At the company..."

"That's why we're having this lunch. I don't want you to tell the clients he died, right off the bat. I don't care what Brighton's direction is. I think it will hurt our image. But I also want you to feel out whether they already know about the accident. Especially, Ms. Svensson. If it's clear the customer has already heard, then a different sympathetic approach should be taken."

Ah, she's already gunning for the Navy Yard project...

"How do you suggest doing this, exactly?" Priya asks. "The feeling out part?"

"I've been thinking all morning. How about saying something like... there's been a change of guard due to promotion and reshuffling, and—Neve Crawford or Shephard Kingsley—pick the right owner of the account, has been reassigned to—insert name of job—and will now be handling your project. I'd love to set up a virtual or in person meet and greet to solidify this partnership." Neve smiles as if she's very pleased with herself.

"So, reshuffling can pass as death?" Talia asks.

"Do you have a word that might fit better given the circumstances?" Neve asks.

"Not off the top of my head. I haven't been thinking about the same things as you all morning," Talia says.

Priya's face screams—*yikes*. It's going to take readjustment not throwing knives at Neve every chance she gets.

"I'm sorry, Neve. I'm not one to move on so quickly. Still processing," Talia says.

"You're right. I shouldn't be talking strategy yet." Neve pulls a tube of lip gloss out of her Chloe bag and reapplies it, using her phone camera as a mirror.

Talia's so shocked she almost falls off her chair. Neve admitted she was wrong. Maybe she isn't so bad, just overly focused with climbing the corporate ladder. Talia will try a little harder to be affable, she supposes.

Priya says, "Enough work talk. Why don't we find out something about each other? Do you girls have siblings? What's your favorite ice cream flavor?"

Oh Lord. This must be what a first date with Priya is like. No wonder she's single.

Drinks are served to break up Priya's lame *icebreaker*. They all ordered mimosas.

Well, at least they have one thing in common.

"I'll start..." Priya continues. "I love raspberry sorbet."

That's not even ice cream.

"I'll play," Neve says. She takes a sip of her afternoon drink. "I have a brother. He's an excellent athlete and overachiever. He makes me look tame." Her face turns sour, and I can picture holidays at the Crawford household rife with competition and spite. "And... mint chocolate chip."

They both turn their attention toward her.

Talia flips her hair off her shoulder and sighs. The sooner she can make this lunch end, the sooner she can get back to

Shep and her pile of new work. "My turn. No siblings here, which is good because I don't like to share."

Priya's face pinches at her comment. Talia's selfishness is a consequence of constantly having things taken away from her. "And butter pecan." She shrugs, not sure if she really even likes that flavor. She can't remember the last time she ate ice cream, and it just shows how juvenile Priya is to ask such a question.

Priya perks up and claps her manicured hands together. "I'm the oldest of three girls. I have one sister in law school, one in pre-med, and I guess I'm following my dad's footsteps in corporate America."

Talia wants to cough into her mimosa—*guess you took the easy road*—but doesn't. *Play nice, Talia. Play nice!*

"How's Shep, Tal? You two looked cozy this morning," Neve says.

Great, Neve did see the hallway peck. "He has one brother. His favorite flavor is Oreo ice cream."

Neve raises her eyebrows. "Come on now. I know you two were in a funk earlier this week. I wore it all over my shirt. Remember?"

"I offered to get that dry-cleaned," Talia defends. Neve doesn't speak, still waiting for her answer. "He's fine, actually, really good. We worked it out. Shep agreed not to talk to his ex anymore, only through the court-appointed lawyer. He also admitted to the fact that Emerson was interfering with our relationship."

"Good, I want that for you. For your relationship to be solid and free of drama. Then you won't be distracted at work."

Priya glares at Talia again, and they're both quickly reminded of who Neve cares about most—Neve.

Lunch wasn't as painful as it could've been in the end. They formed a sort of work truce and clinked their glasses together in a sorority-girl way that made Talia's insides turn in her stomach. She's not a sorority-gal type.

But she knows she should give this new alliance a try. Brighton is like the TV show *Survivor* where only the smartest endure the office politics. Although the analogy hits her differently today as she must choose her allies, and hope no one else actually dies.

She can't wait to tell Shep all about her lunch.

He'll be utterly amused to hear about her first date with Neve and Priya, and their favorite ice cream flavors.

She strides to his office full of pep and stops when she sees he has his door shut, save a sliver. He usually leaves it wide open. He says it makes him seem more "approachable." Shep tries to project a certain easygoing vibe at work, but he's as over-ambitious as the rest of them.

She can see through his window that he has his back to her, sitting straight up in his black leather swivel chair. She slides up to the cracked door and listens to what's got him on edge.

"I never heard my phone ring, Emerson."

Emerson.

"I only checked my messages at lunchtime. We've had a horrible morning. Someone died at a job site. It wasn't even a construction worker, it was a project manager. Like me. One of my coworkers..."

"Well, thank you... Thank you so much. It's nice to hear that."

It's nice, is it? Is she consoling him?

I'll kill her.

"Okay, I appreciate it, but I want to talk to you about your hospital stay. Did you have any injuries? Right." Shep sighs long and hard. "Do you think it was... Uh huh. And who're you staying with now? Brooks? Doesn't he have girlfriend of the week who's upset about that arrangement?"

Long pause. Lot of explanation. *Why is he talking to her for so long?*

"Right. Okay, I'm glad you told me. And I'll pull for you to have our scheduled hearing despite this minor setback. Right, good luck, take care."

She's sure he's hung up before she lightly raps on the door.

"Come in." He doesn't look up right away when she steps inside.

"Shep, who was that?"

He startles in his seat. "Talia. I thought you were at lunch with the girls." He says this as if it's a common occurrence, and he hasn't just been caught red-handed. She's suddenly reminded of the first time they hooked up and how easily he went home to his wife afterward. He's a practiced liar. But he won't lie to her.

"We're back now. Who. Was. That?" she asks.

He knows she knows now, and his stalling question was a way to *feel her out*. Talia should've held back her anger to see how long he would've lied to her, but it's too late now.

"Emerson. She was hospitalized. She called me in the middle of the night and left me a message, but I just saw it now."

Talia gnaws on the inside of her cheek. How didn't she hear the phone ring? She usually has ears like a well-tuned bat. And why is Emerson calling Shep? She's not his responsibility anymore.

"Why was she hospitalized?"

"Someone broke into her apartment. They choked her. Hurt her throat. But her roommate walked in, thank God."

"Oh my, yes, thank goodness. Did her roommate see the man? Did they get a description?"

Shep looks away, out the window at the city. He rakes his

fingers over his face in frustration. "Can we not do all the questions right now? I'm a little worn out on inquisitions at the moment. While you ladies were out, the cops interviewed us one by one. They'll probably be back to get your statement."

Is he serious? Two evenings ago, he promised he wouldn't talk to Emerson. It was a huge fight. Their biggest ever. Now he doesn't want to be questioned about it.

"I'm just wondering if it's possible that she imagined this man. Not unlike the man she imagined when your daughter—"

"Don't, Talia! Not today..."

The hair rises on the back of her neck because she didn't close the door all the way and she knows others probably heard him yell at her. She balls her fists at her sides. "You were supposed to tell her you were only speaking to her through a court-appointed attorney. You promised me," she whispers.

"And when would I have gotten the chance? I certainly couldn't do it today."

"Who's Brooks? Is that the dude from the pictures? Already shacking up?" She can't help saying things to piss him off. He just roasted her royally.

"No. Brooks Stauffer. An old friend from school who lives in the city. He picked her up from the hospital."

It makes Talia wrinkle her nose that Emerson is so close. A train ride away. She was safer in her dump in Hartford.

"I see. Well, my expectations are that the next time you speak to her you make the boundaries we discussed clear. Very Clear." Talia leaves the office and shuts the door behind her.

Neve's eyes are all over her when she leaves.

It's like she's always watching her.

TWENTY-FIVE

EMERSON

I sit at Brooks's thick and smooth dining room table—marble or quartz. I wonder how someone with such exquisite taste can make such poor decisions.

Although, how would he know the art supplies could be used as weaponry?

Sure, sharp-pointed pencils would normally not be allowed at Meadowbrook, but there's only so much damage you can do with those.

I can't for the life of me, or the woman who died, remember what I did with that palette knife. The knife was there, and then it wasn't. Irrelevant to me and my creative needs, I didn't notice it was gone when I packed my supplies away that day and hid them beneath my mattress.

Shep used to complain that I often half-assed it when it came to cleaning up after the kids. He'd find missing shoes and binkies crammed beneath the sofa. I tried to explain that I never saw them when tidying up, but his favorite response was—"No you didn't look, there's a difference."

In this case, he's right. I didn't look.

"Shit, Brooks." How can a human being be so good and bad at the same time?

In the center of the table sits a copy of a hardback book called *The In Between*, with a receipt sticking out of the cover, just purchased today.

I page through it and quickly discover it's a non-fiction resource for understanding dreaming and nightmares. Brooks must've bought it for me. I should grab it and get the hell out of there, but too often I've let Brooks get away with things unquestioned—the boy who was paralyzed after the car accident and the bee sting, the missing attorney. But this time another person is involved who I care about deeply.

Joanna cannot lose her job because of me. I have to at least ask Brooks to tell his side of the story. And warn him about Officer Ramsey.

He won't be home for a few more hours.

I've already read a lot of resources on what happens when we dream and this book seems to have more of the same:

"RBD. Sleep Behavior Disorder, affecting two per cent of the adult population, mostly men."

I feel so unlucky to be an outlier.

"REM. Rapid Eye Movement. Dreams happen in stage 'R', about ninety minutes after you fall asleep."

That's not when mine usually occur.

"Sleep terrors occur during non-REM sleep and are less predictable, specifically during slow-wave sleep."

No one can help me prevent this because they don't know when they'll strike.

"Sleep Studies have proven to be ineffective."

You're telling me.

"Sleep Apnea can cause oxygen deprivation and hallucinations."

I tested for that and—don't have it.

I page through each of these usual suspects with ease, but am stopped by one in the middle.

A new word—Hypnagogia—jumps out.

"It's the transitional state between wakefulness and sleep. Up to seventy percent of people experience hallucinations during this state."

That's higher than I've read in other resources. Makes me feel less of an anomaly.

"There are different brain waves that occur during this time: delta, theta, alpha, beta, and gamma. Beta is predominant. When you become drowsy, Alpha takes over."

I imagine my brain is an ocean, the pink tissue folding over each other in five ripples. Beta is low tide. Alpha is high tide.

During this period your sense of here and now transitions from the real world to the dream world. Some of history's smartest minds have used Hypnagogia on purpose to tap into their creativity—Thomas Edison, Edgar Allan Poe, and Salvador Dali used to nap with a steel ball in their hands so that they would wake when the ball hit the floor. They wished the visions and hallucinations on themselves to inspire their work.

I sit back in shock. Thinking of the bizarre yet intriguing paintings of the artist Salvador Dali, all of the shapes and figures mixed up and put back together in strange places. The brilliant colors. Abstract.

There are people who try to reach the same mental state that's ruined my entire life, on purpose. I wonder if those artists learned how to control it, or if they never wanted to contain it in the first place. It's as I suspected. Fixing the broken wire in my brain would shut off the only gift God has ever given me—creator.

To mend one part is to shut off another. I had a guidance counselor tell me once that no one is ever given an extraordinary gift—art, music, extreme intelligence—without sacrificing something else—personality, aptitude, social awareness, and I get it more now.

My mind is an ocean. I see my children, two and five, sitting at the shoreline. A wave pulls at their tiny feet... *Don't sit too close.*

———

When Brooks returns from Ayada with Chicken Pad Thai—#6 for heat—just how I like it, I wonder if Shep knows my preferred Pad Thai spice number. I'm sure he probably doesn't.

These are the little things that make it hard to be angry with Brooks.

The thoughtful gifts. The way he understands me the way other people do not. How he pays attention to everything I care about, small and large. It's the fabric which makes friendships, understanding the details of how we're woven.

"Thank you." I take my white Styrofoam container and chopsticks and enjoy the moment. Each one with Brooks is like being in a fantasy world. One where I'm given clean spaces to live: salon-worthy treatments, my favorite food, and education on subjects to help me.

Most people just try to shove pills down my throat to get me to shut up.

"You're welcome. So... how was your day?" Brooks asks, unraveling his own container of food.

"Interesting. I walked the High Line and talked to an old friend."

"Nice. How're you feeling?" He motions toward my neck.

"I'm sore, but okay."

"I thought about decreasing your heat level on the order, and then decided you'd be disappointed if I did."

"You'd be right about that." I take a forkful of noodles in my mouth and savor the peanuts and bean sprouts a moment before I chew. "Mmm."

"You make that sound a lot since you've been here," he says, a wolfish grin on his face.

I smile. "I bet that vibration is implanted in these walls. It's like a library of female sounds of pleasure."

Brooks laughs. "My own library of risqué female expressions. Sounds very *Fifty Shades of Gray*. Did you make that sound on your date the other night, Emerson?"

I cough—a little spice, a little embarrassment coming out with it. "Maybe. It's a process, trying to live again after being in the dark for so long. It's like experiencing everything for the first time again."

"So, who's the guy who took your virginity the other night? Because he's just replaced me."

I nearly spit out my food. "His name is Jacob. And no one can replace you."

"That's more like it... Did you find the book I left for you?"

"I did. You didn't have to—"

"That one is supposed to be good. I've actually been searching online for the best resource, and then I found it at the bookstore on my lunchbreak."

I pick up the book with gratitude and almost don't want to say anything to him about his first present—the one found in the body of a woman at a mental hospital.

This makes it so hard.

Not only did he buy the book because he thought it might help me, but he researched it first. It might seem like a small gesture to most, but it's huge to me. Why does he have to be so thoughtful and corrupt at the same time? I just want to see the good. I always have.

"I have something else for you." Brooks pulls an item in a black sleeve from his work backpack and places it on the table.

"What's in here?" I pat the felted pouch. "If I reach inside will I pull out a rabbit?"

"Not a rabbit. A taser," he says.

I pull out the plastic device shaped like a flashlight, yellow buttons on the side, metal ports on the top as well as an actual light.

Brooks places his hands in the air. "Don't try it on me, please. It's pretty self-explanatory. Just aim at your target within fifteen feet and hit the button, and about one hundred thousand volts of electricity will be delivered to your victim."

I smirk at the harmful "flashlight" with interest. Shep didn't allow weapons of any sort in our house. I've often wondered what would've happened if we had one. If I would've made different actions the day Thea died—if she'd still be alive.

"Wow, what an electrifying gift. Truly shocking."

He laughs at my bad jokes. "I bought it for you because you can't kill yourself with it. But if anyone bothers you again, I want you to use it on them. I worry about you out there all alone. Especially after what happened."

"Thank you for believing me that something *did* happen. You're in the minority."

He nods. "And no more random dates. Before you go out with anyone, you give me their name and I'll do a background check..."

I giggle at him, sure he's joking.

"No bullshit, Emerson. You've been out of the dating game a long time. I've seen way too many terrible things happen to unsuspecting women. Social media and the Internet make us all too accessible."

"I'm done dating for a while." I rub my hand over my neck, remembering Jacob's rough hands. *Could he have strangled me? Because I rejected him?* "And thank you for wanting to protect me."

If I get stuck in this loop of gratitude with Brooks, I'll never be able to get out and ask him the hard questions. He's gifted me right out of confrontation before.

At Culver, Brooks actually gave me a diamond tennis bracelet. We'd been arguing, but he said the effortless beauty of the bracelet reminded him of me. Either way I stopped fighting with him after that. But I'm older now. I can't be bought.

"I'll keep it next to my art supplies. I heard those can be deadly too."

I look up at him to see if he grasps the inference, but he just has a goofy smile on his face. "Okay. You don't ask what I do with my toys and I'll try to do the same."

He's got a response for everything. *Lawyer.* He's not going to give up the information willingly.

"The old friend I talked to today was my therapist from Meadowbrook."

He bites on his noodles, nodding at me. "I thought... you weren't supposed to speak with her."

He's brought that up twice now. Is he worried he'll be found out? I'm not sure what for, but it wouldn't surprise me if he's gotten himself into something.

"I'm not, but my therapist, Joanna, has helped me tremendously, and she's in peril of losing her job. It seems the patient who was admitted after me committed suicide inside Meadowbrook."

Brooks stops chewing. "That's awful."

"She... used something I accidentally left behind. She was admitted to my old room."

Brooks shakes his head. "You can't blame yourself, Emerson. They should've been watching her, and they should've checked the room. This is not on you."

But it could be on you.

"Brooks, the tool used was the palette knife you gave me in the art kit."

Brooks drops his fork. "What?"

Now I feel horribly guilty. I was so sure Brooks was in on it, but even the best of actors can't fake the look of astonishment on his face right now. He turns the color of ashen tree bark.

My first instinct is to protect him—like always.

"The officer saw your name on the visitor log. I'm so sorry, but they're investigating the case. I'd expect a call or visit from an Officer Ramsey."

"Shit. I think someone is trying to get me in trouble," he says, and there's more fear in his voice than I've ever heard.

I'm scared for Brooks.

But even more so, I'm scared for the person trying to do him wrong.

TWENTY-SIX
TALIA

As Talia straps Leo into his booster seat like every other day, she wonders what Shep would do if he didn't have her. He'd have to hire a nanny.

Maybe that's all Talia is to him. The babysitter. A roommate to help cut costs. It's a reflection of her mother's romantic relationships. Although she took every shift she could, they still never seemed to have any money. Her quickest fix was to fall into a relationship with a man to financially help her out.

The cherry roots of Talia's hair tingle and itch. This was not the plan...

She doesn't want Shep to rely on her like that. Or the other way round.

She wants him to want her. Need her. To love her. The way a man loves a woman—a wife. And she wants Shep to see her for what she is—Leo's mother.

"Tell me something good that happened today," she says to Leo.

"Uh... how about something bad."

Oh no. Has Emme Mommy made another phantom appearance. "What is it, Leo?"

"We learned they took a planet away."

"What do you mean they took one away?" Talia asks. This little boy has her heart. He's smart and sweet, an even mix of creativity and smarts. He has Shep's dark hair and sense of humor. Loving Leo is pretty easy, and she's not willing to walk away from him just because she's hit a rough patch with his father.

"Pluto. They took it away," Leo says.

"Oh... I heard they demoted Pluto. What is it now? Just a star?"

"What's remoted?" he asks.

"De-moted. It means when you're moved from a higher position to a lower one. Like a planet is a big deal and a star is much smaller." Talia silently steams, unable to separate the planetary comparison from that of her own life. No matter what she does, Shep won't give her the parent card.

And since Emerson's return, she feels like her status in their lives has been downgraded in a cataclysmal way. It doesn't make sense. Neither does Emerson somehow waking up from a long nap and deciding she wants to be a mother again.

No way. Not happening.

Talia has to snuff Emerson out before she gets to Leo.

He appears perplexed at the moment, his brow scrunched up making little kid wrinkles on his forehead.

"What's wrong, Buddy?"

"Oh. It's not... a star. I'm trying to remember what our teacher said Pluto is now." He sighs, and he's so stinking cute she can hardly stand it.

"I'll look it up for you later. Promise. Do you think Dad would rather eat eggplant parmesan or eggplant and red pepper pizza tonight?"

"Eggplant parm tastes like feet. Too snaily."

Ah... she should've guessed he'd say that. "I didn't know you didn't like it. You should've told me."

She's about to voice-text Shep to ask him when he'll be home when he beats her to it.

Won't make it back until late again. Sorry. Things here are still tense.

Talia almost throws the phone. Instead, because she has Leo in the car, she gently sets it down.

"What's wrong, Talia?" Leo can tell she's upset.

Because they know each other. The way two people who have formed a bond can read body language. The way family does.

"Daddy can't make it home for dinner," she says.

"Again?" His voice sounds wilted and defeated. "But it's the weekend."

"Work has been..." she says. And then she tries to think about why it was busy just before Gus's death.

They'd just found out Wickerham fell through. Gus was running around that day and Shep said he had business to attend to when he came home late.

Talia thought maybe he'd shown up after nine o'clock just to prove a point. She never questioned him because he'd confronted her about her false girl's night with Priya. She was so busy defending her lie about sneaking around at night that she never asked him what business could he have to tend to.

Shep had had a Wickerham blueprint tube with him, dirty fingerprints smudging the outside...

Then there was today.

She'd waved at Shep through his closed office door, motioning to her watch, signaling she was leaving to grab Leo. Talia was fine to leave, but all of the supervisors were forced to stay. There were NYPD officers in there questioning Shep at the time. She never stopped to ask why they hadn't let him go yet. She thought it protocol given that the accident happened at a jobsite. But maybe not.

Suddenly, she has lots of questions.

They pull up to a red light. Talia fires Shep a quick text.

That's too bad. Are you still at Brighton? Cops still there?

Yes.

Perfect.

"Hey, Leo. Would you like me to see if Kai's mom would like to have you over tonight? They have a new puppy, and she mentioned to me that Fridays she only works half days."

"Ya! I'd love to meet Ranger," he says.

She can finally see a smile in the reflection of her rearview mirror.

Talia texts Sharon Young, Kai's mom, knowing that, while it was generally rude to try to schedule a playdate last minute on a Friday night, Sharon's only too happy to provide her only child some companionship. It's one of the reasons Talia thinks Kai and Leo are best friends.

Although Leo reminded Kai once, he wasn't always an only child.

He had a sister once.

———

Talia was able to not only negotiate a puppy playdate, but a sleepover for Leo at Kai's house before she drove home and quickly changed into black yoga pants and a dark hoodie.

Now she's stuck on the parkway on a Friday night remembering how different her life was only two short years ago, before organizing playdates and sleepovers. Back when she could skip out of work to a neighboring happy hour hoping she'd meet someone interesting that night.

She'd sit there with her single glass of prosecco, bubbles rising to the top, dreaming of the life she had right now. A quaint home outside of the city with a family and a man who loved her dearly.

It's all she ever wanted, really. Everything she never had.

Emerson didn't deserve Shep.

She grew up with the world at her fingertips and let it all slip away. She probably never really appreciated it to begin with. Shep just pitied her because her parents died when she was *young*.

When Talia talked about where she came from, she felt as though she was just reminding him that she wasn't good enough for him.

Talia parks her car in a residential area near the lot, but it's the kind of close-knit suburban town that makes her feel like someone, somewhere, might be observing her. She meanders along the sidewalk, mindful of any looky-loos peeking through the windows or cameras that might be tethered to a pole.

Most of the citizens are probably just learning about the deadly accident on the news that occurred at the construction site down the street from their homes. She tiptoes into the parking lot, careful to not let the spotlights catch her movement.

The freshly started construction project sits like the inside of a half-molded globe. It hunches over the Hudson River, the open side facing the water, as if waiting for its other half. Yellow caution tape ropes the entire perimeter, the emergency vehicles long gone.

Long flaps of plastic smack her in the face as she enters the building. This is where Shep was the night he didn't come home. He had the prints for the building. There's no other explanation for why he'd need them unless he was there, at the jobsite, inspecting something. But why?

Talia uses her phone's flashlight to navigate the inside, dusty concrete bits making her cough as she finds what she's looking for. One spot on the otherwise dirty floor is completely clean and smells of strong chemicals.

This is where Gus's body must've been discovered.

The crime scene crew has already been in with their solvents to rid the bodily fluids from the cement.

Talia kneels beside it, fighting the urge to touch the surface where her boss landed after his fall.

After Glen died, Talia found herself running her fingers over the wooden siding of her home—over and over again. She read somewhere that blood can never totally be eradicated from wood. Even after extensive cleaning, traces of it can still be found. She lived for years in fear of the wood-paneled walls that lined her mother's house—the secrets they held.

She looks above her at the scaffolding.

The beams that crisscross and bend form a dome that will house a thousand little projected stars to mimic the solar system. She thinks about the fact that Pluto is missing, and how future generations won't learn about it—and how sad that is.

How things can exist, and then one day someone decides they're not valid anymore and they just disappear. She's in danger of the same thing happening to her place in Shep and Leo's life. She's also worried for Shep's existence. Something is wrong with how hard the authorities are looking at his involvement in the Brighton investigation; she can just feel it.

While it's normal for police to investigate, everything about today seemed exaggerated. The conference room shuffle, the urgency to go back to work as usual, the fact that Shep is still being looked at—*why?*

Why else would he have returned so late the same night Gus died?

Where else could he have gone other than this very project site that they were in peril of losing? Scratch that—the site they'd already lost. He had no other pending deals. No other client appointments. She didn't smell the scent of another woman on him, but if he'd thought she'd been messing around with someone else, she didn't think it beneath him to settle the score. Could he have gone to see... Emerson?

She regularly checks his phone, his socials, his emails when he isn't looking, and she hasn't found anything of interest lately. Considering how they came together the first time, while he was still married, she doesn't fully trust him not to stray again, but it seemed more likely he'd come here to investigate.

She knows it's dangerous, but she stands up and walks over to the scaffolding and begins climbing to the top. Her legs are muscled from all the time she's spent lifting at the gym and she's able to hoist herself with ease.

But when she arrives at the top, she's swallowed by a black hole. Talia teeters on the uneven boards and grabs onto the metal sides. The whole building opens into the Hudson like a clamshell. The circular lilt of the building makes her feel like she's pitching forward even though she's standing completely straight. The water gleams like a dark snake winding in the night. It would be so easy to make one misstep, end it all.

Talia's been a little obsessed with death ever since Glen.

The moments leading up to it.

What runs through a person's mind right before they perish? Are they just afraid or are they thinking about all the people they'll leave behind? Is there some relief to ending their pain?

She inhales deeply, coughing a bit at the dust particles. She can totally understand how someone could've accidentally fallen from up here.

Gus complained Five Star wasn't building things to code. He was obviously checking for himself, but what happened?

Gus had his hard hat with him when he left. He was prepared to get his hands dirty. Talia shines her light on the area below, where Gus fell about thirty feet. She heard his neck snapped when he landed. She hoped he didn't suffer.

She strokes the wires holding the scaffolding in place, over-stimulated by thoughts of life and death and what Shep would do to her on this scaffolding to make it sway this way and that.

She pulls her hand away from the roping and her fingers come away with a residue. She wipes it on the white T-shirt she has on underneath her hoodie; and from her cell phone's light, she can see that it's dark and inky, like grease.

She grabs the wire again and almost loses her balance. Her phone slips from her grasp, her breath catching in her throat. Moments later, she hears her cell shatter into a million pieces below her. "*Shit.*"

Her heart races in her ear as she's plunged into complete blackness. She tries to remind herself that she's not leaning forward, it's just the structure of the building making her think that she is.

She closes her eyes and opens them again, less unsteady than before, but it's not the darkness or the height that's got her in a tizzy.

The only thing she can see is her bright white shirt and the black smudge.

She's seen it before.

On Shep's face—and on the blueprint tube he was holding —the night he came home late.

TWENTY-SEVEN
EMERSON

My belongings are boxed up for me and waiting on the stripped clean (well sort of) mattress. Georgie isn't there to see me off, but she did pick up all of my drawings and lay them neatly on top of my art kit beside the boxes. Or at least someone did.

It's sad for us to part this way.

Before I got sick, I had hopeful daydreams of how my adult friendships would turn out, although I was notorious for never doing anything to foster them. I thought once I left the halfway house, Georgie and I would keep in touch, maybe even grab a coffee or lunch once a year; two people from different worlds bonded over our unfortunate circumstances.

But that's not going to happen now.

I pop open the art kit and run my hand over the empty slot where the palette knife used to be. It's not unusual that I didn't notice it was gone, but the recess in the packaging beneath my fingertips leaves me unmoored.

Did that woman really kill herself with a dull palette knife?

The thought makes me silently retch in my mouth. Or did someone have her killed? And why?

Brooks was able to find me employment closer to Leo, and

even though it's not my dream job, I'll take it. He also rented me a car for the day so I can motor to my new apartment. Rent is covered for one month, by him, and then I have to figure it out on my own. All this was his final parting gift to me before I left. He said he couldn't join me to move in because he had—*things to attend to*.

The chill his eyes left me with is lasting and worrisome. I've seen it before. The determination to right someone else's wrong —at all costs.

And I'm concerned his *things* mean more bodies will soon be found.

I close the kit and place it inside one of the taped-up boxes, refastening it as best I can with the masking tape provided. My hands tremble at the weight of it all, my heaviest items—photo albums, self-help books, my sketches. My father once said that whatever you invest in is what you'll be left with in the end. It's one of the reasons he bought the summer home. So he'd have something to leave behind.

I miss him now. He was never warm, but he gave great advice. Mother was cold and the way she comforted was equally deadening. She just didn't want to have an embarrassment for a daughter, and gave up on helping me advance in life when she realized disappointment was inevitable—at least by her standards.

And he was right. All I have left is what is in this box—what I invested in. Wedding and baby albums depicting a life I'm trying to reclaim, self-help books to assist me on my way, sketches to fund the effort.

I could use some of my father's guidance now.

My trunk is popped open on the curb, and I'm not encouraged that broad daylight will sway anyone from stealing my precious items. I fumble with the large box as I place it in the rear of the SUV Brooks rented for me. He got it to accommodate any larger items of mine, but I don't have much.

How can I help but forgive him after everything he's done and everything he's about to do? No one else is looking out for me. I'd give him leniency for just about anything.

A man strides warily near my vehicle, shifting back and forth from one foot to another, as if he can't decide whether he wants to cross the street or do the Irish Jig. As he approaches me, I notice he finally settles on his left leg and that he has a pronounced limp on his right.

"You Emerson Wilder?" he asks. His shifty demeanor extends beyond his defunct leg. His face twists to the side, the scruff on his face uneven, as if he didn't have the care or where-withal to give himself a proper shave.

"Who's asking?" I slam the trunk shut and lock it with my key fob.

"I've been trying to get in touch with you for a while, Miss Wilder. Am I catching you at a bad time?" he asks.

"I'm afraid so. I'm moving today. What can I help you with? Mr...?"

"Bessler. Kent Bessler." He extends his palm.

I wipe my hands on my jeans and shake his hand. "Hi, I received your emails. I'm sorry you made the trip down here, Mr. Bessler, but I'm still not interested in selling right now."

"I see... Well, I'm glad you're doing well. It took me so long to find your residence. It looks like I caught you just in time."

He motions to my vehicle, and I'm officially on alert. Why was he trying to *find my residence*? "I need to be on my way now, but can I ask why you're so intrigued with my family's property?"

He nods, as if he's happy I asked. "I sent you a link in the email. Did you click on it?"

I shake my head. "I haven't. I've been a little busy."

"Okay. I didn't think so. That's why I came down here. I am interested in the property, but I was also checking on you."

The back of my neck tickles the way it used to when I lived

in the city and walked through Central Park alone as the sun began its descent. Why would this strange country man be checking on me? "I'm doing well. I'm actually relocating to a nicer apartment." I gesture to the shithole behind me. If he's in the business of Real Estate he must realize any move from this place is a step up.

"Great. Listen... Can you do me a big favor? When you get some downtime, can you please click the link I sent you. It's about your house. You'll want to give it a quick look." He smiles, overeager.

"Sure." I'll say anything to get him to go away.

Thankfully, he starts to backpedal. "And then let me know if you change your mind about selling." I can already feel the heightened anxiety I experienced in his presence dissipate with each footfall he takes in the opposite direction.

"Send me a message when you do!" he shouts back.

"Alrighty. Bye now?" I wave him along as he crosses the street, climbs into an old Ford pickup truck, and drives away.

New Haven is a half hour closer to Leo, with a bus and train line direct to Stamford—the city where the dragon has my family trapped in a cement box.

The new apartment in the Fairhaven neighborhood leaves a lot to be desired. The tall stacked units that Shep and I used to refer to as—soul collectors—are my new home. At least it's an unshared space. And it's uninspiring, but a judge will consider it a "permanent residence."

My surroundings used to be so important to me.

Now I'm in a shoebox apartment, but at least it's within walking distance to the printing press where I'll be working. Brooks said it would still keep me connected to books and that I could use the experience on my resume when it was time for me to approach literary agents or publishers again. Plus, it's an hour ride on the train to reach Leo.

Brooks thought of everything so I didn't have to. I don't know how people reengage into society without family or a support system. It's like trying to play the game of life with a whole set of different rules, and they're all against you.

Once I've made it up the seven flights of stairs with the last box, heaving it onto the floor, I lock the door behind me, slide down the wall to the chipped linoleum floor. I need a break.

But as soon as I stop moving, there's one thing that plays on my mind more than my new shabby digs.

Kent Bessler's link.

I just don't understand why he'd make the effort to come all the way down here and find me...

I open my email, click on it, and fall down the rabbit hole that leads to Kent's eerie website. He's not a Real Estate investor, as I originally suspected. That doesn't surprise me after meeting him though. Nothing about him screams salesman or—*I'm here to put you in the 4-bedroom ranch of your dreams.*

Nope, Kent Bessler is a paranormal researcher. And he has a whole online show where he livestreams regularly. It says here he began his work after the suspicious disappearance of his stepson in the 1980s. I remember hearing rumblings about the child when I summered in Thompson, Connecticut. I think the boy was nine or ten at the time, rode his bike down some backroad and was never seen again.

Most people assumed he was abducted or attacked by an animal (human or otherwise), his remains dispersed in a way that couldn't be found. But for some reason Kent has apparently been on a kick for all these years that something otherworldly took him.

He gained some notoriety a number of years back for cleansing a house which was so haunted it rained indoors. There is a very complimentary testimonial from the woman involved—although who knows?—those can always be fake. There's been nothing of notable mention on his site since then. My guess is he's a man desperate to make sense of his stepson's disappearance.

We use different things to self-soothe. Mine just comes in the form of pencils and paper.

But then I see the link for my house and a plea to me personally to sell my property to him so he can live-steam his Internet segments from there. *What in the world?*

There's an equally perplexing article titled: "Wilder than Fiction."

I click on it. They warned us in therapy about staying away from social media thirst traps when we returned to the land of the living. But as I peruse the site, further down the hole I tumble...

WILDER THAN FICTION
BY KENT BESSLER

Nestled in the heart of charming rural Thompson, Connecticut, the Wilder house sits like an abandoned monstrosity. The white structure looms atop a forgotten hillside, white paint hanging from the exterior like the loose skin of its victims.

How can a house have victims, you may ask?

Great question. Well, I think this one certainly does.

The first owners, Michelle and Ernest Whitten, Ernest a welder by trade, both died inside the house. The circumstances are murky. They were both in poor health and succumbed to natural causes and, unfortunately, were found in the home weeks after their demise.

The house was deemed a hazard zone.

It's said that a special team was brought in to clean it out, but sparks could still be seen through the window of the top floor at night, representing Ernest's welding torch. The house sat unsold for months, until hedge fund manager Dawson Wilder and his wife, Siobhan Wilder, overlooked the house's eerie history and bought it for their summer retreat from their sprawling estate in Westport.

For years, the Wilders summered uneventfully in the home, until their daughter, Emerson, had a sleepover with three other twelve-year-old girls. The girls played with a Ouija board, a candle fell over, and the house caught fire. All escaped with minor injuries, but what has happened to everyone since then is troubling.

One child from the party is dead.

One is battling a chronic disease.

And the third suffers from post-traumatic stress disorder stemming from the fire.

Both of Emerson's parents died in a car crash on a perfectly sunny day.

And Emerson Wilder has been committed to a mental institute after her involvement in an accident that killed her infant child.

Tell me it's not the house now...

TWENTY-EIGHT

TALIA

Her cell phone sits on the passenger seat like shrapnel from the aftermath of a postapocalyptic bomb, the glass on the front completely shattered, the broken circuit boards pouring out in green and black digital guts.

No one can reach her. Not Shep on his way home from work. Or Sharon Young if Leo needs something.

It's a miracle she was able to climb down the scaffolding in the pitch darkness after she dropped it, using only her hands and feet to feel her way along. Someone who didn't grow up in a way where they had to fight to survive might've not had the steel nerves to accomplish such a feat.

People like Gus.

But Shep made it down the scaffolding...

That's the thing she's convinced of. Shep was at the jobsite the night Gus died.

And now that she sits in complete silence on her drive back, not a text message or social media alert to distract her, she has space to think. There's only one person at Brighton who was motivated for the Wickerham project to fail.

Sure, Shep put up a good front, but that's all it was—a false facade.

Shep didn't want the company to secure that deal.

If they did, Gus would most certainly be promoted. Because he was the lead on it. And if Brighton didn't get it, Shep still had a chance.

Then Gus, learning there was a possible way back in after hearing about Five Star's fumble, rushed to the site in Yonkers to see for himself. And to take his project back without disclosing much to the rest of his team.

If he pulled it off, Gus would be a star. Connie could start counting her escrow.

But just how desperate was Shep to receive the title of senior architect?

Enough that, catching wind of the situation, he followed Gus, to make sure the deal wasn't salvaged? To keep himself as the next in line to be promoted?

"Shep, what did you do?" she whispers out loud.

He told her he felt as though his daughter's death set him back ten years, in every way. How hard would he fight to reclaim what he thought should've been his?

She's positive he didn't drive down to the construction site with the intention of ending Gus's life, but she knows how things can spin out of control in the face of opposition and aggression.

Did Shep and Gus have an argument? Did Shep use the unsafe environment to his advantage? Did Gus threaten him, leaving Shep no other choice but to give him a shove?

Talia holds her breath at the thought until her lungs burn and her ears practically bleed. She knows what it's like. What it feels like to be cornered by someone who wants to take something from you. And the rash types of decisions that can be made in the face of that kind of fear.

Shep had already lost so much. Would he kill to prevent losing more?

———————

Talia's oddly happy she sees Shep's car when she pulls into the driveway. She wants him to ask her where she was.

He must've not been home for long, though, because when she walks through the door he's still dressed for work. He looks absolutely haggard, the half-moon bags below his eyes so darkened, they appear bruised. He sets down his cell phone. "Where the hell have you been? I've been calling you for hours. Where's Leo?"

"He's at Kai's. A sleepover." Talia stands by the door.

She's not afraid of him exactly, but she's also not sure how he will react when she tells him what she knows. She's not mad at him for not telling her about what happened sooner. Talia has secrets of her own. Maybe they can reveal theirs together.

Emerson and Shep are both creators, and Talia often found herself jealous of the fact. She feared there was something missing from their relationship, a connection other couples had that she didn't share with her partner.

She wonders if, once they've told each other their ugliest truths, she would finally feel close to him in the way she hoped. If they will have an unbreakable bond. Much stronger than anything he and *Emerson* had.

"Was a sleepover planned? I don't remember that being on the calendar. And where have you been? You look like you robbed a bank. Why are you dirty?" he asks.

His voice is erratic, the questions so much like rapid fire, she almost ducks. "The sleepover wasn't planned, but Leo wanted to see Kai's new puppy, Ranger. What did the police ask you at Brighton, Shep? Why were you there so long?"

"We had a death at a jobsite, Talia. Connie is suing! The

press are going to be all over this. It's devastating for the company. They had a lot of questions."

She takes a step forward. "Are they coming after you, personally?"

His eyes blaze open. "What? No. Why would they?"

Whew. Good. They don't understand the politics at Brighton, the way Shep could possibly be motivated to end his colleague's life. Hopefully, everyone sees the loss of the Wickerham project as a collaborative failure for the company and all employees involved—including Shep.

"I know, Shep," she says in almost a whisper.

"You know what?" he asks her, and he looks so tired. She can feel his exhaustion. She knows how taxing it is to keep a secret of this magnitude. It's probably the real reason for his brazenness the last few days. Why he couldn't look at her when they were sleeping together the other night.

It was years after Glen's death before she could be in an intimate relationship. Until she could forgive herself for what she'd done. She understands how he feels.

"I know you went to the jobsite the night Gus died."

Shep sways backward as if he's been hit with a gust of wind. "What did you just say?"

She throws her smashed phone on the console table, and then immediately regrets it. If he becomes violent, he'll see that she has no way to call for help. "I was there. I retraced your steps. It's okay. I understand why you did it."

She hopes he'll give her more, tell her everything so that they can move forward together. She'll help him. Talia will cover for him until the day she dies. She'll be that person. No one will be able to break them then.

"W-why do you say that? If you retraced my steps there, others will be able to do the same."

He didn't admit to it, but he didn't *not* admit to it either.

She holds up her hands streaked with black. Even after she

used the wipes in her glove compartment that she keeps for Leo when he dirties himself, it wasn't nearly enough to completely remove the residue. "Scaffolding clip lube. That night you came home late, you had some on your face. You must've missed it when you were cleaning yourself up afterward. It was on the tube you were holding too."

"I don't understand. How did you...?" Shep, stunned, is unable to finish his question.

Talia says, "I went up on the scaffolding to see where Gus fell from. I bet Five Star put too much of the lube on the wires. Rookies. Is that what made Gus slip? I almost did. It's how my phone got destroyed."

Shep gasps. "I don't know... Maybe. You could've died. Why would you do that?"

She takes his hand then, and he examines hers. The lines of black are streaked from her wrist to her manicured nails. "Because I wanted to know what happened. You came home late the night Gus died, but you didn't tell me where you'd been. Shep, I'll be your alibi. I'll say you were here with me. I understand what you're going through. There was an incident when I was growing up... A man died..."

Shep looks at her, shocked. "I didn't know what to do. There was nothing I could do after..." He looks away, petrified. The memory of Gus tumbling to the ground probably more than he can stomach.

She covers his mouth with her hand. "You don't have to tell me the whole story. And I won't tell you mine. That will come over the years... The important thing is the cops don't know you were there. And I won't tell them. I don't care what you did or why. I love you." She says the words she wished someone would've said to her a hundred times over when she was younger. She says the words that set them both free.

"Everything is going to be okay. I love you too," he says. He grabs her and kisses her, deep and slow.

They quickly make it to the bedroom, clothes off. He doesn't turn her around this time, unafraid to be who he is with her now. He peers right in her eyes.

And she can see him for who he is. A man who is flawed and ambitious and tortured and protective of those he loves.

Most importantly, she knows he'll never belong to anyone else now. She's the only one who knows his secrets...

And if he tries to stray, she'll release them all.

TWENTY-NINE
EMERSON

Monday morning brings with it a fresh beginning, and a new job. But as the paper at the press moves from one mechanical plate to the next, hypnotic, I think of Kent and the former residents in Thompson, Connecticut.

As the metal plates clang together, I also try extra, special hard not to imagine my father and mother wrapped around a telephone pole in a cask of steel on a completely clear fall day, just a few months after my college graduation.

As the book jackets flap and turn on the press, it's difficult not to visualize what happened to the Whittens.

Or the three girls who I spent an entire summer with and haven't spoken to since—one of whom is now dead.

During my lunch break, as everyone eats their meals out of colorless insulated bags and don't speak to each other, I read on my phone about Claire Schering—death by drowning on a family vacation off Cape Cod.

It seems the other two, Ella and Jenny, aren't doing well either. Kent said one of the girls has a chronic illness and the other one suffers from a mental disorder. It makes me want to reach out to them—and not. They can't possibly blame me for their bad luck. However, if they've read Kent's article, maybe they do.

I make an effort to shake myself, focusing on details of the press after lunch.

I like the way the white papers pass through the glue dispenser and adhere to the pages, binding them together.

The glossy book cover features a fox and a hen leaping happily off their wooded path to greet me as they run around the conveyor belt, over and over again. This particular title, *The Great Chase*, is a wonderful depiction of animals on the hunt. It's harder to create than it sounds. The illustrator used a two-dimensional pencil drawing for the cover, similar to my style—the outlines thick, the insides wispy to mimic motion—clever.

I enjoyed demonstrating the trouble my character, Silly Suzie, got into with every color in my pencil box. She was the modern day Junie B. Jones, always up to something, and she filled me with excitement.

Here, my work is monotonous yet steady, and my fellow employees quiet, but amicable. Most importantly, I've knocked two things off my list for the upcoming hearing in the last two days.

Employment—done.

Place of residence—done and done.

Certainly, the courts will see my efforts as major progress, so my visitation at the end of the month will be unquestionable. Now all I have to do is share my personal story in therapy, and convince Klinefelter I'm ready for a monitored visit with Leo. I haven't seen him in person since I was in the hospital.

And I have no idea what I'm going to say to him.

———

"Thank you for agreeing to meet me after hours." Maybe if I'm extra nice to Klinefelter he'll grant me my checkmark sooner.

"Certainly. Good to hear you found a job—" he pages through some papers "—at a printing press."

"That's right. They print primarily books. Paperback and hardback. This morning I did a run for a children's book I could've designed myself." I smile at the memory. "And I think the experience, understanding the manufacturing process, will give me extra insight into illustration and the publishing industry in general. Resume builder." These are all Brooks's words coming out of my mouth.

He nods. "Very good. And how much does this job pay?"

"It pays forty-five thousand a year, plus benefits. Not a ton, I realize, but enough to cover my rent and afford the fare to and from Stamford on the bus or the train."

"Eventually, if you want partial custody, you'll have to live in the same school district as your child, or be within geographical range to drive him in every day. I'm assuming you won't be able to afford private transit. I think it's great you found a position in your field. I'm just preparing you for what's ahead."

"Do you think it's not enough? This job?" I ask.

He shrugs. "It will probably be enough for a visitation. They usually want paystubs for at least two months to show stable income, more for custody. You'll only have one for this hearing. It may be enough, but if we don't get it this time, we could prepare for—"

"No. It has to be this time. I want to see my son at the end of the month. I've waited long enough." The sharpness in my own voice surprises me. "It's all I've been focused on. I've been working so hard."

Klinefelter twists his lips. "I understand. I'm not sure that's going to be possible given your most recent hospitalization."

I feel my throat close around my vocal cords. I try to channel Joanna and remember what she told me to say. "Dr. Klinefelter, I only followed your advice about attending the therapy sessions and I think they were a trigger. Or not. The break-in at the halfway house was also in a terrible neighborhood and is still under investigation. I don't think we can make assumptions about what happened that night."

"No one else saw the intruder, Emerson. I'm trying to see this from the court's point of view. What if I release you and you have an overnight with Leo where you think there was a break-in and something happens? Your roommate reported erratic behavior. There was disarray in the room. I have to be certain you're fit to care for your son."

I pull on the hem of my flannel shirt. "Not for this visit! It's supervised. And during the day. Surely the fact that I've established employment, moved on my own, and am sitting here right now talking to you in complete sentences should be enough for a supervised visit. *Please.* I need to see my son."

Klinefelter appears almost sympathetic. "We have one more appointment before the end of the month. I have to think about this long and hard if it's best for Leo to see you right now—at this juncture in your journey. Do you want to talk about this intruder? How it made you feel? Who you believe this person was?"

"I don't want to talk about it. You have the police report." Because if I do talk about it, he'll think I imagined it. It will sound like a carbon copy of the story I told the night my daughter died. And maybe it was a terror. But either way, talking won't help my case. This is why therapy is bad. Sometimes the truth works against you.

"Okay, well, then do you have any other assets? I'm looking ahead, if I push forward visitation and it goes well. It's important to establish financial stability before your court hearing."

"Yes, I have my family's summer home. It's not in great shape, but I actually had a man approach me recently about buying it. He's a paranormal researcher. He wants to tape segments for his Internet show there. It's weird, but a lot of people who've lived in that house have wound up dead."

"Is that right?" Klinefelter asks. *Sensationalist.*

"Yes, he wants to use the house's history as ambience for his show, apparently."

"So he thinks it's... what... haunted?" Klinefelter laughs, and I can't really blame him.

"Perhaps. And he thinks my haunted house is worth fifty-thousand dollars. I can bring in his email with the offer to the courthouse and just use it as leverage if they need to see more assets."

"It's an offer. It's not money in the bank," he says.

I'd love to wipe Klinefelter's smugness right off his face, but I know he's right. "I could just sell it. I could use the money to put a down payment on a decent place for myself and Leo. I'm freaked out about the house's history anyway."

"No, I don't want you selling your property, just yet. It's the only asset you can use if this first hearing falls through. But I do want you to bring the deed if you have it and an appraised value, if possible."

"I can do that." *I think I have that somewhere.*

"Okay, work on that..." He thumbs through some more papers. "And then... I need the sign off from your group therapy." He squints at it, uncertain. "Have you been going? It says you're incomplete here."

"Yes, she wants us to share our experiences before she'll pass us, but I haven't felt comfortable doing that. I will tomorrow. I'm ready. For everything."

Klinefelter's face sours.

"There's something else I want to talk about too," he says, his lips turning down. "Emerson, Meadowbrook made me aware of an incident with your palette knife from an art kit that was brought in but not approved by the hospital."

I play dumb. I can't let him know I spoke to Joanna. "Oh... I noticed the knife was missing from my kit, but not sure how or why that happened."

"It was left behind in your room. Shoved under the mattress. A patient is dead because of it."

"Oh my god." I don't have to fake the shock in my voice. I still can't believe a woman died. In my old room.

"There was something else discovered with the knife." Dr. Klinefelter passes me his phone.

I gasp and almost drop it on the ground. It's a pencil drawing of a man—*the Man*—who's plagued my nightmares.

The one who chased me down the stairwell.

The one who showed up in my bedroom.

I couldn't be sure of what his face looked like before—but I am now.

The paper is unfolded and lightly speckled with tiny flecks of red. *Blood specks from the dead woman?*

Bile rises in my throat. I cover my mouth with my hand. The emotional response the man in this sketch elicits is strong and raw.

The face is drawn entirely in pencil, startling in its realism. His eyes are so angry and demonic, it's hard to look at him, as if his gaze is boring right through me. His laugh lines are filled with slick anger, a stubble on his face that appears as coarse as sandpaper. There are colors in the corners—yellows and oranges—as if he's emerging from a desert with the hot sun behind him. It's hard to believe this man doesn't exist in real life. I feel like I've seen him before, recently, but I can't place where.

Klinefelter's office phone rings. "Excuse me." He picks it up and squabbles something back to who I can only assume is his wife. It seems she didn't get the memo about him working late tonight.

I quickly take a picture of the drawing while Klinefelter is distracted, arguing with his wife in hushed whispers.

He eventually hangs up, frustrated. I hand him back his

phone. "Sorry about that," he says. "Where were we? Do you recognize that picture. Is it yours?"

My heart beats wildly in my chest. "It could be." It's a simple pencil drawing. Any artist could've drawn it. Although, it came from my room. The chances of it not being mine are slim. "I... I don't remember drawing it."

The image gnaws at me. Both the familiarity and something else. But I can't put my finger on it. "Who did you say shared that with you?"

Klinefelter rifles through some papers. "A Justine Blaskowitz."

"She's an intake nurse at Meadowbrook. She's been there forever," I say.

"She must've found it when she was readying the room. When she went to find your file, there was a note to forward everything to me," Klinefelter reveals.

I was hoping Meadowbrook wouldn't offer up incriminating information to Klinefelter—the palette knife, the patient. This.

I guess it's important for disclosure.

But it hinders my chances of seeing Leo again.

"Have you drawn things you haven't remembered before? Perhaps in your sleep? Do you know who this man is?" Klinefelter asks.

I swallow an imaginary gumball in my throat. How do I answer him? Sure, I know who this man is. *He's the man who killed my daughter. He's the man who tried to strangle me the other night.*

But I can't answer that way. Passing the buck on who killed my daughter only makes it sound like I'm not taking accountability and that I'm less likely to care for my other child. "No, I don't know him. And I've never drawn anything in my sleep before."

I've heard of an artist who has. Lee Hadwin had an entire gallery display in south London. But I am not him.

Klinefelter smirks at the picture. "This drawing is quite good. If it's yours."

"I can't be sure it is." He's trying to compliment me into admitting I drew it. Won't work. Although it's likely that I did, something tells me this picture will be admissible in a custody hearing. Klinefelter can serve as witness if I admit that I did or did not draw it. But not if I don't answer him definitively.

Did I draw him? My whole body is chilled.

Did I make this man leap off the pages and come after me in my bedroom in Hartford?

It is slightly reassuring to put a face to the perpetrator—the killer—but more disturbing than anything. I'm ready to crawl out of my skin. It takes every measure of reserve I have to remain seated, calm and collected.

"Okay, I'll see you back next week and we'll discuss final steps."

"Fine, but I want to go for it at the court hearing. The visitation." My voice is wobbly, but he has to understand my intentions are firm.

"Let's see how your first week of work goes. I'm very happy with your progress though."

The timer for our visit clicks. Klinefelter looks tired, eager to get back to his cranky wife. This will all be over soon.

I keep remembering Joanna's words to ensure my release: "He's just as eager to check your boxes as you are to have them checked."

I sure hope so, because I don't know what I will do if I don't get cleared to see my son. I'll have to attempt another drive-by. They can't expect me to wait for a piece of paper to be signed before I can see my son again. It's been over a year.

I woke up one day and lost a daughter. Leo woke up and lost us both. Does he think I disappeared along with Thea?

Thea, taken from me by that haunting shadow...

The unsettlement of that picture lingers like a bad rash as I sit, waiting for the bus. I know I'll never get it out of my head.

The striking contrast of that little bit of color in the corners is bothersome too, and then I realize why...

It was created with paint, which made up the bright yellow and orange background.

It's a mix-media drawing—pencil and paint. Whoever drew that picture used the knife to cut the paint and spread it on the paper.

THIRTY

TALIA

Days fly by in a delightful state of normality. There's beauty in simplicity again—setting the timer on the coffee pot in the morning, pouring Shep his first cup. The fresh flowers Shep picked up from a vendor on the way home, just to brighten her day.

But... Talia's also brutally aware they're getting closer to a very important date—Emerson's court hearing.

She and Shep have spoken little about her since Gus's death.

Gus's funeral, the Wickerham bid, and the Svennson art gallery bid—which they're in the process of closing—have been all-consuming. Talia's been Shep's absolute bedrock, and he, hers.

Talia picked out Shep's suit for the funeral and answered all his questions:

"What do I say to Connie? Should I mention that I understand why he went down there. To the site? How I might've done the same thing given the same information?"

"No. Just tell her you're sorry. None of those details matter now. He's gone."

"You're right. What would I do without you?"

"Hopefully, you never have to find out..."

She's someone Shep turns to now for advice. It's like she's rounded a corner from girlfriend status to honorary wifey, even though she has no ring yet.

Talia's careful not to give Emerson airtime in their conversations now.

Ever since they had their little "talk", he's softer toward her, indebted.

She can feel the unspoken words they share in every moment, like an unbreakable force pushing them together. When he looks at her and kisses her cheek after he returns home at night, he's drawn to her instead of away. When he moves inside of her, they're one; when he breathes Talia's name in her ear, she's his. Only his.

He's not thinking about anyone else now.

She owns him in a way she's longed for.

She no longer checks his phone for secret texts or second guesses herself. She's heard of couples going through difficult times and coming out stronger for it, and she thinks that's what's happened here. Tragedy has made them closer.

But as perfect as everything seems, the pull of each calendar day as it turns from one to the next, closer to the hearing date, is a stressor she cannot ignore.

Emerson was never supposed to leave that damn hospital.

Talia finds herself whispering those exact words to herself sometimes, in the dark, when she's by herself, waiting for Shep to come home.

When she's alone in the break room.

Sometimes the words just tumble out in a rush because she's been trying with such force to suppress them that her mental dam breaks, spilling over.

Emerson's return has wrung her from the inside out.

No one has any idea how hard Talia's worked to leave her

small town and find this wonderful family. She will not let Emerson back in and ruin all her plans.

They already picked out Leo's costume for Halloween. Leo wants to be Chase from *Paw Patrol*. Emerson doesn't get to be a part of it. She didn't help him try it on. She didn't see how excited he was when Talia found the exact one Leo wanted. Talia took the day off work to volunteer at the daycare and make cobweb cookies. Emerson can't just step back in and steal away these moments from her, or future ones.

Forget Thanksgiving and Christmas.

Talia's never had a major holiday with the two of them yet. She wasn't officially with Shep last year until almost spring, and she already feels as though this woman is trying to ruin two holidays she's spent endless hours thinking about. Celebrations she never got to have with her family growing up.

There's no way they'll give Emerson visitation after she was placed in the psych ward in the hospital for the night a week ago. The rules were clear.

Thirty days episode free.

Talia's read the requirements for visitation rights, even if Shep doesn't know she has.

But what about the next evaluation period? Talia can't live like this.

Every month is a new threat that her family will be taken away from her or shaken up, her little Leo left at the hands of a woman Talia doesn't trust in the dark. How will she ever release him to Emerson for an overnight visit?

It would be better for everyone if Emerson just went away and never came back.

It reminds Talia of the last person she wanted to make go away.

And how her father helped make that thought a reality...

Then there are the meddlesome people who *fell* to their own demise.

Brighton is finally fully operational again now Gus's funeral has taken place. With no cameras inside the Wickerham planetarium, the authorities are none the wiser of what occurred inside.

Talia and the team have moved on, and are just making the last finishes on the contract for the art gallery.

"Did you file the revisions from the architectural department?" Neve appears at her desk, and she moves so quietly, Talia is startled by her stealth.

Gus liked to make his presence known.

"I did."

The shift in supervisors has been smoother than anticipated, nonetheless, and Talia would even verge on calling their relationship friendly.

"We need Shep to close this for us," she says.

"He's on it," Talia says, even though she's never thought it fair to put so much pressure on someone who merely wanted to sit at his desk and design buildings. The zigzagged ladder here isn't a logical one.

"I noticed you and Shep are both taking Thursday off and then Shep is headed to Boston on Friday for the weekend," Neve says. "Are you sure you don't want to off-load some of your responsibilities?"

Oh no. Neve can't pull the project from her. She's the one who found it. But Talia can't miss the court date either. It is coming at an inopportune time.

"Svensson knows these bids can take a while. She has her prelim bid, and she had a few questions which we're waiting on. I don't think she's expecting an answer back this week."

"If it comes back on Thursday, I'll let you know," Neve says.

Talia grits her teeth. She'll let me know... *she's pulling it from me.*

"I'll be back Friday and contact her first thing if that's the case." Because Emerson is not getting visitation that day. Her lawyer put in a request for next-day visitation after the hearing on Thursday if they rule in her favor, and for some reason Shep signed off on it without fully reading it. Shep's also sure there isn't a chance that Emerson will get visitation the first time around either.

But... that's the problem.

There'll be a second time.

And a third. Unless... Talia figures out a way to eliminate her for good. Shep got rid of Gus to advance his career. Talia can't see how it would be any different if she did the same to Emerson to secure their family.

"Good. Keep me posted." Neve saunters away. She owns management. She's the kind of woman who's suited for it, really. As much as she'd like Neve's role, sometimes Talia wonders if she'd really be able to hack it.

Domestic issues are already hampering her current position. Gus lost his life trying to lobby for a house for his wife and kids. Family matters have no real place in the workplace and especially upper management.

Maybe Neve is truly the better choice for the job. Fine. Let her have it. Let her win at work.

Just as long as Talia doesn't lose at home.

She must be first. She must come out on top.

She must... get rid of Emerson Wilder.

THIRTY-ONE

EMERSON

All I wanted was a suit or something decent I could wear to Leo's visitation hearing. But now a crystal dangles above me in the dank backroom of a drycleaners/laundromat.

One of the women at work told me the owner has a "sale" every six months for items left unclaimed, but the cashier, a woman named Halia, asked if she could "read" me before I bought the items I'd found.

In an accent that sounded like it's from the Caribbean islands, Halia explained her second occupation is a reiki healer. Even though I told her several times I have no money, she insisted I try it for free. I haven't found my "peace" since I left Brooks's apartment. Maybe reiki will clear my mind, lighten the nerves that threaten to overcome me. Help me find my center, which I so desperately need to win my son back.

Easier said than done.

As I lie on a long table that doubles as a workstation for employees, the smell of chemicals is thick in the air. I cough a few times, adjusting to the pungent fumes. I wonder what I've gotten myself into.

I'm lying completely still, but I can't relax. Much like the scenario at Jacob's, the walls feel like they're closing in.

"I-I don't think I can—"

"Shh..." Strangely, her shushing works a little. I don't say anything else.

Halia turns on gentle, tinkling music—a light mix of chimes and drumming. It must be coming from Halia's phone, because this place doesn't look like it's equipped with an audio system. "Close your eyes. I offered to do this for you because you need to clear your bad energy."

"Bad energy?" I wonder if it could be true. Or if this is just some scheme.

Why do you do this to yourself?

It's like chaos follows me. Or I seek it.

Or I overthink every situation to the point that it becomes something it's not.

How did I get here?

"I want you to stop thinking..." *Ha!* "...And let your mind unspool. Your thoughts, let them travel..." Her accent makes me want to head somewhere that has clear blue water. The kind where I can look down and see my toes. I can't see my toes at all right now, lying flat on this table, and relaxation does not come.

"I know I'm not supposed to talk, but how does this work?" I peek and see Halia, hovering over me, eyes closed, hands outstretched over my body like she's pushing on an imaginary countertop above me.

"Reiki rebalances your body's energy, which can be upset by outside forces. It reduces stress and promotes healing."

Well, that sounds nice. But I'm still uncomfortable and tired of being viewed as a specimen instead of a human. Even the drycleaner cashier can tell there's something wrong with me. How will I ever fool the judge?

Halia continues, "I'll try to find out what you need to become more spiritually stabilized. I entered this business to heal people who need it, and yes, I like to be paid. But occasionally, I'll meet someone I just know I need to help."

I smirk, because it's hard to trust people. "I'm your pro bono case of the week."

"If I took one every week, I'd go broke. Shh... now."

I bite my lip so I can't speak. At least I get the gist of what's going on here. But it all sounds like a bunch of new age hocus pocus.

"Quiet your mind."

My mind laughs back at her. She doesn't know who she's dealing with here.

"Miss... in order for this to work, you must believe in the process."

Oh shit. All I wanted was pants or a skirt and a matching jacket. Now I feel like I might leave here without my soul. I try to concentrate on the music. It's soft, like I'm lying in someone's backyard and the windchimes are blowing above me. I imagine I'm at my summer home, in the early days, when I used to chase Freddie the Fireflies through the sky.

My thoughts run like a movie reel:

Me as a child laughing and playing.

My mother painting in the privacy of her attic studio.

My father trying not to work, but inevitably on his phone in the office.

And then...

The girls. Three of them. I can barely recognize their faces now. One is completely blank, a hologram reflection, like the sun has burned her out.

It must be Claire's face that I cannot see. Claire who is dead. Drowned.

I feel my heart accelerate.

"Relax," Halia's words flow in and out.

The images continue.

*The sleepover. All four of us playing a game—**find Michael's bone**—displaying on the Ouija board.*

"Where do you think his bone is?" Ella asks.

"In his pants," Claire says of her summer crush, Michael.

Claire giggles. Surely she made the Ouija move the way she wanted. We all giggle.

Candles are lit. We sleep. Until the fire alarm goes off. Everything is in flames. We run for the door.

Everything starts speeding up, flashing before me.

My parents—dead in a crash.

Me holding Thea. Shep and Leo by my side.

The man. The same one from the drawing.

His eyes draw me in. Hollow. Black. I'm falling...

I jerk up with a gasp.

"Easy does it," Halia says. Her eyes are warm yet concerned. I'm sweating like I've just birthed a baby.

"Could you see what I saw?" I ask, because the pictures were so vivid, I'm not sure how she couldn't have.

"No... but I could feel them."

I shiver. "Can I sit up now?"

"Yes." She pulls on my hands until I'm sitting upright. My feet swing over the table, and I have to grab onto the side so I don't fall off.

"What was that?" It didn't feel like healing. It felt as if she'd ripped off a bunch of tiny scabs. My body tremors increase, consciousness hitting me, the outside world now touching all my fresh wounds. I wipe a stray tear from my face.

Halia hands me a bottle of cold water. I gulp at it greedily.

Her speaking voice is as soft as her shushing voice. "You have a wide open third eye." She points to my forehead. "You're like an emotional sponge. You feel everything everyone is feeling, see people for who they really are. But you absorb their pain and stress too. Be careful who you surround yourself with.

You've probably made mistakes trusting those you shouldn't have in the past."

"Doesn't everyone make that mistake at least once?"

Halia wipes off the station where I was lying, as if she's eager to decontaminate my bad juju, when just a moment ago she was enthralled to help me. What's changed?

"Yes, they do. But it's what you attract. I think you might have had something attached to you... or still do. Bad energy. I felt it the minute you walked in. Maybe you can figure out what it is from what you saw."

"So what did you do? Did you heal me?"

"No. That would take many sessions and I know you don't have the funds to come back."

Ahh... she wants me to come back. First one is free. "I see."

"But I did rebalance your energy so it's not filling your head."

Overthinker. "Okay."

"And I would strongly recommend not hanging around people who drain you, even if you feel indebted to them or are unhealthily dependent on them somehow."

I think of Brooks—my emotional vampire. "I'll lookout for that."

"I worked your solar plexus. Your middle. You had a blockage. It causes analysis paralysis and stress. You might also be worrying about the wrong people, placing blame where none belongs, ignoring the real problem."

I do feel horribly guilty about Claire, although I'm not sure why.

I want to tell Halia that I was in analysis paralysis for a year in a mental hospital and that I just came out of it, but I don't. That will only scare her more.

She hands me a plain black, yet tasteful, woman's dress and jacket and a white silk blouse in a plastic bag, wire hanger. "This should fit you," she says.

"Thank you. How much?" I ask.

"It's on the house. Just don't tell the owner." She winks.

"How can I repay you?" I ask.

I'm not sure I buy into anything she's told me, but she's not wrong about her brief assessment. I do overanalyze. I have trusted the wrong people. And I am definitely stressed. The music is still playing from her phone, making me feel loopy.

"Just promise me you'll try harder to remain centered. Focused. Imagine yourself a tree. Your feet are your roots, and they keep you firmly planted."

I take the bag from her hands and nod as if this is a completely sane piece of advice. "Thank you so much. Your kindness means more than you know." As I say the words, the vision of a burning man with eyes the color of coal fizzle in my memory. Who is he?

THIRTY-TWO
TALIA

Shep might think they have the hearing all hemmed up, but Talia has to be sure. It's visitation hearing week, and she's feeling a bit unhinged.

But if she wasn't a dot her i's and cross her t's kind of person, she wouldn't have graduated top of her class in high school. She wouldn't have ridden on a full scholarship out of her one-horse town. She wouldn't have gotten a job at Brighton. And she wouldn't have landed one of the company's most promising up and comers there, Shephard Kingsley.

He may not realize it but in letting her sign a legal custody paper, Shep signed off on Talia to be a custodial guardian for Leo after his divorce. Now she has access to the legal team representing Leo and the authority to ask all the questions she wants. By law, she has the same rights and obligations to Leo as a biological parent.

She stands in the corner of the breakroom between the refrigerator and the counter, cupping her hand over the receiver of her cell. "Hi, Jan, just checking in to see if the paperwork from Ms. Wilder's lawyer has come in yet? The one from her therapist and the other paper that needed— Oh. It didn't." A smile sneaks up her face. She fights it, tamping it down. "Okay. Thank you." She hangs up, the confirmation all she needs to feel safe for the time being.

Emerson hasn't been cleared by her doctor yet.

She can't so much as touch a hair on Leo's head if she doesn't have the final say from her psychiatrist. There's another smaller checkpoint she has to meet, but the doctor is the biggie.

Next on her list: Confirm Shep's travel for Friday. Most women might not like being relegated to their boyfriend's admin, but they've had good fun with the subjugation theme in the bedroom as of late. Date night next week might feature a naughty secretary... she's not sure.

If they can just make it to next week.

November is her Opus.

Things will slow down around Thanksgiving. Government proceedings, like court hearings, will be pushed. Workers will take vacation. And Emerson will just have to wait until next year. Talia's sure.

It will give Talia some time to figure out how to extricate Emerson from their lives for good. It's the only clear solution. It's not just for Leo's safety, although that's her biggest concern. It's the stability of their home. *Their* family.

What Emerson's return would do to the beautiful cadence of their lives.

They're in a groove now, she and Shep. And Emerson is the spoke in their wheel.

Talia absolutely cringes when she thinks of how a custody arrangement will completely screw all of her careful planning.

From the little things: Leo's drop-off and pickups at school or his extracurricular functions; every other weekend, lugging their crap from one home to the next, with something ultimately getting left behind.

Then there were all the big things: the splitting of important events. Missing birthdays and holidays—having this other, deranged, woman hanging around while she carves the turkey was not what Talia had in mind for her future family.

Talia doesn't want to share.

It was never something she thought she'd have to do. But the threat is imminent.

Her thoughts keep circling back to Gus's death.

Shep is being seriously looked at for the senior architect role now. If his intention was to push Gus off that ledge, in part so he could further his career, it worked.

And the authorities are clueless.

They've truly moved forward, right along, as if he was never even here.

What if they did the same thing with Emerson?

Leo doesn't really remember her. He knows what she looks like and remembers she sang to him—but that seems to be about it. If Talia can prevent the visitation, and make Emerson disappear before Leo ever gets to re-meet her, that would be ideal.

With the winter months coming, the roadways will be slick...

It would be a shame if something happened to her. If she lost her life in a crash it would be a dark poetic justice, mirroring how her beloved parents died.

An unfortunate slip and fall could be an easy out too, a la Gus Romeo.

The only trick will be getting Shep to partner with her on this one.

How close Shep would feel to her then...

They'd have only each other, cemented together forever by the lives they've taken and covered up.

———

Lunch with Neve and Priya has become this odd, weekly thing Talia has come to simultaneously like and hate.

Like—because she's forming a closer relationship with Neve, a woman largely responsible for her upward mobility at the company.

Hate—because she knows Neve's goodwill is fake, her interest in Talia solely based on how much she can do for her at work.

Priya is like this small, intermediary buffer between their resounding, sometimes clashing, voices.

"What're you guys doing over the weekend? Any fall parties?" Neve plucks a beet from her goat cheese salad and drops it into her mouth. Talia can picture Neve sashaying around in a slinky Halloween costume, the type of partier who doesn't take off her mask until the lights turn down.

Talia knows that type of girl. She used to be just like her.

"My sisters will be in town. We're having dinner with our parents," Priya says.

"Shep will be in Boston closing up the Liberty Trail project. It's just Leo and me. I think we'll try apple picking or visit a pumpkin patch, not sure. His school Halloween party is Monday, and Tuesday is Halloween." I take a spoonful from my cilantro chicken bowl and glance up to find Neve inspecting me.

"You said you had a doctor's appointment Monday. Are you really going to Leo's party?"

Shit. And this is why she and Neve can't really be friends. Talia will never be comfortable telling her the intimate details of her life because sometimes they interfere with work, and Neve will never understand that. She doesn't have the same attachments.

"I do. The party is a bit after school, so I'm able to do both," Talia says quickly.

"Right. Whatever. Well, my family has an annual pumpkin carving contest I have to suffer through this weekend." Neve pulls up some elaborate carving designs on her phone. A pumpkin carving contest family tradition is the most humanistic thing she's expressed to Talia since she's known her.

"I like the fairy," Priya offers.

"Scary pumpkin," Talia says, pointing at a carving with pointy teeth. She's a firm believer that Halloween decorations and costumes should be frightening. People who try to make it anything else are missing the point.

"I like the demon," Neve says. Talia knew she'd pick something with horns. "I'm due for a win. Haven't had one in years," she seethes. And there it is. The competition.

Talia's mind switches from Neve's family warmly sipping apple cider next to a roaring fire, to a circle of individuals voraciously gutting pumpkins with knives, racing to make the winning design. Neve mentioned her brother was super athletic and more competitive than her. Talia can't imagine what their sibling rivalry must be like.

"Well, good luck. I hope yours is the best."

Neve smiles. "Thanks. We could all use a little extra luck this week."

Talia looks away, catching Priya's frightened face in her periphery. Priya knows Leo's visitation hearing is this week. It was hard to keep it completely under wraps with Priya sitting right across from her, because of the incoming phone calls from the law office. But Talia had done everything in her power to make sure Neve wasn't made aware.

"What do you mean by that?" Talia asks.

Priya slurps her soup.

"Oh... just the closing of the Liberty Trail, and hopefully winning the bid for the art gallery. It's a big week for us," Neve says.

"Right!"

Work. Of course she's talking about work...

THIRTY-THREE

EMERSON

The first thing I see is Jacob part his lips in a mix of wonder and relief as I walk down the dusty steps of the Methodist church, for what I'm sure will be the last time.

I missed the prior session because I was in the hospital. Klinefelter gave me a pass, but I never felt the need to explain my absence to Jacob.

Nevertheless, I sit down right beside him, his familiarity drawing me in, a moth to a flame. "Hi."

Halia is right. I am a sponge for the emotionally wounded.

He whispers in my ear. "Hey, I was worried about you. I never got your phone number. I heard there was a break-in at your place." His forehead creases with concern. If Maggie shared my personal details with the group, she really shouldn't have.

"There was. I wasn't too hurt, but they never caught the guy."

I've thought for a week that the man in my apartment could've been Jacob. Maybe he was upset with me for rejecting him and tried to kill me in a—*If I can't have you no one else will* —sort of way. But if it had been Jacob, I'm guessing Brooks would've already had him disposed of... It makes me nervous Brooks hasn't called me back. I haven't heard from him since I left his place.

Jacob's face doesn't match the man from the drawing. The drawing makes everything about that evening seem so much more real. But I'm still not sure what it means. I keep going back to the night Thea died, and the fact it was the first terror where the shadow touched me. I remember his glove on my arm, the way his fingers wormed into my skin. I convinced myself I imagined it, but my throat was definitely injured. And now—the realistic drawing.

"Are you sure you're all right?" Jacob asks. I'm reminded he's a nurse. However, his bedside manner is a lot gentler than his manner in bed.

"Ya, I'm okay," I say, and strangely, I am. Since I left Halia, the words that normally get stuck between my head and my mouth flow freely now. The idea that bad energy was clogging up the spiritual pipes, and has now been cleared, still sits oddly with me, but I'll take what I can get.

"Who wants to share today?" Maggie asks.

I raise my hand. Throat chakra clear.

The details of Thea's death come slow. I realize after a moment it's because I'm not speaking from memory. I'm recounting the events that other people have told me have happened and it rattles me to the core—not being able to fully feel the loss of my child.

The single, most life-altering event of my life.

My voice, my whole body wobbles, but I'm able to get it all out, and I'm more confident I'll be able to do the same at the hearing.

After I finish telling a crowd of strangers the most awful experience of my entire life, the whole room is silent. Some people are quietly sobbing. Jacob remains stoic and still. Maybe in the near future it will feel therapeutic, but right now, it doesn't. It's pure hell.

Maggie is mumbling something, but I can't make it out. All I can do is hold out a form for her to sign. She nods, scribbling her signature on the dotted line, and I turn away and sit back down.

Jacob places his warm hand on my shoulder. I let it rest there as my insides turn with unrest. I nod, letting him know— *we're okay.*

He may be an intense guy, but the mistakes I made with him are not his fault. I'm not ready for a relationship, but I realize he's not the horrible person I probably made him out to be either. We're all just trying to find our place in the world. And I still haven't moved on from my last relationship.

What will Shep do when he sees me for the first time since he visited me in the hospital?

Competent. Cleaned up. Coherent. All my fight back. I've finally found my words.

But am I too late? I hope I say the right things.

When our session concludes, I walk hurriedly toward the steps to the exit, a huge weight off my shoulder as I send Maggie's sign-off memo to Klinefelter via an Insta-fax app. I remind him that I need all of the paperwork in this week before the hearing.

I think Klinefelter was warming up to me during the last session after I said, "Since I've been seeing you, I've noticed an improvement in my overall mood and judgment."

These words streamed from my mouth yesterday after my session with Halia, and Klinefelter gobbled them right up. He might've even smiled.

His final comments to me were that if I completed the bereavement group requirement, he saw no reason why I wouldn't get a pass for supervised visitation. It's everything I needed to hear.

He emails me right back:

Received

No promise of anything else, but I have to believe he'll keep his word.

Jacob appears beside me, waiting by the curb for the bus. "Will I see you again?"

"Not here, you won't."

Jacob sighs. "It gets easier after you've told your story."

"I don't like group, Jacob. I don't need to hear more bad stories. Only the good ones."

Jacob grins. "Can I trouble you for a quiet movie, preferably a comedy, where we only speak to each other briefly before and after the show?"

I giggle at him for trying. "That sounds nice, but I need to get myself together first. Rain check? My court hearing to see Leo is this week. Lots to figure out."

"Sure. Well, good luck... And when you've got yourself sorted, you have my number."

"I do." I pat my wallet in my pocket—in control of my future. For the first time in a very long time.

THIRTY-FOUR

EMERSON

No voicemail or text messages from Brooks when I check after leaving the church and search my phone. I texted him and asked him just to reply to me so I know he's all right—nothing.

He's gone dark. It's the scary stealth mode where he's up to something and doesn't want me to know about it. It's one thing when he's getting justice for others. It's a whole other animal when someone's coming after him.

I sigh and try to remember what Halia said.

In some ways, the one therapy session with her was more beneficial than all of Klinefelter's. I cannot absorb Brooks's issues. I have my own to worry about. My only focus should be the visitation hearing and seeing my son again.

I give Joanna a quick ring. I need to know this visitation is really happening. She has the inside lane on all-things-mental-health.

"Hey, I've been thinking about you..." she says in a low voice, which tells me she's still at work. "Things here have been rough with the investigation."

"I'm sorry to hear that. I'm just calling to let you know that I feel good about the hearing. I finished group therapy today, and

I should have Klinefelter's final sign offs soon. My lawyer hasn't said much, only that he'll use everything he has to secure me a visitation date."

"You're still pushing for Friday?" Joanna asks. "For visitation?"

"I am," I say.

"Don't be surprised if that doesn't happen. Usually these things take a while."

I clench my eyes shut. *It has to be Friday.*

My fingers press into the phone. I have to at least see Leo. If only a spin by Shep's townhouse again. I can't take it anymore. "I wonder if we can use the drawing Justine sent Klinefelter to prove that my apartment break-in could've been real. If they bring that up."

"What drawing?"

I open my eyes. "Justine didn't show it to you? It's a picture they found in your patient's room. The one who died. They think I drew it. But I don't remember creating it. It has paint on it too. The palette knife... Why didn't they show it to you? Your boss... Rupert? Surely he'd know?"

"I'd ask him, but he's late getting back from vacation. There's a stormfront coming through. He was on Nantucket, probably got stuck. Emerson, do you have a copy of the picture?"

"I took a screenshot so I could place it side by side with my other drawings to determine if it was one of my own. It looks pretty close, but I can't be sure. But why would Rupert not show it to you before he sent it to Klinefelter?"

"If Klinefelter said Justine sent it, Rupert might not even know it exists. And as it's part of a live investigation where I was the supervisor on the floor, I probably would have been left out of the loop for now. But your treating psychiatrist may be allowed to see it. Can you send it to me?"

"Yes."

"Okay, do that, please. I've got to get off the phone. Let me know how the hearing goes."

I hang up and send the photo. Maybe Joanna will be able to make sense of it all. I'm still worried she's somehow going to be held responsible.

Rupert is in Nantucket... Nantucket makes me think of Cape Cod and Claire Schering again—her one hand reaching above the surface as something else pulled her down. Her burned-out face. *Dead.*

I take a deep, ragged breath. Maybe if I contact her family, it will give me resolution.

Sponge. I can see myself as so, absorbing everyone's problems.

Focus on Leo.

I push away the damning thoughts and try to find the light. I've envisioned all the things I'm going to say to my little boy, who's not so little anymore.

I'm going to tell him where I've been.

Something took Thea from us, and I was so sad I had to go to my special place to feel better enough to be his mommy again.

We've always had an understanding, Leo and me. I still remember the very last day he belonged to me.

It's a memory I treasure, one I played back a hundred times in the hospital.

Just a simple day, but it's the last memory I have of my family—me and Leo and Thea...

———

We're playing at the park, and I've almost finished my revisions for the latest Silly Suzies chapter book, high on childlike creativity, success, and my son's hysterical giggles. I could roll around in the sun with him all day, but my deadline looms. I hope Shep makes it home on time tonight so I can finish my work.

Thea naps happily in her car carrier beside us. Her lips are rounded like she's blowing me a kiss, her cherubic cheeks rosy from the sun's rays. She's fallen asleep holding her feet, and she does it so often I'm already convinced she's going to be a gymnast.

I've laid a patchwork quilt on the ground that I made when Leo was in my belly.

Scissored pieces of my father's favorite ties I couldn't part with, Shep's old shirts too. Shoelaces, patterned fabrics, a potpourri of odds and ends. The blanket is a combo of every man I've loved and the boy my son is to become; but he's too busy running around to sit on it.

Leo brought his action figure "guys" along with him, a bunch of muscleheads with dented armor whose names I can't remember.

"Who're you going to be today?" I ask.

"This one." He points to a superhero with a red cape.

"Okay. What's our story?" I ask him, because our scenarios must always have a plot. Leo cannot have a mother who works in publishing and not understand the art of story. "There must be a conflict. A problem for them to solve," I explain.

Leo nods and says, "My guy lost his magic shield, but the villain finds it first and tries to smash it."

"Ooh, that's great conflict." I hide the toy shield beneath the blanket. We play out the decided script.

Leo and I lie there and crash our characters together, the reflection from Lake Lillinonah, a perfect backdrop to our early fall day. The rich colors of the autumnal leaves bounce off the ripples like a watercolor painting.

Shep wanted to purchase one of the lake houses with the premium vinyl siding, but there'd be no budget leftover for rehabbing the property, my favorite part. When I met our two-

story Victorian in Newtown it was like finding a hidden Monet in a sea of fakes. There were other New England beauties that looked much the same, but none had the striking, original bones of that one.

Leo picks up his figures, and I can see the villain's eyes bulge out of his green sockets when he's struck in the head by the shield Leo recovered unbeknownst to me.

Thea cries, and I pick her up, trying to thrash my character into Leo's action figure at the same time I rock the baby. He giggles. "The battle's over, Mom!"

"So it is. And you... are the winner!"

"Ya!" he cheers.

"I'm glad you belong to me, kiddo," I tell him.

"I'm happy you belong to me too."

I give him a squeeze, wishing Shep was here to enjoy some of these tender moments with us.

THIRTY-FIVE
TALIA

Given the circumstances of Emerson's case, one that was in the news and drew a ton of media attention, they brought in a big dog instead of a hearing officer.

That's what Jan, the paralegal at Frederick & Roy, had said when she tipped Talia off that Judge Curtis Willoughby will likely be overseeing their case today.

And what a pit bull he is, according to Talia's Internet search.

She reads Willoughby's profile with pleasure.

Willoughby is a fifty-something divorcé. His ex-wife Jocelyn (Willoughby) Proust, cheated on him with *their* financial planner—who was found guilty of tax evasion and fraud six months after Lawrence Proust and Jocelyn wed.

Articles on Lawrence Proust's arrest are suspicious and loaded with possible collusion. Talia has no doubt Pit Bull Willoughby used his powerful jaws to orchestrate a monetary bribe to the presiding judge in the case in exchange for Lawrence's sentence—five years in white-collar jail.

Willoughby shows little leniency on drug and alcohol

offenses. He's also known to be stringent when doling out custody arrangements.

And... he will hate Emerson Wilder.

He will love Talia though.

She's wearing a smart navy suit today with a conservative pale pink blouse, simple pearls, and gold jewelry. Talia pulls up her breasts in their cups to give her ample cleavage, but not so much that she doesn't still appear like a class act. An independent career woman with not so much as a parking violation on her record. Willoughby will eat her up, promote her from custodial guardian to permanent parent once he gets a load of Raggedy Emerson.

And if he doesn't, Talia has an arsenal of inflammatory evidence in her tote bag she can toss the judge to sway him her way. She doesn't mention any of these things to Shep, of course. She's only saving them for the worst-case scenario.

Shep seems out of sorts this morning, and she doesn't want to upset him anymore. He has a major deal to close for the company this weekend, and she can't have him distracted. Neve will never forgive either one of them if he messes it up.

But first... this.

Emerson is just a blip on the calendar.

The hot ash of a long, nasty cigarette Talia needs to stamp out.

The courtroom is small and unassuming. It reminds Talia of the tiny made-for-TV set she's seen on tacky shows like *Judge Judy*, which gives the whole proceeding an informal feel. But nothing about today is casual.

Their lawyer hasn't arrived yet, and neither has anyone else.

Maybe Emerson won't show at all.

Talia squeezes Shep's arm. "Are you okay?"

"Yeah... I just haven't seen her in so long. It's hard, ya know?" he says quickly. But Talia feels the threat in his every word. He's not stressed about fighting for his son's welfare. He's worried about *Her*. Seeing his ex-wife. It means he still cares.

Talia pulls on his lapel and gives him a little kiss on the lips. "I love you so much," she says. He opens his mouth, and she's sure he's about to say it back, but they're interrupted.

Their lawyer, Attorney Damon Roy, arrives with a coffee in his hand, and a—*this ain't no thing*—expression on his face.

"Hey guys, you ready?" Roy asks.

Talia doesn't realize how nervous she is until he asks that question. They've only met with him a couple of times, and they've only had one phone call leading up until this point. All of a sudden it doesn't seem like enough.

Talia wonders about Emerson's prep work. What with all her doctor's appointments, therapy sessions, rampant dating life, and hospitalization, Talia can't imagine she'd squeeze in the time. But what if she has?

She grinds her teeth together. That woman does not deserve Leo. Talia doesn't trust her to tie his shoes.

The judge appears next, and it is not Judge Willoughby. *Shit.*

It's a woman, with short-cropped hair and a face more suited for an elementary teacher position than that of a hard-nosed judge.

Instinctively, Talia looks behind her and spies through the paned glass, Willoughby, all robed up for the day, and she thinks maybe there's been a mix up. He seems fired up, talking to a man who Talia recognizes, but can't place. Maybe another lawyer at Frederick & Roy? They march off down the hallway together as the woman introduces herself as Judge Priscilla Holcomb—she even sounds like a pre-school teacher.

A man in a burgundy sweater vest and matching socks walks into the room and takes his seat on the defendant's side. A witness for Emerson, but Talia can't imagine who he might be. The owner of the paper printer where she works? Talia examines his fingers, looking for stray print stains and comes up empty.

It's someone Talia hasn't accounted for and she doesn't like it.

Another man in a suit struts in and takes a seat on Emerson's side. Obviously, Emerson's lawyer. He appears uninterested as he studies his watch and even a little bored. Unimpressive, but Talia guesses Emerson went for the first available public defender.

The door swings open, and there she is—Emerson.

Talia almost cries out loud at her polished black dress and blazer look, white-collar shirt folding over her collar in cute Wednesday Addams fashion, and low but tasteful heels. Where did she find such an outfit on her salary? The judge smiles at her even though Emerson's five minutes late.

"The train, my apologies," she says as she takes her place, and completely ignores Shep and Talia.

Talia can feel Shep's eyes burning through her shoulder, taking in his ex-wife.

Emerson looks great—in a bookkeeper kind of way.

"Very well, now that we're all present, we can discuss the matter at hand. We're here today to determine initial visitation rights for Leo Kingsley, biological son of Shephard Kingsley and... Emerson Wilder."

The gut punch of the word—biological—bowls Talia over.

"...who's been estranged from her son for the last year due to mental health issues. Leo has been in the care of Shephard Kingsley and custodial guardian Talia Davenport."

Talia feels Emerson jerk at Talia's title. *Yes, you need to realize who's been taking care of your son!*

But Shep doesn't. Because he knows she's earned it. And should continue to hold that title.

Holcomb speaks. "Ms. Wilder, tell us a little bit about how you've spent the last year and what your recovery has looked like."

Emerson glances at her lawyer, as if she's not sure. "Go on," he mutters, as if he doesn't have time for this. Neither does Talia.

"I've been working very hard on recovery. I've attended regular weekly psychiatry appointments as well as group grief therapy. I was sick because I lost my second child unexpectedly."

The judge flips through her files. "When you fell down the steps with her and she unfortunately died."

The sting of sympathy in the judge's voice unnerves Talia. It was not a simple accident as she says. Willoughby wouldn't have seen it that way.

"That's right." Emerson's voice is tight, but she's holding it together.

"That is a considerable loss and I can understand how it's taken you this long to come back from it."

"It was. It has been..."

Talia's gaze floats over to her lawyer, Roy. He needs to speak up and mention that this wasn't just a clumsy trip down the steps. Both Talia and Shep were clear about their concerns regarding Emerson's mental stability to handle Leo, yet Roy says nothing.

"Shep," Talia whispers.

He glares at her. "Let her finish."

Talia flinches as if she's just been slapped.

"But I've been working very hard since the accident, and I feel quite capable to care for my son now."

No. no. no. This is not going right. She has to do something. "Judge, if I may. I think we have to be careful about using the word 'accident' here. Emerson was chasing a hallucination in her sleep when she fell. It wasn't a simple misstep down the stairs."

Talia locks eyes with her, and Emerson's face drains of all color, her cheeks pulling in like Talia has reached across the room and yanked the air right out of her. *Yes, the truth hurts.*

"I have the full file, Ms. Davenport. I'll ask for you to refrain from speaking until Miss Wilder is done."

Shep shoots Talia a cursory glance, annoyed. But she's rattled Emerson. That's all that matters. The judge needs to *see* her for what she really is. And why she's not in the right state of mind to handle Leo.

"Of course. Please continue," Talia says.

The judge sweeps Talia up and down quickly, the way unattractive women do when they're envious. This will not work out in Talia's favor.

"I have made progress with my therapist, am able to verbalize and understand what happened so that it won't happen again," Emerson continues, and it's only then that Talia sees the paper in her hand. Her list of qualifications to be a mother, which are probably half fabricated. "I have a job. I have a deed for property I can sell to buy a new place, and am currently living independently." Emerson looks up and makes eye contact with the judge.

Talia can see her life fall apart as Holcomb practically ingests her pain.

I hate women.

And then... Emerson says the words that seal Talia's fate in a breathless, pleading gulp.

"Please, I just want to see my son again."

THIRTY-SIX
EMERSON

She is evil.

I knew the first time I saw her through the window, yelling at my son. And it was confirmed when I saw Brooks in the courthouse. I wonder what he's up to. He only shows up at times of danger.

She's the dragon—a treacherous illusion—one minute beautiful and still, the next a contorted mix of fire and brimstone.

She taps her long nails against the table, CLICK, CLICK, CLICK, and...

You stand by pretending not to notice her agitation. You've always been a tolerant man.

Tolerant of the babies' cries.

Tolerant of my rampages through the house, scraps of paper here, paint chips all over our dining room table. Tolerant of my middle-of-the-night jabbering.

But this is different.

Klinefelter takes the stand. I can barely comprehend his boring drawl because my ears are still ringing from how she's verbally assaulted me. My hearing tunes in for the important part...

"During our time together, Emerson indicated that since my therapy she's noticed an improvement in her overall mood and judgment," Klinefelter says, but he's rudely interrupted.

Her fingernails make a wretched sound.

TAP. TAP. TAP.

She touches our son with those claws.

"And I concur," he says. Klinefelter is taking a while to get to the point, but he's saying the right things.

This is going to happen for us, isn't it? It's been a terrible year, but you don't want to be with her. Not really. Sure, she's young and pretty, and I'm sure she's done okay with Leo, but my brief observation tells me she's not a natural with kids.

You're what she wants.

But what she doesn't understand is that you need a lot more than just a young pretty girl on your arm.

You and I are hammer and nail, practicality meets art. I'll stain the door after you've measured twice, cut once. It'll swing just right.

What do you build with her, Shep?

"Is that your formal opinion, Dr. Klinefelter? Has Miss Wilder been able to complete all the tasks on the designated evaluation?" Judge Holcomb asks.

"Yes, that's correct, on both accounts," Klinefelter confirms.

Her lips twitch. It's subtle, but I can sniff out her terribleness like a dead animal stuck beneath my tire. She probably thinks she's good at her deception, but I know what she is. I can see her now. Not just a monster, but the kind who wants to take our family all for herself, cling to them, control them. She won't stop until she's sucked them dry. The worst emotional vampire of all.

Klinefelter drones on in a very noncommittal way about my progress.

But all that matters is that *You* hear a professional's acceptance of *Me*.

Then, maybe you can accept me too.

It's the first time we've looked at each other in a very long time and I can still... feel you. Our connection doesn't cease to exist just because we do.

And I caught your dirty side-eye at her, at the way she spoke to me.

Somehow, she still seems irrelevant. Like I was lost at sea for a year, and you presumed me dead, but now I'm here... very much alive... and it changes everything, doesn't it?

She knows this too. That's why she feels so threatened. She should...

I notice my lawyer, Harry, glance at his watch, and I wonder if he has a hot date after this because it's the second time he's done it.

"Dr. Klinefelter, have you come to a formal medical opinion on whether you feel Emerson is fit for a supervised visit with her son?" Judge Holcomb asks.

"I have. I believe given the extensive therapy that Emerson has exhibited under my care, that with a court-appointed social service worker, it's in my medical opinion that Emerson Wilder should be cleared for a supervised visit with her son, Leo Kingsley."

I sway to the side because hearing it in person is so much more gratifying than words I've only imagined in my head. I can't help but smile—at *You.*

You smile back. You're happy too.

And then I glance at the thing next to you, her face snarling. Her fingernails clattering on the wooden bench in front of her.

TICK, TICK...

I flinch at the clatter of her nails on the wood. It's like no one else can hear them except me. But then I see her open her mouth and I know the real explosion is on its way.

"Your Honor, while I respect Dr. Klinefelter's opinion as a professional in the psychiatry field, I do have some concerns about Emerson's mental state and her interacting with Leo, and evidence to back up those concerns."

"What're you doing?" Shep asks her.

You're stiff as a board. Infuriated with her, aren't you, Dear? Maybe I should let this play out so you can see what she's really like.

"That would've needed to be disclosed before the hearing," my lawyer says.

"New evidence can be added if the judge deems it fair and both parties agree," Talia argues.

"Now she thinks she's a lawyer too," my lawyer says. *Go Harry.*

"Ms. Davenport, what does this evidence contain before we entertain your unorthodox request?"

She removes a labeled envelope from her briefcase.

Sweet Jesus. What can she possibly have in there? I'm in the clear...

Shep sighs and places his hand up, begging her to stop.

I don't know what it is, but I imagine it's a paper bomb of some sort, threatening to undo the decision that has already been made. I can't allow it.

I want to leap over the table, shred the papers she holds, throw them in her face. I think of my torn sketches on the floor in Hartford and how damaging that was. I can't imagine this could be worse.

"There're elicit pictures in this envelope of Emerson and a man she couldn't have known more than a week after leaving the hospital."

I was wrong. The sound that leaves my mouth is somewhere between a hiccup and a yelp. "You had me followed!" I blurt out.

I see how you flinch. This is how she will keep you. This is how she will win.

You've seen the pictures and now you'll see me naked with

Jacob every time you look at me. She understands how to manipulate you, but she doesn't really understand you—only how to trap you...

"While that shows Miss Wilder might've not exercised the best judgment, it doesn't mean she presents a threat to her child. And did you have Miss Wilder followed, Miss Davenport? That poses its own concerns," Judge Holcomb asks.

"I didn't. I knew someone who lived in the area, and they took the photos."

"I saw a man with a camera slung around his neck when I exited that man's building. I thought it was odd. He was clearly hired. But you should probably spring for a professional next time, he was hardly hidden," I say.

"I didn't hire him. And you can prove no such thing."

"Again, while this shows possible poor judgment, I don't see how it prohibits a visit where Miss Wilder will be accompanied by a court-appointed chaperone," Judge Holcomb says.

"What you'll also find in this envelope is camera footage from my Ring doorbell. It's dated from the night after Emerson was released from the hospital. She's there, in front of my house, staring into my windows like a lunatic, violating her explicit orders to stay away from us until this date. She's clearly a danger and a flight risk."

"That's a stretch!" Harry argues.

"If it's such a longshot, do you give permission for Miss Davenport to include this evidence in the proceedings?" Roy asks.

"I didn't know anything about this, but very well," Harry says.

"Neither did I," Shep offers, loud enough for me to hear. Loud enough for her to know he sees her as a monster. What kind of woman wants to keep a mother from their child?

A bailiff, who's been a mostly silent party, walks swiftly to take Talia's envelope and delivers it to the judge.

"Given this new information, a breach of the no-contact policy as well as the impulsive sexual behavior does show a pattern of questionable behavior..." The judge starts.

"Are we going to also ignore the recent hospitalization for her nightmare? Thirty days episode free is what I was told before I'm supposed to entrust her with Leo?" Talia asks. "I'm sorry, but I've been primary caretaker of this boy and I can't just hand him over if there's a threat to his safety."

"We're just talking about a supervised visit here," Harry says. "Counselor, can you get control of your clients and offer your own objections?"

Roy nods at Talia. "Please leave the objections up to me, Ms. Davenport."

She's got a mouth on her, and I can't see how it's helping her case.

"Then please do your job," Talia says.

Roy bristles. "Can you address the breach in the thirty-day policy, counselor?"

Harry clears his throat. "Dr. Klinefelter has already given his professional opinion regarding Emerson's mental state, which includes the time following her... nightmare. We also need to take into account that Emerson's visit will only be a brief meetup, and she will not have Leo overnight nor impose a threat of this type."

Roy rebukes. "I've had clients in the past who've exhibited these behaviors and have posed a flight risk the moment they saw their child. Another month of close observation or two can't hurt."

"Absolutely not! I've waited long enough. I just want to see him!" I shout.

Harry grabs my hand. I'm acting every bit the loose cannon she's made me out to be. I hate her for doing that to me.

Roy flips through an envelope of photographs. Talia must've made copies. There's disgust spread on his face that tells me he's reached the ones of Jacob and me. *How embarrassing.*

But I won't apologize. To him or any of them. For just trying to be human.

And I won't let any of them stand in the way of me seeing my son. Court ruling or not.

She's waged a battle, this awful woman.

The judge puckers her lips. "I appreciate the love and concern you both share for Leo. Something I've learned after presiding as a judge in the family court system for over twenty years is that in most cases it's in everyone's best interest that the child be reunited with their mother or father."

She opens her mouth to object, but the judge holds her finger up to stop her.

"I don't appreciate the way in which these pictures were attained, by a hired hand or not. I'm throwing them out of my decision-making process. Miss Wilder, you will be granted supervised visitation, but you will also follow the rules."

"Yes, ma'am. I shouldn't have gone to the residence. I just wanted to see where my little boy lived and—"

"Uh, huh... I don't care what you wanted. You will follow the rules from here on out."

"Yes, ma'am."

Harry pulls out a paper. "I have visitation set up already for tomorrow with a court-appointed supervisor for Miss Wilder and Leo. Either Shep or Talia will have to drive him to our specified location at Bridgeport's Seaside Park—"

"That location is unsafe. There was a stabbing there last week," Talia spits.

"Enough now," I hear Shep say. "Don't interrupt."

Harry continues, "The location was a midway point between the two residences and has already been predetermined."

"I won't put Leo in danger just because Miss Wilder can't afford to travel to a nicer—"

The woman just can't help herself.

"That will be enough from you, Miss Davenport!" Holcomb says. "One of you will deliver him to the designated location tomorrow or you will be held in contempt of court. Do you understand?"

"We do," Shep answers for both of them.

Talia seethes beside him.

THIRTY-SEVEN
TALIA

"I can't believe you're mad at me," Talia says, watching as Shep tosses clothes in a carry-on suitcase. He moves around Talia as if she's not even there. "Our lawyer said I had a good point given the evidence that Emerson might try to run."

He stops in his tracks, his face sweaty. She's never seen him so angry before. "That's because you put our lawyer in an awful position by presenting evidence he never knew existed. You don't think Emerson is a flight risk. You offered up those pictures to humiliate her!"

He's calling her a liar. She can't allow that type of disrespect from him. She also can't let him leave mad at her. He has to understand she presented that evidence for them. To keep their family together. But that's not the part that bothers her the most. "I didn't know you still cared so much about her."

He doesn't respond, continuing to pack the clothes *she* picked up from the drycleaners, for the trip *she* booked.

Today was supposed to go differently. She called their lawyer on Tuesday and Emerson didn't have clearance from her doctor.

"The pictures demonstrated instability and the Ring

footage showed a chance she'll try to kidnap Leo and flee. You can't leave and put me in a position to bring him to her tomorrow. It's too soon. I'm going to ask to push the visitation date. We can do that."

Shep holds up his travel shaving kit and turns to face her, livid. She flinches. "You *will* deliver Leo to his mother tomorrow. The judge made it clear you have no other choice. She's not going to steal him. If you're so worried, make sure he has his watch on with the GPS tracker. Not that I think it's necessary."

She exhales, trying not to take offense at the way he said— his mother. *I am his mother!* "We haven't even told him she's out, Shep. He's too young to process this so quickly. We can't just be like... hey... Leo, remember your mom? She's back now and you're going to see her tomorrow!"

Shep's mouth creases into a thin line and she knows she's got him on that one. He's in such a hurry for this all to be over, he hasn't thought about Leo's feelings. *He's* the bad parent here. She won't dare say that though.

"It's court-ordered. Emerson's done her part. Now, you have to do yours."

"It's not what's best for Leo. It's what's best for Emerson."

"What is your problem?" He's shouting now.

"We were supposed to have Judge Willoughby. How did we end up with that bleeding heart female judge? She already made her decision before we even got there. It was the wrong one, and I won't let Leo suffer because of it. He's not ready," she says.

Shep exhales. "Because Brooks fixed it so we'd have Holcomb."

Talia remembers seeing Brooks now. The man she thought looked familiar. She'd searched for him online after she learned Emerson would be staying with him. He doesn't participate in social media, but his work headshot was attractive, and he did have an impressive career. A successful lawyer who now dabbles in politics. "Well, that's criminal."

"He probably used his connections to get her a more sympathetic judge."

"You know she's sleeping with him then too, right? Probably has been this whole time. Even when you were married. He wouldn't make such big strides for her if he wasn't."

Shep cackles now. "Now you're just making shit up. People can have genuine relationships without it being physical. They're old friends. Maybe if you had any of those, you'd understand."

Ouch. "Too far," she says.

The way he insults her reminds her of the way Glen talked to her mother. She can't allow it. She won't.

"Well, I don't like the wild assumptions you're making."

"I don't like the way you're speaking to me. Remember, we go into everything together. We're a team. And I'm not ready for her to be a part of ours. And I think you know that Leo isn't either." She's already thought about this speech when the time came. "Leo needs counseling, Shep. It's unsafe for him to see Emerson without weeks, maybe months, of speaking with a professional to prepare him first. You just can't drop this on him."

"How do you know this? Are you a child psychiatrist? I'm pretty sure a judge who's worked in family law for twenty years wouldn't have agreed to something that could destroy him."

"You can't trust the justice system to make decisions for your child. They don't know him. Leo is a sensitive boy. He was crushed they took Pluto away as a formal planet."

"Ah yes... Pluto. Let's compare that to the importance of seeing his birth mother," Shep says sarcastically.

"Shep, let's request to have the meeting pushed and tell them our son isn't ready. It's not all about what Emerson wants."

He pulls his phone out of his pocket and starts flicking his finger over the screen. Shep makes wheezing noises that sound somewhere between swearing under his breath and coughing up a hairball.

"What is it?" she asks.

"I'm going to cancel my trip. You're impossible! I can't trust you to follow the judge's orders and that could implicate me too."

Talia can see the office outlook icon populate his cell screen. *No.* He cannot cancel the trip. The company needs the Liberty Trail deal to close, and if they find out it didn't because she was being difficult—the final seal on a major deal killed over a domestic spat—her career there is done.

"Don't do that. You can't cancel, Shep," she says. "Fine, okay. I'll take him."

He glances up, and he looks like he hates her more now than he did when they started their argument. She's confused. "I just said I'd take him. Did you hear me?"

"Oh, I heard you. It's only when work was threatened that you changed your stance."

She crosses her arms at her chest. "I don't agree with it one bit. And if she pulls something wild, I want you to remember this conversation."

"I'm fairly certain she's not the crazy one at this point."

Talia falls backward, catching herself on the end table. It feels as though he's struck her even though he's standing completely still. *You're going to be sorry.* "Take it back, right now. I've done everything for you. Sacrificed so much. Apologize to me."

"Or what? What're you going to do, Talia?" he asks. He's so pissed and she doesn't understand why.

"I'll tell her everything. All about how you kissed me at the Christmas party when she was pregnant with Thea and couldn't give you all the love you desired."

His mouth drops open. "You wouldn't. That was a mistake. You came on to me. And... it was just a kiss."

"Was it? Would she see it that way—a mistake—considering where we ended up? Together?"

"Why're you doing this?" he asks.

"Because you're letting her come between us. You care more about her feelings than mine. We're bonded by what we've been through together. Don't make me want to tell-all, Shep. If you don't watch your tongue, and remember how to speak to me, you're going to have a lot bigger worries than whether I drive to Bridgeport tomorrow or not."

He steams, silently, but he knows she's got him. The fact that he cheated on Emerson, Gus's death—these are secrets he doesn't want out. He forgets these ties that bind them when he talks to her with such spite.

"Fine. I'm sorry. You're right. I'm being unkind. But you've reacted terribly to this situation. What's best for Leo is healthy coparenting and this isn't the start of that."

She hates that he's using that word—coparent—in regard to Emerson. Talia doesn't want to copilot their family with anyone other than Shep. And there's no way Emerson can just sit down in their small intimate cockpit and take the controls.

"I'm going to have to take the afternoon off tomorrow for the visitation. I'm already taking a day Monday and a half day on Tuesday. This isn't going to look good for me."

"Do you want me to cancel? I'll cancel and try to reschedule for next week," he says, much calmer now.

"No. It's just, once again, I'm taking steps backward at work so that you can grow."

He appears taken aback. "Wow, for someone who says they're in this for the long haul and most interested in putting our family first, you seem pretty resentful. I've offered to cancel my trip twice now. And my next promotion will be because of circumstances I can't control."

"Or ones you can. Just like Emerson's presence in our lives. We can push back."

Shep grimaces at the word—push. "You need to think about what you want, Tal. Emerson is going to be a part of our lives. If you can't handle that, then I get it." He moves around her one last time, zips up his suitcase, and places it near the door. "I'm going to pick up Leo from daycare today." He slams the door behind her.

The door rattles on the doorframe leaving her shaken. She was hoping he'd take the hint about Gus.

Then maybe they could begin a dialogue about making those thoughts a reality. A plan. And Emerson could be gone before the new year.

But no. She's not going to have his agreement on this one.

He didn't tell her it was a bad idea either though. He just doesn't want to be a part of it.

THIRTY-EIGHT

EMERSON

On the way home, I stop at a shopping mall I've never visited before and walk aimlessly through stores searching for a gift to buy Leo. Still dressed up, strangers smile at me in a way that validates me.

I'm respected. Worthy of acknowledgment and praise, like the American flag flapping in the wind.

Solid, a necessary material to this world—like wood or cement.

The way I was treated in that courtroom today did not make me feel any of those things.

She looked at me like I was subhuman. She spoke to me like I was invisible.

How could you let her behave that way? How can you be with someone who'd rather possess you than love you?

I try not to think about Shep as I buy something for our son.

Leo. Think about Leo...

What does he like these days? He's probably out of the action figure stage by now.

I bet *she* knows.

Yet somehow she still doesn't seem like a real threat. There's no way Shep will marry that woman. There's something so unauthentic about the way she conducts herself, there's no way Shep can be serious about her. I know him too well.

Now... I have to get to know my son again.

I pick up a plush stuffed animal, then place it back down, the fuzz leaving an unpleasant residue on my fingertips. He's older now. A stuffed animal isn't right.

Leo is both parts, Shep and me—artist and builder.

I grab a paint kit, and think maybe we can create something together, but I don't have the funds for the supplies, and I want to give him something he can fiddle with at our visit in case he's nervous.

I place the kit back down.

I hate the fact that being with me could make him uneasy. It's not really anything I've considered before.

In my mind, nothing has changed and the victory in the courtroom today was for both of us—Leo and me. It felt more like a fight through quicksand, everyone pushing me down, trying to suffocate me, but—I did it. I made it out, victorious. The corners of my eyes are wet, and I blink the moisture away, too stressed about tomorrow for happy tears just yet.

He's still my sweet little boy. He came from me, bound by a bundle of blood vessels in a flexible, clear sheath until he was removed from my body. Everything about our connection is second nature, but he might feel differently about me now after all this time.

How much of the day that Thea died does Leo remember?

Did he wake up and find me before the medics arrived? Surely someone would've told me if he had. It was the middle of the night. He was sleeping. Has he been to counseling to deal with his sister's death?

Does he even really remember me? He must...

"Can I help you?" A store associate is in my personal space.

I step back. "Yes... I'm looking for a gift for a four-year-old boy. Any ideas for me?"

She smiles and I notice the thin gold necklace she's wearing has two charms—an A and a D. Her necklace probably represents her children's initials. It makes me want to buy one with an L and a T.

"Oh, well, what kinds of things does he like?" she asks.

"I'm not sure. Where did you get that?" I point at her charms. "I really like it."

"Oh, thank you! We sell them here. In jewelry." I may just be asking the question to distract myself—from not knowing what my own son likes. But I won't make myself feel like I don't deserve to wear a necklace just like it.

The sales associate continues, "My nephew is around that age and likes Legos. Not all kids do, but even the ones who don't seem to appreciate the novelty. Or you can't go wrong with Matchbox cars."

"Legos? He likes to build," I say, in almost a whisper. Does he still? I've failed him in so many ways. But there's still time to turn it around.

"Aisle five. Good luck. There's a lot to choose from."

When I leave the mall I have a shopping bag with a tiny skyscraper—my favorite oxymoron—in a plastic bag, and new jewelry on my neck, the first present I've bought for myself in years. A celebratory gift.

Celebrate the small milestones... I hear Joanna's voice echo in my head. It makes me wonder how she is. What she thought when she received the image of the man I sent her. She's probably happy I'm someone else's problem now. I think about baking Klinefelter a zucchini bread or something equally deca-dent. He did okay today—for him.

My phone buzzes in my pocket as I wait for the train.

I missed Brooks's call. *Damn.*

I call him back and he picks up on the first ring. "Hey... where have you been? I mean, I know where you were this morning, but in general? And why were you at the court-house? At my hearing?" I ask.

There's a woman boarding the train looking at me like the bumbling idiot that I am.

"Sorry, I've been out of touch." He says this often when he's up to something. "I think I cleared things up with the cops. The palette knife used was manufactured into a shiv, the way pris-oners sharpen things once they get inside, and make weapons out of them."

"Jesus." My mind runs in a thousand different directions. How could that have happened inside of Meadowbrook? *I didn't do it, in my sleep, did I?*

"I had a receipt to show them I bought the kit earlier that same day, and my attorney argued there's no way I could've created the altered version in the timeframe it was used, even if that was my intention."

"I pulled the knife out at least once in its original form, unaltered. You delivered the kit to me in its original form. I unwrapped the plastic, for God's sake. It was brand new. What's going on, Brooks?"

"Right... I'm still not sure. I trust the hearing went all right this morning?" he asks in that way where he already knows the answer.

I knew that's why he was there. I don't care what he did to fix my case. After what I endured in that courtroom, I see now that I needed a helper to pull me through to the other side. Harry wasn't enough. I would've fallen all the way to the bottom without Brooks. *Dead*. It would've killed me not to win today.

"Good! I got visitation. It was a fight though. They had naked pictures of me... with the date I told you about."

"*What?*" He sounds more angry than I would expect.

"I think Shep's girlfriend had me tailed." As I say the words out loud, they hit me in the gut. She really has it in for me. I've never seen her as a real contender where Shep's love is concerned. I could practically breathe his conflicted feelings for me across the room.

Stronger than any he's likely had for her.

But a new fear creeps up in my throat—a sense of danger as I remember her face as the judge made her decision. She looked like she'd actually harm me.

"What's her name? The girlfriend?" Brooks asks.

I press my lips together, because I've made a point not to say her name out loud. Once you name something, that gives it relevance. "Talia Davenport."

I can hear him tapping the name into the Notes section of his phone.

The Notes section of Brooks's cell phone is one of the scariest places I've ever traveled—and I've been inside of a mental hospital.

I hope he'll do a background check on her and find something more damning than she has on me. Nothing so awful that she's a threat to Leo, but a wakeup call for Shep which seems about six months overdue. She is not who she pretends to be.

"She looks like a bitch," Brooks says.

I laugh out loud. The lady on the train who had a problem with my senseless mumbling on the platform stares at me again. It's good to laugh loud enough in public for people to get annoyed. "That's accurate. She just can't be the bitch who steals my family."

"You don't want him back. He's spineless. And he's using her as his spine," Brooks says.

"I love the way you talk to me. I don't want to know what you were doing there this morning, Brooks, but thank you, in any case. This one meant more than all the rest."

"You don't need to know the whys or the hows. All that matters is that the appropriate ruling was made for the right party."

"You're like the Robin Hood of the Justice system."

"Something like that... Listen, I may need to disappear for a bit. I was calling you to make sure you can take it from here. And that you don't get worried if you don't hear from me in a while."

Shit. I hate when he goes dark. "Everything okay?" I fight nausea, the unsteady train rail giving me motion sickness, Brooks's own bumps in the road more concerning than my own.

I need Brooks in my life.

I may want Shep, but I need Brooks. He's like the umbrella I can hide beneath if the world truly comes down on me. Everybody needs a shield.

"I'm okay. I just have to figure out this mystery of who's targeting me and why, and I can't do it the traditional way. Did anyone not like you at Meadowbrook? You were there a long time."

"Too long. They like to turn beds quickly. I think they make more money that way. It has to do with their billing system. But Joanna knew I needed more time. I don't know what would've happened to me if they released me any sooner."

"I'm glad you got the help you needed. And I'm going to get you back up to speed when I return. Enjoy your time with Leo tomorrow. Take care, Emerson."

"Bye, Brooks."

My call ends and the woman on the train eyes me with disdain. Her jowls overpower her face and I imagine they are curtains I can turn inside out to block her out. I stare right back at her, so hard, I can see the flecks of orange in the pupils of her eyes.

She glances away, uncomfortable, as if I've just climbed through her skull and bored out her insides. I'm already tired of people judging me.

Inside of Meadowbrook, I was safe.

I give the woman another dirty glance, and remind her—out here, no one is.

THIRTY-NINE

TALIA

The conversation with Leo goes worse than expected. Shep is impatient with him because he has to hop a flight in the morning. He just expected Leo to adjust to the news that he'll be seeing Emerson—*his mother*—who he hasn't so much as heard a word about in the last year, and barely even knows—tomorrow afternoon.

Talia tried to tell Shep this wouldn't be easy.

Leo's little face pales in comparison to his dark hair. "No. Emme Mommy is sick and isn't coming back," he says, for the third time.

Talia winces, her own words repeated back to her through Leo's mouth. Shep doesn't know that though. Shep sighs, for about the hundredth time. "She was sick, buddy. But the great news is, she's been in the hospital, and she's finally well enough to come out."

Leo shakes his head. The poor kid's in shock.

"She's not coming back." He hugs his middle. His nose is red and his eyes are watery. He's sneezed a few times since he's been home. A seasonal virus is all they need on top of everything else.

Shep kneels in front of Leo and rubs his shoulder, but Leo is tensed against the living room couch. Talia can see him swallow, uncomfortable. *Is he going to be sick?*

Talia's just noticed the photo album in Shep's hand. She's never seen it before. It's leather, but it has little airplanes stitched across the cover in blue and red leather strips. Emerson must've made it for him.

Leo pats the airplanes.

"Your mommy made this for you." Talia feels the subtle jerk to her system when Shep calls Emerson Mommy.

Mommy was just in the hospital a week ago because she saw imaginary predators in her bedroom.

Mommy is not fit to have you in her care.

But that's not actually Talia's biggest issue. It's the fact that Leo doesn't want to be in Emerson's care. He touches the album, but doesn't open it. He's not responding to the news of his mother's return with excitement or even guarded curiosity.

Because he's four years old, and he doesn't understand what's happening.

Shep flips open the album, and inside is a picture of Emerson holding Leo as an infant. "That's you."

"I'm so little," Leo says. It's clear he's never seen these pictures before. Talia hasn't either. They slash into her sideways. These are family memories she should be making with Shep, not revisiting ones he created with another woman.

"You are little, but you get bigger with each page," Shep says.

Talia sits there beside Shep, knowing he expects her to be the supportive girlfriend. But looking at photographs of Emerson, who appears to be healthy and happy, and knowing deep down what she's capable of, is the absolute worst. And she can't stand being complicit with Shep as Shep lies to their little boy— all while he's having trouble processing any of it.

"That's your mommy after she got her Silly Suzies deal. She was so excited."

Leo smiles at a photograph of Emerson standing next to the author of the series, Natasha Wales. Natasha holds up their first book that would be one of many. Shep forces Talia to keep the books in the house so Leo can have some reference of—*who Emme Mommy is and what she used to do*—and Talia hates it.

"Emme Mommy is an artist," Leo says out loud, like he's trying to identify her species in science class. He probably uses the same tone when he says Saturn has seven rings. It's just a fact to him.

"That's right," Shep says. "And she's so excited to meet you tomorrow after school. I have to go away for work, but Talia is going to take you to see her."

"Tomorrow?" he asks, terror on his face like the time they took him on a Ferris wheel at Playland Park and crested the top.

Shep glances at Talia briefly, and this is so fucking hard.

"Ya, bud. It will be a short meeting, this first one. Don't worry."

Today is step one—the announcement that Emerson is back. It's too soon for them to move on to step two—meeting in person. They can't rush this.

"He's not ready," Talia says.

Shep glares at her, disappointed.

Leo shakes his head. Tears streak his face.

"Leo, I know you're scared, but Emme Mommy is feeling better now and she just wants to see you. She misses you very much, sweetheart," Shep says.

"But tomorrow is movie day. We're watching Charlie Brown's pumpkin patch. And my nose is runny. I don't want Emme Mommy to get sick again." Leo says all these phrases in short rasps. Especially the last one.

Poor guy. It's all kid-speak for—*I don't want to go. I'm not ready*.

"Shep…" Talia nods at Leo, as if there's any more to say here. "He's not ready."

He gives her a stern look, an order to cooperate, which is just ridiculous.

She's always thought he was a good parent, overall. She does most of the running with Leo, but Shep's always been able to talk to him on a level that she could not. But today, she's not so sure he's being a good parent at all. He's just doing what's easiest. What the court told him to do. Not what's best for his child.

Leo can't tear his eyes away from the photos in the book. Shep shuts it. "Leo, you'll still get to watch the movie. Talia is going to take you after school to meet your mom. It will be quick. She just wants to say hi. And Talia will give you your allergy pill. It's that time of year when you get the sniffles."

He looks a bit stunned. "I want to go play on my iPad now." Which is code for—I've reached my full childhood mental bandwidth for the day.

"Go ahead, honey," Talia tells him.

Leo bolts from the living room, and once he's out of earshot, Talia whispers, "Shep… this is a mistake. I think you can see that now."

"If you do not take Leo to meet Emerson tomorrow, we will be held in contempt of court. We will get fined, Talia. And most importantly, it will delay our efforts in eventually getting the custody agreement we desire later on down the line."

There won't be a custody arrangement. Emerson will be gone by then.

"Are you denying the fact that your son is extremely uncomfortable with this decision?"

Shep blows out more hot air, plays with his hair that could use a trim. "Sure. It's uncomfortable for everybody. But it will teach him life lessons about how to push through when things are difficult. Might as well rip of the Band-Aid."

"No. You cannot treat this like a minor cut. This is major stuff. And listen... you know I've always been here for you guys, but I don't think I should be the one to deliver Leo. You should."

Shep pulls his phone back out, flustered. "So you do want me to cancel my fucking trip? Why can't you be straightforward if that's what you want?"

He's cursing at her again. The disrespect makes her want to throttle him.

I've killed a man before. I'll do it again.

"That's not what I want at all. If I have to remind you how to speak to me again, we won't be having *any* future conversations. I want you to push the visitation."

He bows his head, beyond frustrated.

She wants this relationship to work, but not badly enough to be treated like garbage.

"Here's the thing, Shep. I lived with a woman who forced me to be around men who made me feel uncomfortable, all the time. She told me it was for my own good, and that's just the way it was. And I still have never, ever forgiven her. It's the reason I don't speak to her now. Leo may be a child, but we can't disregard his feelings. He will remember this later. All of it."

"Talia, I'm sorry..." He hesitates, but doesn't finish.

Talia's told him a little bit about her upbringing, but hasn't gone into great detail.

Shep says, "Look, I know I lost my temper. It won't happen again, I promise. But I need to be able to count on you to take Leo to meet Emerson tomorrow. Can you do that? If the answer is no, I understand, really. You have done a ton for us. And I appreciate everything and I get it if this is one thing too many. I can reschedule Boston or ask Neve to take it."

He cannot ask Neve.

She'll take the Liberty Trail account and then try to steal Shep's promotion. It's hard to be mad at him when he's being so understanding. His life is in a tailspin, and he's being perfectly considerate. She has to help him find his way out, not pile on.

"Okay, I'll do it. But for the record, I think it's a huge mistake."

"Noted. And thank you." He kisses her on the forehead.

She remembers a long time ago reading something about forehead kisses meaning a warm gesture that symbolizes a person will be there for you no matter what.

She wonders how far that devotion stretches, because over the next couple of days... that sentiment will be tested.

FORTY
EMERSON

Dear Miss Wilder,

I'm sorry if I startled you the other day when I drove into town to find you. The last thing I want is for you to feel frightened by me.

I know you're not willing to sell your property right now, but I did want to give you a soundbite of what I was preparing to use it for, in case you change your mind. Please click on the link and respond after you review it, so I know that you got it.

Kind regards,

Kent Bessler

Oh boy... Maybe it's because I've just won my hearing.

Or perhaps it's the fact that I just watched my husband's new girlfriend reveal herself as the sociopath I suspected she was in front of a room full of people. Hopefully, I get the same judge for the custody hearing too.

In any case, I tear off my suit jacket and decide to humor ole Kent Bessler.

The springs of the hand-me-down couch my colleague gifted me sink with the weight of my body. I click on the link and disappear into Kent's weird cyberworld.

Kent's stubbly face appears on my cell screen, my old farm-house in absolute tatters behind him. I try not to scream out loud. Like something out of *American Horror Story* the weeds and brush overpower what used to be a walkway, leaving no clear path for a person to reach the front steps, which appear as though they're sunken in.

It's evident Shep hasn't paid the landscapers for the upkeep on the property. He probably hasn't had anyone go inside to turn on the water to make sure the pipes haven't burst, and he sure as hell hasn't had the property manager come by for routine maintenance.

You took all my money and then let my house fall to shambles.

Every day I have more doubts about Shep's place in my life. Reuniting our family might be what's best for Leo, but it's unfortunate proof like this that makes me realize, much like my house, that Shep really did leave me to rot.

Brooks is not wrong about that.

I wonder if Shep even paid the property taxes before we divorced.

Maybe my house is in foreclosure, and Kent needs to do nothing more than waltz into the county clerk's office and make an offer. "*Sonofabitch.*"

I have to rewind Kent's link, because I haven't heard a word he's saying in his ultra-weird, ghost-chasing voice over my own thoughts. If Kent is still offering fifty grand for that house, in that state of disrepair, maybe I should take it. It will probably cost me way more than that just to make it livable again.

The beginning of the recording starts again:

This is Kent Bessler, paranormal researcher based out of Thompson, Connecticut. At the Wilder property, again, which we discussed on our last segment. I'm standing as close as I can to the property line without trespassing. Thank you to all who've inquired about the survivors. I believe I've addressed what I could in the comments section below.

Today, we're headed east on forty-four toward Providence, near the location of where my sweet stepson went missing.

Kent throws images up on the screen of a quaint New England town, large bodies of water, serene music. But then, his music changes to something closer to the *Psycho* theme totally cheesy, but the intended heartfelt message is not lost on me.

This road is where his bike was found abandoned, tire tracks dug in as if by an abnormal force. The tire tracks were actually two inches deep. Doesn't make sense.

Unless it was raining or the ground was soft for some reason, I think to myself. Or... someone hit him with their car, causing the bike to dig deeper. A person could've sprung from the woods, grabbed the boy while riding, caused the thick indent. I hate where my mind takes me, but it's anywhere but the occult. Kent is a bit cracked, that's for sure.

And then—Kent's face—too close up—appears back on the screen.

The show closes with the camera's pan up to my house's upstairs. There's a fabricated flame transposed over the window. A closer look, and I can see there's also a shadow of the man who used to live there, Ernest Whitten, holding his welder's torch.

At the bottom of the video is a picture of Kent's stepson, about ten, a quick blurb about how he mysteriously vanished while riding his bike. There's also a Venmo donation link to

Kent's show, asking viewers to help bring justice to the paranormal cases no one else wants to touch.

I click on the comments section, and surprisingly, Kent has
a following. Over one hundred thousand subscribers. The
naysayers are equating Kent's theories surrounding the missing
boy to anything from a lack of mental faculties to drug use.

I don't buy into the occult, my own demons are hard enough
to fight.

Kent seems like a poor man who never got over the disappearance of his stepson, using his show to assuage his own hurts
by trying to solve other people's unsolved mysteries. The
videography is poor and the music is hokey, but I can't help but
feel sorry for the guy. If he really wants to unload that eyesore
of a house from me, I should probably let him.

There's a lot I could do with $50,000.

Buy a car. Place a down payment on a condo.

I received exceptional news today. I got a "yes" on something I worked so hard for. Something, I direly needed in my
life to move forward.

I shoot Kent a message right back.

I have a feeling my "yes" might do the same for him.

Joanna calls my phone as I slide a chicken potpie into the oven.
I've been saving it for a special occasion. Sad really. I'm going to
need to really up my game if I'm to ever feed my child.

"Hey, how did the hearing go? You never called me."

"I'm so sorry. It's been a busy day. I won the case. I'm going
to see Leo tomorrow."

There's a pause on the other end, but I can hear the silent
glee. No one knows what this means to me like she does.
"That's so wonderful, Emerson. I couldn't be happier for you."

"Thank you. So much. I'm nervous about seeing him again,

and I know we have to ease into everything, but I just can't help thinking about our future together already."

"Wonderful. And Shep? How was he?"

I could scream out loud when I think of Shep. "His girl-friend came at me during the hearing. Had pictures of me. Had someone follow me. Had Ring doorbell footage of me near their house. Attacked me for being hospitalized."

"Oh my god."

"It was terrible. Shep didn't do a lot to defend me, although he did tell her to quiet down a few times. She's a handful. And she's going to be a problem."

"Well, ideally you want someone you can coparent with and she doesn't seem like she's the right person for that. Maybe he'll figure that out."

"She does not want me in their life. At all."

"Well, that's too bad."

"That's right." It's good to hear the resolve returning to my voice. "I can't wait to see Leo tomorrow."

"Fantastic. I hope you're meeting inside. The storms that have Rupert delayed are moving our way. We've only received an email from him. Emerson..."

"What's wrong? This isn't just a courtesy call, is it?"

It's the inflection in Joanna's voice. Strained. Sure, she was curious about my case, but there's something else. Something bad.

"Do you know the picture you shared with me, the one Justine sent to Klinefelter, but not me?" The fact that the picture wasn't shared with Joanna is such a sticking point. I can only think about his fingers clenching my arm, around my neck, since the drawing was discovered.

"Of course," I say.

"I gave it to the police. To Detective Ramsey. He's the only officer who's advocated for you. He thinks there's more to your break-in. He's been following the case."

"Oh good. What did he say?"

"Well... they ran facial recognition on the man's face. They haven't relayed all the information to me yet, but... They might have a match."

"What?" I ask, dumbfounded.

"It matched a man in their database. A former convicted felon."

The Man... Is real?

FORTY-ONE

TALIA

Storm clouds smear the morning sky. The temperature dropped about ten degrees overnight, and Talia wonders if it will snow before Halloween, like it did last year.

Even though she pushed him to go, Talia also secretly hopes Shep's flight to Logan International Airport is canceled so he can deal with the Emerson and Leo exchange. But she checks his flight and sees that it still shows—*On Time*.

She thinks of their evening last night, after their little talk with Leo. They called him down for dinner, and he just sat there, pushing his food around.

But Talia knows that look, and it's far more than a loss in appetite.

Leo is a thinker. "Why isn't Pluto a planet anymore? Why doesn't Mercury have rings?"

And when Talia picked Leo up from Kai's house. "Why does Mrs. Young use vinegar to make pancakes. Pancakes are sweet. Vinegar is sour." He is constantly examining things—the why behind them. Talia thinks he's going to be a scientist of some sort.

What did his tiny brain wonder after their photo album

discussion? *Why is Emme Mommy back? Why did Talia tell me she wouldn't get better?*

Talia can't even imagine, but she knows what it's like to have those types of thoughts at a very young age. She was that kid. Shep doesn't understand what it's like. That she is trying to protect Leo from everything that hurt her when she was younger.

And she failed...

"Earth to Talia!"

Neve is leaning on her desk. For how long, she wonders?

"Sorry, I was... just worrying about whether I checked to make sure Shep's seat had a carry-on option. I made that mistake once before with Gus." She clicks shut her browser windows—all displaying searches on child custody law.

"Well, did it?" Neve asks.

Whew. She shut the windows in time. "Did it what, I'm sorry?"

Neve makes a face like she's frightened. "Have the carry-on? The ticket? Are you okay?" She laughs now, and Talia pretends to laugh too.

"Oh! Yes, it did," she says, her cheeks warm with embarrassment.

"Okay... Great news. The art gallery project bid came in from financing. I'd love to have something over to Svensson by the end of the day." Neve's teeth gleam so white Talia wonders if she's just had them bleached.

"Um..." She stalls. *Shit.* Talia has to leave a little early today to scoop Leo off the bus at four, which means she needs to leave by two forty-five at the latest to avoid rush-hour traffic. If she sends the bid over, Svensson may want to discuss it, likely later in the day once she's had a chance to look it over.

"What is it?" Neve asks. "Hey, how did the hearing go? Wasn't that this week?"

THE WIFE AT THE WINDOW

Priya pops her head above the partition. "I was actually wondering that as well."

Jesus. Priya's so quiet Talia always forgets she's there. "So... Emerson is getting visitation."

"Ooh. You didn't want that." Priya states the obvious.

"Right. But—"

"She's his mom. And I told you this would happen and not to fight it or it would cause problems between you and Shep. And it has, hasn't it?" Neve asks.

"It's fine."

Priya and Neve communicate a look that says—*we know you're lying.* "When's the big visitation day?" Neve asks.

"Well, that's the problem. It's today."

"Today?" Priya asks, shocked. "Wasn't the hearing just yesterday?" It's hard to surprise Priya. So Talia knows she's not off base here that this is all happening way too fast.

"It was."

"And how's the little boy taking it?" Neve asks.

"Leo... is not taking it well at all. He's not ready. He broke down yesterday," she admits.

She won't tell them about her fractured relationship with Shep. That serves no one if she plans to stay with him—which she does.

"Well, are you still taking him today? File an injunction or something?" Neve asks, as if she knows anything about the legal system or the proper definition of the word—injunction.

"Can't. The judge has it in for me because I pleaded on Leo's behalf that it was too soon, and she said I'll be held in contempt of court if we don't show. He's not feeling great on top of it. Sneezing yesterday, woke up with it again today. Which is why... I might need an extension on that bid to Svensson until Monday."

Please say yes. Please don't give it away to Priya or take it yourself.

"We'll just... not tell Svennson the bid is in until Monday," Neve says.

"Really?" Talia can't believe her ears.

"Ya, whatever. It's Friday. She's probably practicing early hygge or shearing a goat or something else very eccentric and therapeutic. And I can't have you distracted drafting the bid. God forbid you miss a zero."

"Thanks..."

"So leave or whatever, when you need to get the boy. If he's sick, you could probably get out of the whole visit though."

Priya seems to be preoccupied on her phone, which is unlike her. "That's what I'm looking up?"

"Why?" Talia's confused as to why these two are helping her. She feels something strange welling up inside of her. Has she made actual... *friends*? She's not sure, she's never really had any.

"It says here, all you need is a doctor's excuse or a note from the school, and it's possible to push your visitation or custody date," Priya says.

"Can you please forward me that link?" Talia asks.

"Already done," Priya says.

"Thank you, guys. But she knows where I live. What if she shows up if I don't deliver Leo? It'll be a whole thing. I've caught her on my Ring doorbell stalking us already."

Oh crap. Talia overshared. Neither Neve nor Priya will make eye contact with her now.

"I'd invite you to my parents' house, but both my sisters are in town, and it will be insane," Priya says.

Talia can't fathom bringing Leo to a place at Halloween time that doesn't believe in distributing candy. Everyone should have chocolate at this time of year.

"Come with me. To my parents' country home. She'll never find you there," Neve says.

I give her a hard stare to see if she's serious. "I'd have to bring Leo with me."

"No kidding," Neve says.

"Do you even like kids?" Talia asks.

Priya covers her mouth, stifling a giggle.

Neve places her hand on her hips. "I'm fine with kids. I just don't want any of my own. He'll get along with my niece and nephew..."

"If I can call off this meetup, I'll take you up on the offer," Talia says, although she doesn't really think that will be possible.

"Sweet. I'll call my mom, and let's reconvene after lunch." Neve claps her hands as if they've just adjourned a work meeting instead of making plans to spend the weekend together. This must be what being friends with Neve looks like.

First, Talia goes online and finds the logo for Leo's school. She right-clicks on it, saves it, then pastes it into the masthead of one of their standard business letters, and voila, she has the start of an official school letter from the nurse.

She writes:

Date: October 27, 2023

To Whom it May Concern:

Leo Kingsley was excused early from school today because he was ill. Leo had a fever and complained of a runny nose and sore throat. We require a minimum of twenty-four hours before he can return to class.

Sincerely,

Kimberly Columbus, School Nurse

(insert fake number close to the actual school's)

(insert fake electronic signature)

Talia calls the courthouse to find out who the contact is for supervised visits. She writes down the information. But won't send the email until right before she picks up Leo.

That way Emerson won't have time to catch a train to Stamford if she decides to go *Single White Female* on her and show up at her doorstep.

Shep will be in flight and in meetings. Even if Emerson tries to call him, he likely won't pick up. And if he does try to contact Talia, she'll be long gone. She'll explain Leo was too sick to see Emerson, but that she didn't want to ruin his entire weekend, so she took him out to the country for some fresh air.

He'll be pissed. It might end their relationship.

But when even Neve, the ice queen, thinks it's heartless to make Leo see his mother so soon...

She knows it's the right thing to do for Leo. And in the end, that's all that really matters.

FORTY-TWO

EMERSON

The train ride to Bridgeport is filled with hope and terror and anticipation.

I hold the Lego set in a giftbag, colorful tissue paper poking out of the top. Maybe Leo will save building the Lego for our time together. We can build it and our relationship back, brick by brick.

I wonder if he'll even like it.

I wonder if he'll like me...

After all that time with that... woman.

I'm so mad that Shep's not here today to hand off Leo to me. That it will be that hateful dragon instead.

In the paperwork, it said he couldn't attend the meeting today because of a prearranged work trip. What could possibly be so important that it couldn't be rescheduled? He never put his work before his family when we were married.

Well, maybe that's not true...

Maybe if he would've come home at a reasonable hour the night I had my terror, Thea would still be here. But *this*. Today. His son's first time reunited with his mother. He should be here for this.

Maybe she's arranged it this way. To try to get me to back down.

She'll figure out soon enough that she can't push me aside like unwanted trash. Yesterday's hearing was my foot in the door, and I'm here to stay now.

My phone rings. It's my lawyer, probably calling to check on me. "Hey, Harry."

"Emerson, have I caught you before you've left for your meeting?"

"No, I wanted to get there a little early and settle my nerves." My hands grip the present like it might fly away from me.

"Look, I have some bad news."

No. I need this day. Do not give me bad news. This has to happen. I must see my son. "What is it?"

"Leo is ill. Nothing major, but he does have a note from his school that he went home early today."

"Bullshit, Harry." My throat is squeezing itself shut. *I cannot*... with this woman.

"There's not a lot I can do. We can ask for the doctor's note too, but today will have to be postponed. If this happens again we'll file for contempt of court, but we can't make Leo attend the meeting if there's proof he's sick. And there is."

"You've got to be kidding me."

"You know... yesterday was a lot. This is one of the tenser cases I've worked. Maybe a little break in the action to collect your thoughts might be beneficial."

"I don't think so." My fingers dig into the bag. I need to see my son today.

I *will* still see my son today.

FORTY-THREE
EMERSON

Change of plans.

So Leo's not well enough to meet me. Okay, well, then I'll come to him. I can drop off his gift and I will ask to see him.

He has to be home. He's sick.

If she refuses, I'll scream his name until he comes to the door, throw pebbles at his bedroom window. Whatever it takes. I cannot make it another day without seeing Leo's face. It's all I've thought about.

An officer can try to arrest me, but I'll explain I have planned visitation and that Leo didn't show up. I was worried, so I took the train to check on him. Maybe I'll lie and say I never received a call from Harry. Why do I care if I have to lie to get what I want?

She sure doesn't.

There's not a bone in my body that believes she didn't make up Leo's illness.

And she waited until Shep was gone to do it. She's sneaky and horrible.

And she's not doing herself any favors with Shep. His last

girlfriend lied to him about their finances, and while he's tolerant of a lot, lies, even small ones, aren't on the list. This will end them. He'll know all about it when he returns. I'll make sure of that.

And then he'll leave her.

I saw the way his face twisted in that courtroom when she wouldn't shut her trap. I'll let that doomed relationship self-destruct, but not at the expense of my relationship with my son.

I walk from Stamford station. The clouds look like over-stuffed gray pillows ready to burst at the silvery seams. Every time I come here it's raining. The landscape here is gray and filled with sadness.

It's also where my son lives.

Not for long...

She's done everything she can to ruin me, and it's time to turn the tables.

I think about the photographs of me and Jacob, and the complete vulnerability of those private moments. There's also the fact that the court has them sealed up somewhere. There're naked pictures of me floating around the legal system, and it's all her doing.

She said she had a *friend* who took the pictures. Everyone in that courtroom could tell she was lying.

When I reach the townhouse, it's like a fortress and she has Leo locked inside.

But all of the lights inside appear to be turned off. There's no car in the driveway and Shep's car fills the small garage. He probably flew or took the train to whatever work venture he was attending, which means she's not here. And neither is Leo. Everything about this feels off.

If Leo had a note from school, he likely is really ill, but then where is he? Is he so sick that she had to take him somewhere—an urgent care maybe?

Is she at the grocery store picking up supplies before the storm, and she had to drag Leo along because Shep isn't here?

Or is it something more sinister?

My heart burns in my chest. I just want to see him again. That's it.

It's unlivable, being separated from him. I can't do it anymore.

The brazen surface of the outside brick brushes against my cheek as I push myself as close to the building as possible to avoid the freezing spray of water. I make sure to stay clear of the video recorder inside the front entrance doorbell, but I need to get inside of the house and make sure my son is okay. If he's not home, maybe there's a clue as to where they've gone.

I creep over to the keypad beside the garage, and try to think of what the code could be.

People are creatures of habit. Shep used his birthday at our old house, so I try it now.

It doesn't work.

The rain grates at my skin as I attempt Leo's next. The red light flashes, denying me access, and I wonder if I'm going to have to throw a rock through the window to get inside.

I'm worried they have an alarm system. Surely, a broken window will trip it. The police could be an option. I could ask for a wellness check on my supposedly sick child, but I'm breaking the law just standing in their driveway.

How could I explain I suspected they weren't home without admitting that I was on the premises?

I cover my phone from the storm with my hand and scroll through Talia's Facebook page. Her profile is set to public, her social media posts, a complete highlight reel. She looks perfect in every post as if she posed and retouched her makeup before each one. People who try that hard make me wonder what they're overcompensating for.

I find her birthday listed clear as day.

My slippery fingers punch in the date—0428—and the garage light turns green and begins to lift. The garage code is set to *her* birthday. Shocker.

FORTY-FOUR
EMERSON

Once inside the townhouse, I slip my wet shoes off in their immaculate home. My house never looked this orderly, even when I tried. The white walls are so bright they hurt my eyes, reminding me of the hospital, the decorations sparse and uninspiring.

The books on the shelf are all classics—*War and Peace, Gone with the Wind, The Old Man and the Sea.* I know she's never read them. They're just for show, like everything else about her. That's what's missing from this space—a sense of character.

"Leo!" I shout, just in case he's here.

No one answers. I keep the lights off, the pre-dusk sunlight still enough to make my way around. I don't want the neighbors to know I'm here.

I find Shep's office and sit in his leather chair, inhaling his leftover cologne. I rifle through the papers on his desk and see a flight itinerary for Logan International Airport. *Boston.*

I check the time and it looks like he's still in transit. My guess is that Shep can't pick up for me right now anyway, and I have a better shot of making contact with him if I wait.

His itinerary says he won't be back until Sunday, and I wonder what Brighton has him doing over there. I miss hearing about his work stories, watching him get excited over new projects—dreams to build. He used to say that every building or business started as someone's vision, and he was the creator to bring their dreams to life.

For a long time I thought he was the one to make mine come true too.

What if I just sit here until Talia and Leo get home?

Swing around in the leather chair. *Mommy's home.*

She'd lose her absolute shit. We'd end up in a fist fight. Not the best way to reinsert myself in my son's life—in the same way I was taken out—with violence.

And handcuffs.

Because I'll definitely be arrested for trespassing then.

I dig around on Shep's desk for clues as to where Leo might be, and I come up empty. Shep has a heap of overdue bills. He was awful at money management. It's the reason he didn't know his ex-girlfriend was stealing from him.

I rise from the desk and dig for clues as to where they went.

I see a bottle of allergy medicine, tissues, and cough drops on the kitchen table. Leo has seasonal allergies. I'm also guessing they'll be back to retrieve these supplies if they're headed somewhere. If they were going away for the weekend, wouldn't they take those items with them?

There's nothing downstairs, so I take the steps to the second floor. I open up the door to Leo's immaculate room, save a couple of tissues on the nightstand.

Maybe she wasn't lying about him being sick...

It's hard looking at all of his things, a snapshot of how much he's changed. Action figures are replaced by dog characters with different working uniforms I've never seen before—police officer, fireman, a garbage truck driver. His Halloween costume hangs on the doorknob, a replica of one of the dogs.

He has a couple of Legos built and displayed on shelves in his room, so my gift isn't a complete miss. I'll just have to wait to give it to him. I glance at the sad wet giftbag in my hand and shut the door, leaving it as I found it.

The bed in the master is made, the drawers in good order.

I find their Jack and Jill closet. As I flip through her clothes, all expensive name brands—*now I see why you're with Shep.* She's as bad as the girl before me.

I find drawers and open them, looking for clues as to who this woman really is. And where she might have taken my child. The first drawer has enough lingerie to fill a Victoria's Secret store—*and now I know why he's with her...*

This relationship is nothing but surface material, as I thought.

There's a banker's box inside one of the drawers. A weird place for storage. I open it and find the first cluttering, a mish-mash of items—an old Yearbook, a few photographs, an address book.

I pull out the address book and discover a host of passwords.

She's so organized, she has every single one written down. When she updates the password she places a date beside it, a level of detail that annoys me. I take the book downstairs and find her laptop closed on the countertop.

I open it and discover the password for—laptop—a bunch of numbers and letters that mean nothing to me. I type them in and have access to her files.

I open her email and see one from her colleague, Neve. I remember Shep seemed to like her. I never got the chance to meet her because we never made it to the same Brighton functions.

Hey, after you pick up Leo, meet me at the train station. We'll leave and go to my parents' house from there. They even bought an extra pumpkin for Leo to carve. He'll love a little time in the country.

Can't wait!

Xx,

Neve

Thanks, see you as soon as I can snag Leo. Thanks for the idea to call him in sick. It worked!!

~T

570-555-5555

I take a picture of the emails with my phone for my lawyer. I'll tell him a "friend" from Shep's work who knows me took the picture and sent it to me.

My hands shake to the point I'm sure I could strangle her if she was standing right in front of me.

Talia Davenport has kidnapped my son.

FORTY-FIVE
TALIA

"We're going on an adventure!" Talia screams over the pelting rain as they make a run for it across the train station parking lot. Talia tries to hold an umbrella over Leo's head, but it's kind of impossible to carry a child's booster seat, roll luggage, and effectively handle an umbrella at the same time. Leo does his best to stay beneath it, his stuffed backpack weighing him down.

"I thought we were going to see Emme Mommy," he says.

"No, the school said you were coughing. We don't want her to get sick again."

It's mean to make him think his cold could set Emme Mommy back to the state she was in before, but it's also absurd to force Leo to see Emerson before he's ready.

"I wasn't coughing. I was sneezing," Leo corrects her, and he sounds mad about her mistake.

"Yes, that's right. Sneezing," she says.

Water drips down his cute face as he gapes at her in confusion.

When they reach Neve's vehicle, to Talia's shock and amazement, Neve hops out of her Range Rover and opens the backdoor for Leo, then climbs back into her driver seat.

Leo jumps inside to stay dry as Talia leans, half in half out the car, trying to fit the complex contraption that is his car seat, swearing under her breath as the rain drenches her back from every angle.

She thinks she can hear Neve laughing at her from the front seat.

By the time Talia sits in the passenger seat, she needs a towel. "Sorry!" she apologizes.

"Tell me again why people have children," Neve says.

"Hey!" Leo shouts from the backseat.

Talia shoots Neve a dirty look. "Try harder to be nice if we're going to spend the weekend together. He's a sensitive kid."

"I was kidding! It was a joke."

"Didn't sound funny to me," Leo peeps.

Talia and Neve stifle a shared laugh. "This is going to be a trip to remember," Neve says.

"I told Leo it was going to be an adventure."

"Ya... well, our adventure would normally take about two and half hours to reach from here, but I'm guessing it's going to be closer to three with this weather. Do any passengers with small bladders have to use the restroom before we leave?"

"I went already," Leo says.

"I was talking about Talia," Neve says. "She takes a lot of bathroom breaks at work."

Leo laughs, because potty jokes are always funny in their house. "Miss Neve thinks she's so funny." Little does Neve know, Talia visits the bathroom more frequently than most to check her appearance, not to use the facilities. Can't have Shep seeing her looking anything but her best.

"What're we going to do on our adventure?" Leo asks.

"My parents have a pumpkin carving contest. Do you want to play?" Neve asks Leo. Talia appreciates the fact that she uses her best "kid" voice.

"Ya. I'm going to make a ghost," Leo says.

"Ooh... Scary," Talia says.

Talia's phone rings. *Unknown number.*

"Who is it?" Neve asks.

"I don't know." She's worried it's the police, because if Talia was Emerson the first thing she would do if her visitation meeting was canceled is call them and file a complaint, something that would be on official record in case it happened again. But Talia has a good excuse. A written one, actually. Cleared by the family law department. "This is Talia."

A woman squawks at her, and it takes a minute before she realizes who it is. "Emerson?" Talia's guessing she retrieved her number from the courthouse paperwork.

"That's right," she says, breathing too heavily into the phone. "I know you have Leo and you're fleeing with him. After you claimed he was sick."

"Are you near my house? Because if I catch footage of you on my camera, you're in way more trouble than I am. Remember what Holcomb said? I have a school note. Leo's missed appointment is an excused absence."

"Your note is bullshit!"

Talia wonders if she's bluffing. Does Emerson really know that the note is fake? It's impossible that she called the school to verify. Talia was careful to wait until just before the family courts and the school closed before relaying her message. The school administration building would've been closed for hours by the time word got to Emerson. "It's not, actually. He hasn't been feeling well. It's not the best day for you to meet him. He was nervous to begin with and he's not his best self."

Silence on the other end. Talia thinks she may even hear a little panting. "I want to speak to my son," Emerson says.

"Hang up the phone and put it on airplane mode. You shouldn't have to deal with this while Shep's out of town," Neve tells her. And she's absolutely right. She had to let Shep attend the meeting, but she shouldn't have to deal with Emerson while he's gone.

"See you at the next visit. Provided you don't have any more bad dreams." Talia hangs up, and Neve cackles beside her like a witch. Maybe Talia's one too. It is Halloween season after all.

"This rain is the pits," Talia says. They're moving at a snail's pace on back country roads. It doesn't take long before Leo starts to complain.

"My iPad is almost out of battery."

Talia looks behind her at Neve's charging situation. "There's a port back there. Take your charger out of your backpack and stick it in the charging port in front of you."

"Huh?" he asks.

Talia sighs, still a little unnerved from Emerson's call. She hasn't figured out what she's going to say to Shep yet. She promised him she would take Leo to the meeting. She thinks about texting him a screenshot of the fabricated note from the school. But it's easily refutable, and if Emerson really gets on to him about it, he probably will validate it. He already surprised Talia once by confronting her about her make-believe spin class with Priya.

She can hear Leo whimper in frustration as he looks at the plug end of the charger, not understanding how to make it work with the USB port.

"Give it to me," she tells Leo.

He hands her his charger and she plugs it into the port for him. Neve watches her curiously.

"It's like their minds aren't fully formed yet," Neve says.

"Precisely. They're still developing humans," she says.

Neve nods, and it's fascinating—teaching the phenomenon of children—to Neve. Talia wonders if she's ever had a child in this vehicle. It's so pristine, her SUV looks like it's never seen a sticky lollipop or a crushed Goldfish cracker. "So how many nieces and nephews do you have?"

"Just two, one of each. My brother always wanted a boy and a girl, and that's what he got. He's one of those people who decides what the world is going to deliver him, and it's granted."

"Seems to run in the family." Talia grins, not exactly stoked to be spending the weekend with this over-accomplished bunch.

"Oh no... he puts me to shame. He went all-state for football, scholarships for crew, played pick-up hockey for fun and ended up with a minor league offer without even trying out. Academic honors. Devastatingly good-looking. Irritating, is what he is."

"I don't have any siblings. I wouldn't mind one."

"He could be worse, I guess. The rain has finally let up a bit. Why don't we pull over at this rest stop? Your little dude can use the restroom. You can grab snacks and I'll refuel."

"Okay, sounds like a plan. Leo, we're going to take a potty break. If you go, you get to pick out a snack and a drink."

"Yay!" He cheers.

As they enter the store, debris from the road, branches and leaves are all over the parking lot. She wonders how Neve even made it this far.

Talia pulls Leo into the ladies room.

"I don't want to go in there. It's for girls."

"Well, your dad's away, and this is what we do when he's not here, remember?"

"No. I don't want to go in there." Leo holds his crotch. He *really* has to go.

"I have to go too. You can use the stall right next to me."

"No. Dad's let me go in by myself before. At McDonald's once. I'm a big boy. You go on your side, and I'll go on mine. You meet me out here."

She wants to fight him, but she's exhausted and losing

patience. "Fine. Wait right here when you get out." She points to a kiosk, where packs of Swedish fish hang from small hooks. It makes Talia think of Svensson and everything she has to prepare for Monday that she didn't complete.

They disperse into the restrooms. Talia's thoughts are in a million different places.

Did she upload the reports for the Svensson account to her cloud so she could access them remotely over the weekend?

Did Shep land okay with this weather? He hasn't texted her to confirm like he usually does. How will she respond to him?

Who has Emerson contacted about her disappearing act? How much trouble is she in?

Talia exits the bathroom and is surprised to find that Leo isn't waiting by the fish. The rain has started back up again and it's coming down in sheets that obscure her vision of the parking lot. There's no way he went out there by himself.

She hollers back into the men's room. "Leo, are you still in there?"

There's no reply. The convenience store is empty except for her and the cashier. Talia does a lap around the store, wondering if Leo became enamored with a snack or a toy; or if he's hiding. Although he's never done it before.

"Leo!" she calls again. She doesn't see him anywhere. Talia approaches the cashier, a male teenager playing on his phone, earbuds in. She motions for him to take them out.

"Can I help you?" he asks.

"Did you see a little boy in here? He used the bathroom and I can't find him now." Talia's eyes scour the rows of day-old bread and Halloween candy.

"Ya, he left with his mom."

Talia's eyes cross and she can't see for a moment.

How did Emerson find us?

"What? Did she say she was his mom?"

"No... but, it looked like it. The woman had dark hair like

him. They checked out some snacks really quickly and then they drove away in a Rover."

"Oh my god."

Talia runs to the store window and squints to see through the storm.

Neve's SUV is gone.

FORTY-SIX

EMERSON

I silently fume as I scour Talia's email for information that might lead me to Neve's mother's house. A last name will usually do the trick, but nothing comes up under Neve Crawford. It's like she doesn't exist on the Internet or the White Pages. She's the opposite of Talia who enjoys posting her every waking moment. I wonder how the two women are even friends.

Talia has it coming when Shep returns. He won't tolerate her behavior. He's going to break up with her over this. He has to. Especially when he finds out she doctored a school nurse's note. What about when the school finds out? The nurse? Leo could be thrown out. Someone needs to call this woman out for what she is—a lying maniac.

I try to phone Shep and it goes straight to voicemail.

"God damn it."

I try him once more, and it goes straight to voicemail again. Our son is missing. Sure, I know who with, but it doesn't mean he's not in danger.

Maybe he's dodging my calls.

I call Joanna—voicemail.

Talia and Neve have no idea I'm aware they're headed to Neve's family home. I just have to figure out where that is, exactly. I sigh.

I try Brooks and am surprised when he answers. "Hey, what's up?"

"Everything went to shit, Brooks. Shep's girlfriend didn't show for the visitation and she ran off with Leo and one of her colleagues. I need to track this person's family home and find my son. I don't know what she's capable of."

Brooks answers with one word, "Name?"

"Neve Crawford."

"Hold on..." I can hear him tap some keys. "N-E-V-E?" he asks.

"That's right. I think."

"Well, the colleague doesn't have a criminal record, so that's comforting. I can't find her on any other searches. Where're you right now?'

"I. Um. Broke into their house looking for Leo."

"*Emerson*. You need to get out of there. It might even be a trap. She might be doing this so you come after her. She'll use it to show you're a threat, so you eventually don't get custody of Leo. Ever. Have you thought of that?"

"Oh my god. But she's the one who lied about my son being sick at school, faked a note from the nurse."

"That's bad behavior, but she'll likely just get a slap on the wrist for it. Your offense is much greater. Breaking and entering..."

"That's what Talia said." *Is she setting me up?*

"What're you doing there?" he asks.

"Going through her computer, looking for a way to track them."

"Is it her work computer?" Brooks asks.

"I think so."

"If you can hack into it, you might be able to find something on the company intranet. HR usually will ask all employees to fill out an emergency form. A lot of employees place their parents down for that." Brooks doesn't have a strong connection with his parents because they're awful, and I don't because mine are dead. It's just one more thing that binds us. "I'll look around a little more and then I'm out of here. Hey, what about you? Did you figure out your situation?"

"Too soon to tell."

I don't like the sound of that. "Take care of you."

"The storm looks like it's moving out, but be careful of fallen trees if you figure out where they are. Not that I suggest that you kidnap your child back from her, because that's what it is, Emerson. If you take Leo, the police sound an Amber Alert. And you would be a criminal."

"I get it. Be careful. Be good." It seems ridiculous that finding Leo and bringing him home is kidnapping, but I've seen more Amber Alerts where the kidnapper was related to the victims than not. And now I understand why.

I fish around in Talia's computer until I find Brighton's HR intranet. There's a disclaimer that says—*for internal employees only*.

I can't imagine they post addresses, let alone parents' addresses, but I quickly find Neve's profile and click on it. Displayed is a photograph of a gorgeous brunette with a daring uneven bob and a look of defiance, even in her corporate headshot.

It only lists Neve's company email address and phone number, which I already have.

But beneath each employee's name is one casual personal detail.

Under Neve's: *Favorite time of the year and why?*

Answer: *Autumn. I love visiting my parents in the country for hot drinks, pumpkin carving, and getting lost in the corn maze that is Fort Hill Farms.*

Fort Hill Farms? I've been to Fort Hill Farms. I've gotten lost in that maze, the largest I've ever seen. It took my parents and I an hour and a half to get through it once. Fort Hill Farms is way up north in—Thompson, Connecticut.

I was supposed to be the first person to show Leo that town.

But why is he there, now?

I think of Kent and his presumption that my property is cursed, those who lived there damned, and while I don't believe in the afterworld, a warning lurches in my body to keep my son away from that place.

FORTY-SEVEN
TALIA

Neve won't pick up her phone.

At first Talia thought it was some kind of prank, and she expected them to whip right back around and pick her up. Leo would be cracking up from the backseat. *Got you, Tal!*

But Neve hasn't reappeared. The gas pump where she parked her vehicle is vacant. The SUV is like an apparition that was never there to begin with.

Talia doesn't understand what's happening.

Neve doesn't even like children. Why would she take hers?

"Would you like me to call someone? The sheriff?" the cashier asks.

She stands so close to the window, her face is almost pressed to the glass. "No, that's all right... They'll be back."

If Talia decides to call the cops, she'll do it herself.

Her body races with nerves and uncertainty. She doesn't know what she wants, but the police don't seem like the best option.

Surely there has to be a reason for this.

Did Leo get sick in Neve's car? Did Neve get him a carbon-ated drink, only for it to explode all over her spotless backseat, and now she's so pissed off, cleaning it at some roadside car wash, that she won't answer her phone? If Talia calls the cops, they'll issue one of those jarring phone alerts, and everyone within a few miles radius will see it.

Then—someone—will contact Shep and tell him his son has been reported missing.

"*Shit.*" She broke her promise to Shep and lied about where she was taking his son, and now he's missing. This will destroy them. He'll come home and tell her to pack her bags, and she'll lose everything. The irony is that she was worried about Emerson taking off with Leo, and now *she* somehow managed to lose him.

Talia spins around in the store, searching for a better cell phone signal. The rain has stopped outside, but it's still dark and wet.

"What town is this?" she asks the cashier. She doesn't even know where she is.

"Planfield. Where're you headed? Could you Uber if your friend left by mistake?" He sounds so innocent. He doesn't realize that sixteen-year-olds may leave each other by accident at places like fairgrounds, concerts, or gas stations, but adults do not.

"I don't even know where I'm going!" she says, and now she's panicked.

"Oh-kay. Let me know if you need anything else." The boy places his earbuds back in.

She doesn't know where Neve's parents live. She just jumped in Neve's car with promises of pumpkin carving and a fun fall weekend with herself and Leo, and trusted Neve to take her to their destination. She has no idea where to find Leo.

Talia calls Priya.

"Hey, Talia, how's it going?" There's noise in the background, girls chattering, most likely Priya's two sisters.

"Not well. Listen, Neve left me at a gas station and took off with Leo."

"What? Why? Call the cops."

"I can't, Priya. If Shep finds out, it's over between us. Besides, I don't think Leo is in danger. It will be a whole missing kid thing, on the news... Neve will never forgive me for that. I'm sure there's a reasonable explanation. I just don't know what it could be."

"Have you tried calling her?"

"Of course. No answer. Listen, do you know where Neve's parents were from? I thought maybe she mentioned her home-town when we had lunch, but I can't remember. I need to find them, but I don't even know where we were headed."

"I don't. Somewhere... in rural Connecticut."

"Shit."

"Have you left the store, to look around?"

"No, why?"

"I don't know... Weird stuff happens at convenience stores. It's storming. Maybe she got into an accident. Go check and call me back, okay? I'll try to see if I can figure out where she's from. This is very strange."

"Okay, thanks, Priya. And whatever you do, if Shep calls you, do not tell him about this! I'm trusting you this time."

"Got it. Good luck. Don't worry. Neve wouldn't hurt Leo."

"I know." She throws her phone in her purse and charges outside.

The pavement is slick, the night air crisp and unforgiving. She walks around the perimeter to where Neve was parked, looks in the garbage can and sees wrappers inside from snacks that Leo ate in the backseat on their trip there.

Neve took the time to clean out her car.

That doesn't sound like someone who would make a split-second decision to steal a child. Was Neve... hijacked? Did someone, in the midst of the storm, see her luxury SUV and decide they wanted it, and take Neve and Leo hostage?

Talia told Leo to—"stay right there." By the Swedish fish. He usually listens. He's not the rebellious type to run off and he's not defiant, by nature. Leo probably trusted Neve because she was their ride, a friend of Talia's.

Emerson. Did Emerson somehow follow them out here and take back what she thinks is hers?

No, that can't be it. The cashier said a woman with dark hair left with Leo.

Talia rushes back into the store. She motions for the store clerk to take his earbuds out again.

"Ya?" he asks, reasonably annoyed.

Talia shoves her phone in his face and scrolls to a picture of Neve on the Brighton website. "Was this the person the little boy left with?" She has to make sure it's Neve who took Leo. Emerson has light hair, but teenagers mess things up all the time. He could've been looking at a picture of Oliva Rodrigo on his phone, glanced up and thought he saw a woman with dark hair when he really didn't.

"That's her," he confirms.

"Do you have video surveillance of the outside of the store."

"Not that I can pull up for you without my manager."

"*Damnit.*" *What do I do?*

"Can you track her phone? With an app, maybe?"

"No..." *But I can track Leo's watch!*

She knows she made Leo put his watch on because Neve said they might go to a corn maze and she was worried he could get lost. The question is—did she turn the watch on?

Sometimes she'll not power it up until they reach their destination, to preserve the battery. Small watch. Small battery. But no matter how hard she tries to remember if she pressed the button, she can't.

Talia was preoccupied, afraid Emerson would come after them. She still is.

She knew she was still dangerous. She should have predicted this. Recourse, for that fabricated doctor's note. She mixed Neve up in it all. Neve knew what she was getting herself into, but if something happens to her, Talia will feel awful.

Her hands shake as she logs into the tracking app on her cell phone.

Her eyes scan the long, desolate country road before her while it loads, still looking for Neve's silver SUV.

Where the hell did they go?

FORTY-EIGHT
EMERSON

It's dangerous—me behind the wheel of the car for the first time in over a year. Shep's BMW is older, but well kept, and still handles like a racecar—gliding along the slick late October roads like I'm accelerating for takeoff.

But something is horribly wrong and Leo is in danger. I can feel it. She's going to do something terrible to Leo.

It's like Halia told me—I breathe in the emotions of others, a wide open third eye—I can feel things about my surroundings.

I sensed it when I watched the two of them through the window—a stranger reprimanding my child. My son, shrinking back. Perhaps he did something to deserve a lecture, but it was the energy between them that was bad, like a substitute teacher put off by a student.

I've finally pinpointed the negative energy in that room.

She was agitated by Leo. That's how she views him, with annoyance. It didn't make sense until I saw her in the court-room. Talia is out for blood. And she will do whatever it takes to get what she wants.

But I'm the one chasing her. I couldn't protect Thea. I won't make the same mistake with Leo.

She wants Shep. The lifestyle. The things he can afford her. The pretty pictures on social media for all to see: Leo's just a way to hold on to Shep and his pocketbook.

And Talia could probably tell after a few moments in that courtroom, seeing me mentally sound and strong, that the link I have with Shep is stronger than hers. It's palpable, the connection we share.

What might Talia do to sever that link? How far will she go?

At first I didn't think she'd hurt Leo. That would make Shep hate her.

But if she thinks she's already lost Shep, would she do something to Leo to get to me? To get to both of us? Talia waited until Shep left to make her move...

That fact makes me push my foot on the accelerator even harder.

Shep still won't return my calls. I texted him letting him know it's urgent.

I'm guessing he's silenced all of my communications upon seeing the photographs of Jacob. It's exactly the kind of resentful crap he'd pull. He can have a whole other life with another woman, and I can't have a one-night stand, or I'm written off.

Maybe Talia is trying to trap me like she did with those pictures...

I have an inkling that she somehow knows I'm driving out there right now, stealing her boyfriend's car, so she can vilify me. She can have something else for her case file to tell Judge Holcomb—*not only did she break into our house, but she stole our car, and chased me and Leo over two hours away.*

She'll use it against me in court to show I'm unstable, but I don't care.

I need to find my son.

My phone rings—Joanna. Finally.

"Hey, Joanna—"

"Emerson, where are you?"

"Talia never showed for the visitation. She ran with Leo, but she has some bullshit nurse's note from the school, so I can't call the cops. Apparently, she had it cleared with the court, but something is up, Joanna!"

"Emerson, Rupert is dead."

"How?" I want to have more of an emotional response to his death, but Rupert constantly made comments about cost right in front of the patients, as if they were just cash machines to him, not people. I suppose it was part of his job, but I have no personal connection to him whatsoever because of it.

"He never returned from his vacation at the Cape, and they found him, drowned."

Same way Claire died. Same location.

"That's awful. I'm sorry."

"The detective... wants you to come in. He has questions for you. About Rupert."

"Joanna, I have to find Leo. He's in... Thompson, Connecticut. The same place I used to summer as a child."

"Why did she take him there?"

"I don't know."

"Well, I'm sure she won't put him in harm's way. Please turn around and come into the police station in Hartford? Detective Ramsey would like to speak to you."

"Not until I find Leo." I end the call and turn off my phone.

Nothing will stop me. There's a force moving me along, an urgent inertia that makes me wonder if I might be too late.

If I lose another child, I won't survive.

FORTY-NINE
TALIA

It's on!

But the relief at Leo's tracker appearing on the app is short-lived. The blinking dot that is the little boy has stopped in the middle of a place in rural Thompson, Connecticut.

Talia tries to find an Uber that will take her there, but her ride has been canceled twice. "God Damnit."

She's going to have to call Shep soon and admit defeat here if she can't figure this out. She can't believe Neve still has not called her back. Priya texted her that she also tried to call Neve, and that she wouldn't answer her either.

The only scenario that makes sense is that Neve was hijacked with Leo inside of the vehicle, and is unable to use her phone.

And the only person who would possibly do that—is Emerson. She'd have to come with a tag team to hold Neve down, but who knows what sorts of humans Emerson's met living in East Hartford. Maybe she brought her boyfriend along, the tattooed thug from the photographs. He looked like he had enough muscles to restrain a thrashing Neve and a little kid.

Talia's desperate, on the side of the road outside of the gas station, her cell phone battery quickly depleting. She tries to do the math. Would Emerson even have the time to catch up with them if she left her place at the same time she called Talia?

There's not a chance in hell.

How would Emerson know where they were going when Talia didn't even know where she was headed herself?

Unless... Emerson was closer to them than she thought when she made the phone call.

Maybe she had a tracker on *them* somehow. Perhaps Shep gave her access to Leo's watch too. Talia goes back through her courthouse documents in her email and can't find her own cell phone number listed on any of them. Emerson has an "in" to her personal information somehow. Talia's cell phone isn't listed on her social media sites either.

Shep, or her lawyer, could've shared it with her—coparenting communication and all that crap—but maybe she reached it a different way.

But it does mean she could contact Emerson... No, that could make the whole situation worse. She doesn't know how erratic a state she is in.

She can't call Shep either. Not yet.

The police are still out too, unless she decides to call Shep. Because he'll tell her to call them right away and yell at her for not doing so already. Both choices seem like such defeat. There's no imminent threat to Leo's safety, which is the only thing that gives her comfort.

Neve wouldn't hurt him. And Emerson wouldn't hurt Leo either. At least not on purpose—in a conscious state.

What she doesn't understand is why Emerson is doing this. It will ultimately diminish her chances of ever getting custody of her child if she steals him. But that's the thing about crazy people—they operate without logic.

And sometimes those irrational moves lead to people getting hurt.

Neve is a live wire. If they have her tied up somewhere, she'll raise a fit until they set her free, and then she'll tear their faces off and use them as dinner plates.

Neve's parents are also expecting them for dinner.

If Neve doesn't show, they'll realize something is wrong and report them missing.

Talia's phone dings. Her Uber *is approaching*.

Finally. It's been over an hour since she was left at that gas station.

And the last half... waiting for a ride.

Talia just hopes it takes her to Leo, because if it doesn't, she'll never forgive herself. And neither will Shep.

FIFTY

EMERSON

I pull into Thompson, rows of cornfields swaying in the October wind as I refill Shep's gas tank. I hope to God Leo is doing something to enjoy himself like making caramel apples or bumping along on a haunted hayride somewhere, but something deep in my gut tells me he's not.

Someone has taken him and does not want him to be found. I double over at the thought, my whole body coursing with fear and adrenaline.

On top of my anxiety for Leo, it makes me sick being back here again. All I can hear are the sirens of the past from the fire trucks pulling up to my house as it was engulfed in flames.

Memories of this place come back in patches.

Chasing fireflies and making blanket forts, mostly by myself, while my mother painted in the attic. Abstract and beautiful, but she hid the only part of herself that was like me.

It made me feel ugly so many days. Like she was ashamed of my creativity, as she was of her own. Ashamed of me.

Although I think when she was painting, she was the happiest. If I snuck up on her, I'd catch her humming along as the paintbrush swooshed over the canvas, and that's how I really knew she was at peace. You can't hum and be unhappy.

My father's contentedness was spent passed out drunk on expensive liquors—brandy and bourbons—in the backyard. If he wasn't in his office trying not to work, you could most likely find him in a hammock or on a chaise lounge with a novel he'd never finish.

There was restless energy in that house. A slowdown from our urban life. Some days—too slow. Boredom that led to exploration and fits of fancy into town, where I'd miraculously, even as an extreme introvert, befriend others. I was interesting to them, a species from somewhere in "the big city."

"Where's Westport?" Claire asked. She had thin, blonde hair that hung to her shoulders.

"Just outside the city. On the coast."

"Why do you come all the way out here? If I left this place, I'd never come back." Jenny, goth style with a fake magnetic nose ring, asked.

"My parents' choice, not mine," I said.

"So, you don't like it here?" Ella, small and skittish, asked.

"I do like it," I said, partially a lie.

"What about your house? It's kind of... creepy, don't you think? Set back in that field. It was for sale forever, you know?" Claire asked.

"I didn't know that. Just looks like a big white house to me," I said.

"I can bring my Ouija board over. We can see if it's really creepy," Jenny said.

"Isn't that... bad luck?" I asked.

"It can be, but I'll have special candles to ward off the bad spirits," Jenny said.

"Okay, then. As long as you bring them," I said, *trying to be agreeable.*

"Are you allowed sleepovers? I'm not. My house isn't big enough," Ella said.

"I think so. Let's see what my parents say," I said, *because I'm not sure. I've never had enough friends for a slumber party.*

It's hard to be back in this town and not think of them, my summer friends. The fire was toward the end of the summer season, right before we went back to school. Nothing was the same after the blaze...

No one in town, including a barkeep who's lived there thirty years, has heard of the Crawford family. It's possible everyone here doesn't know the Crawfords, especially if they're the sort who keep to themselves. But when the Internet and a local library search come up empty too, I start to get worried.

Where are you, Leo?

I stare into the cornfield, imagining he might walk through the other side.

I could try again in the morning, with daylight on my side, but I fear I'll be too late.

I have a text from Joanna that just says:

Did you find him?

I text her back that I didn't.
She sends me a link with no context.
I click on it.

HOSPITAL ADMINISTRATOR DROWNING MARKED SUSPICIOUS

Rupert Mansfield, 52, an administrator at a mental

*health facility, drowned off the Cape near a vacation
home, marked suspicious. The case is still under investigation. Follow the story here for updated posts.*

I swallow the spit budding in my throat, wondering what
this has to do with me. I wasn't anywhere near the Cape when
he died. They can't suspect me.

I text Joanna back:

Sorry to hear. I'll be in touch when I get back.

If I get back.

FIFTY-ONE
EMERSON

This place is where all my problems started. Everything in my life, although not perfect, was normal for the most part, before I started vacationing in Thompson.

It feels like an ending place.

And if something has happened to Leo, it will be mine.

I drive aimlessly and decide to visit my old house. Maybe I can resolve some of these horrible feelings if I face their origin spot. Clear my head so I can find my son.

The country road to reach my old summer home has no cars on it, and the gravel driveway leading up to the property is unkept, giant holes in some places that make me fearful I'm going to bottom out the Beamer.

I can see the house looming in the distance like a decrepit overlord, shutters falling off, vines growing out of the windows like sprawling spider veins. "Ugh." It's going to be so much work to fix it up. I'm more certain than ever that I should sell to Kent.

I notice that he emailed me back—

Let me know when we can make a deal!!

Tomorrow, I want to tell him. Any aspirations I had of making this home a special place for my family have disappeared. I just want to move forward with my son. I want to make new memories in different places. I'll be happy to unload this eyesore.

As I pull up to the property, my headlights illuminate another vehicle parked out front. The cloud cover from the storm has made it an inky black night, not a star in the sky, so I didn't see the car at first.

Why would anyone be out here at this time of night?

Shaking, I'm about to turn the car around, but then I see something else—a stuffed animal lying on the ground beside the car.

It's one of those superhero dogs that was in Leo's room. *Leo?* Why would he be here?

No one should be in that house. But especially not him.

I throw the car in park, and dash out toward what I can see now is a luxury SUV. I pull on the handle, but it's locked.

"Can I help you?"

I whip around to find—Neve—Talia's colleague standing right in front of me.

"Neve? I'm—"

"I know who you are. Do you know who I am?" She wipes rainwater from her face and tucks her hair behind her ear to reveal a nasty scar on her cheek.

"No..."

"Are you staring at my face?" Neve asks. She's aggressive, close up, in my personal space now.

"No, of course not. Where's my son. And Talia?"

"*Of course not.*" Neve mocks me, using a snotty voice, and I don't understand why. She seems deranged.

Neve's too close. I give her a shove back, pissed, and scream at her. "*Where's my son?*"

Neve's hand flies back, but I'm still surprised when she

slaps me so hard across the face, I slam against her Range Rover. *Holy shit.*

The right side of my face lights up with pain.

"W-what is your problem?" I think about the taser that Brooks gave me which is—*at home in my apartment.* I hold my hand to my face. It's still stinging.

"Do you know who I am, Emerson? Take a good look."

My eyes pull at tender flesh as I try to focus on her face. "Neve Crawford."

"No, you dumb bitch. Who am I really?"

Oh no. It's not her real name. No wonder Brooks couldn't find her when he ran a search—and neither could I. I don't recognize her, and I have a feeling that's going to be a major problem. I slide sideways, trying to wiggle my way out, but where will I go? Nowhere without Leo.

I peek in the SUV. He's not in there.

"I-I don't know. Where's my little boy?"

"You won't get him back until you answer my question."

I knee her as hard as I can in the abdomen and shove her away from me, then barrel toward the house. Leo has to be in there.

I can hear her breathing behind me as I shine my flashlight app on my phone around looking for him. "Leo! Leo, where are you?"

The house creaks beneath my feet, floorboards jutting up every which way. When I scramble through the front door it smells terrible, like backed-up sewage. Empty containers of food and used needles litter the floor everywhere.

Great, someone has used this place as a stash house.

I hear Neve, right behind me.

I turn to find her with a fire poker in her hand. I recognize it as an original piece from the house's stone fireplace. *Oh shit.* The look in her eyes reminds me of some of the sicker patients I came into contact with at Meadowbrook. I'm terrified. What has she done with Leo? Where is Talia?

"Where is he? Just tell me. I don't want any trouble. I just want my son."

"Well, I wanted a lot of things... Like a pretty face. This is your fault, you know?"

I have no idea what she's talking about. "Leo!" I yell again. I try to move away from her, and trip over a nail that's come up from the boards. "Ow, shit."

"He's in the attic." The poker at her side now, she looks almost lethargic, like someone has hit her with a paralysis dart.

I don't have any choice. I have to see if he's up there.

I run up the stairs, careful as the wood yawns beneath my feet. The steps could give way at any moment. The attic, where my mother used to paint. When I reach the top, I use my flashlight app to scan the room and it's a mess, but Leo isn't there.

I feel Neve's presence before she appears.

The door to the attic slams shut. I turn and hear chains and a clanking sound. I know long before I try the door that it's locked behind me. A quick inspection of the room shows boarded-up windows—no way out.

I'm trapped. I spin around holding my phone in the air—no cell phone reception way out here in the sticks. And definitely no WiFi.

I'm so angry and confused, all I can do is scream. I sound like a fucking animal, and I don't care. "Where is my son, Neve? I'm sorry. I realize I'm not the best judge of character, but you need help. I know a good therapist."

"All those times I missed my own corporate parties because of you, and you wouldn't even know me to see me. You need to remember me. Look around and you'll figure it out. If you don't, you die. And so does your son." Her voice echoes through the door.

"I don't know what you're talking about! *Please.* He's just a little boy."

"Ya... well no one wanted to have little boys with me because of my face! Except for one guy, the only one I could get, and he's crazier than all of us!"

What is she saying? I spin in disbelief.

There's a mess of papers everywhere, a mix of fast-food wrappers from whatever squatters have been invading the place. I shine a light on another scrap of paper to reveal a used piece of toilet paper. "Oh, Jesus God."

On the far wall—I see it. My mother's paintings are displayed. Someone has hung them over the boarded windows, but there's something wrong with them.

My mother's favorite abstract impressionist artists were Monet, Renoir, and Degas. And my mother loved painting people going about their everyday lives. It was one of the reasons she never showed them to anyone, embarrassed her work wouldn't be interpreted correctly. But they were beautiful pieces.

I completely forgot they were still here, or I would've had Shep place them in storage with some of her others, long ago.

And now... they're destroyed.

I remember the one on the wall in front of me—the ballerina.

Speckles of pink and beige and yellow make up the swirled background, and in the center is the dancer. She holds up her leg, flexible and graceful, her beautiful face—marred by giant black exes.

Someone has taken the time to cross out her eyes with paint.

The ballerina's mouth has a black X over it too. It's so garish, I place my hand over my mouth, sure I'm going to be murdered now.

The other paintings have similar markings, totally defaced.

A fisherman in a boat with a black line that stretches from his cheek to his casting line.

A mother and daughter with Xs over their eyes.

A baby girl—with an X over her entire body.

I shriek at that one. *Thea.* Is the defacer representing my baby in that one? I feel myself come apart. I throw empty containers at the boards, hoping it'll bust through to the windows, but it's no use. I'm sealed in here nice and tight.

She planned this.

Neve has been here before, barricading windows and destroying my mother's old paintings.

"Why did you do this?" I scream through the door.

Neve's voice is small and eerie. "Your mother was a terrible human being."

I close my eyes trying to think how Neve knows my mother. I can't recall her from my Westport days. I would remember a little girl with a scar on her face. "I'm sorry. I know my mother could be callous. I had to grow up with her, but that's not my fault. Just please tell me where my son is."

She doesn't answer.

Please God.

I can hear Neve descend the steps. *No.* Where is she going? She can't leave me up here.

I spin around, feeling claustrophobic. I check my phone. Still no service and only forty per cent left. What will happen when it dies and I'm in here, alone in the dark. I'll lose my mind.

My flashlight catches a wooden chest on the floor with painted flowers on it. I recognize it as my mother's. For some reason the lid is open. With all the junk and litter in the room, it shouldn't seem out of place, but it does.

I walk over to the chest and kneel beside it.

On the very top, I see letters bound by a rubber band addressed to my mother: To: Siobhan Wilder.

A dead calm falls over me, around me—swallows me whole. I've seen these letters before. They were the ones from the townspeople of Thompson that my mother was so agitated by during the house rebuild.

"People in small towns make their problems, our problems," she'd said.

I have a sinking feeling they weren't small problems at all.

I pull an envelope from the pile and remove the letter.

Dear Mrs. Wilder,

My previous letters have gone unanswered. We're still seeking financial retribution for the fire that scarred Genevieve's face. The physicians are saying that with multiple surgeries, while she's still a child, they'll be able to restore it, but we don't have the funds because the hospital says the surgeries are considered "cosmetic." Even though Genevieve still has difficulty chewing on one side of her face. She's grown quite thin and the kids at school are really giving her a hard time.

I know that, legally, you don't owe us a dime. Those fancy Westport lawyers made sure of that, but I'm asking as one mother to another, please help, while there's still time to repair the damage that occurred at your house.

Sincerely,

Aida Conrad

I bowl over in disbelief that my mom, a benefactor of so many charities, wouldn't help this woman and child. The next letter, though... is leveling.

Dear Mrs. Wilder,

Please find it in your heart to help.

The scar tissue on Genevieve's face is thickening, although the doctors say there's still time for a positive outcome if we move quickly.

My husband was so torn up that he couldn't pay for Jenny's surgery that he took too many pills with his beer last month and... well... he didn't wake up.

We're in a bad way here. If you can spare us anything at all to help Jenny along I'd really appreciate it. She's beside herself over her father's death.

~*Aida Conrad*

No. *No.*
Genevieve is—Neve.
Neve is Jenny.

That's why I couldn't find a Neve Crawford. She doesn't exist. She's Genevieve Conrad. Did she change her name?

"I'm sorry, Jenny! I know who you are now. I read the letters. I didn't know they were sent. My mother never told me!"

Her voice is farther away now. "But you knew I was hurt. You never even once called to check on me."

I close my eyes trying to remember. One of the girls did leave in an ambulance. "The news said everyone left the fire with minor injuries. I didn't know yours were bad and I didn't think you'd want to talk to me. I was only twelve—"

"I was only twelve too! With a disfigured face. But it could have been fixed. Your family ruined me. You made me bring those candles. You were worried about evil spirits."

I look at the artwork, and now I understand what Neve was doing. They represent her—once beautiful, but twisted by the fire. I think of my own pictures, torn apart and spread all over my room.

"I was a kid, Jenny. I don't remember what I said. I'm sorry. I have money. I can help you."

"You don't have money. That's why you were begging Quigley Tree to hire you. I had dreams once too, Emerson. But no one would hire me because of my scars. Not until I learned how to cover them."

"You called Quigley Tree?"

"I did. It couldn't be that easy for you to start over again. I've had to fight for every little thing I ever had. It's not just about my face. You killed my family. My mother's at a home much like the one you were in the last year. Couldn't deal with her losses."

"I'm sorry about your family. I lost my parents too. We can—"

"No, we can't do any of those things. Because nothing is worse than what you did to my brother. The only one to make it out of this godforsaken town. He showed such early leadership skills. He was destined for the military. Even went to a military prep school. On a full scholarship."

Oh shit...

Finally, I hear the chains on the door unravel. I search for a weapon to use against Neve, but I can't find anything. Maybe she's opening the door to reason with me.

All I want is to know Leo is okay. Maybe she'll just tell me and I'll sell this place and give her every last penny.

Just let me go.

Let *us* go.

She opens the door.

"Jenny, Please let me—"

I don't get to finish my response before the fire poker comes crashing down on my head.

"Ugh." I place my hand on the hot, searing spot, the blood seeping into my palm. I hunch in pain. "Please," I croak.

"That was for me. This one's for my brother."

And down comes the poker again.

FIFTY-TWO
TALIA

The white farmhouse in the distance has no lights on inside. Talia thinks maybe she's gotten her location mistaken, but the driver is already in reverse at the end of the long driveway before she can second guess herself.

The potholes leading up to the property are like craters. Her black fall boots have a small heel, and they sure weren't made for walking on these backroads. But Talia's so worried that this is a decoy, that maybe Leo's kidnapper just dumped his watch to throw her off course, that she barely notices.

She shivers as she approaches the driveway and is relieved to see Neve's SUV there. But it's not the only vehicle.

"What?"

Shep's car is in the driveway. *Oh fuck.* He is here too.

She knows what happened now. She's so stupid to have not figured it out sooner.

Emerson called Shep and told him everything, and he came straight home. Emerson knew Talia was in the car with Neve, and while they were in the gas station—Shep called Neve.

He didn't call Talia.

He was too angry with her. Who knows what he said to Neve to get her to leave that gas station. He's very persuasive. His threats were most likely career-related, and so Neve, being the workaholic that she is, left.

Talia didn't bargain for any of this.

And now, they're all inside. Preparing to do what, exactly, she doesn't know.

Maybe they're figuring out how to punish her.

Talia texts Shep. One final ditch effort for forgiveness before she goes in and faces the music.

Shep... I'm so incredibly sorry. Things spun out of control. Can we please just talk?

Talia, what're you talking about? I'm at a work dinner, do you need me to leave?

Oh shit! He's either lying to her, or he's still in Boston. Of course he's in Boston. There's no way he could've driven here this fast, even if he flew home the same night.

But that's definitely his car.

My mistake. No worries! It was an old text that sent by accident.

He's too smart to actually buy that, but she shuts off her phone to cut off communication. It's almost dead anyway. Talia quickly bounds up the busted steps and is disturbed to notice this house is in such bad shape. There's no way anyone can actually live here.

She opens the door and couldn't be more surprised.

Neve stands before her, but she doesn't look like Neve. Her perfect makeup is smeared from the rain. She has a gash on her face, and the curl in her lips is even more pronounced than usual. Neve looks like she's going to bite her.

There's a lantern on the ground illuminating a woman tied to a chair—Emerson. She must've had a spare key to Shep's car.

"What is this, Neve? Where's Leo?" she asks.

"Everybody keeps asking me, *where's Leo*? Who cares where that brat is. This was supposed to be a girls' weekend anyway."

Emerson screams through the fabric strung across her mouth—*help*—as if there's anything Talia can do for her. Neve is the one holding the fire poker and a gasoline can.

"Neve, what is going on? Why do you have Emerson? Did she come after you and Leo, and that's why you're so mad? Why does your parents' house look like this?"

Emerson shakes her head—indicating—*No*.

Neve laughs at her. "Never were the smartest, Talia."

"I don't know what's going on here, but I want to see Leo. Right now. I called Shep," she lies. "He's on his way back now."

The grin slips off Neve's face. "Well, it takes a long time to get here from Boston, and by then, this will all be over. Leo's in the attic. Why don't you go find him?"

Emerson starts her moaning again. She's shaking her head vigorously, telling Talia not to go up there. And Talia's watched enough horror movies to know how this one ends.

"Go upstairs and get my son, Neve! *Now*. There are people on their way," Talia says.

Neve drops her gasoline can and charges Talia. She swings the heavy metal poker at her head, and Talia ducks.

"What is wrong with you?"

She swings again and lands it on Talia's shin.

"Ow! Why're you doing this?" Talia gives her a solid kick to the abdomen with her good leg, and Neve flies backward.

Talia gets up to run away, but her foot catches on the uneven boards.

"Ah!"

She trips and looks behind her, but it's too late. The fire poker is already coming down on her head.

FIFTY-THREE

TALIA

The smell of gasoline wakes her up.

Talia's head throbs like half of it is missing. Her vision isn't quite right, spots that shouldn't be there dotting the air. She's sure of something—she's concussed, positioned in a chair, hands tied behind her back, a gag in her mouth.

And she's practically rubbing up against her former nemesis in the same condition—Emerson Wilder.

Talia chews on the gag. It's material and she thinks she tastes bleach. If she chomps enough, she might be able to break through.

Talia releases a guttural sound to let Emerson know she's conscious.

Emerson makes one back, but it's weak, like she's lost hope.

Talia can't imagine Neve's motivation for any of this, but she's most worried about Leo. Something's happened to him, and it's her fault for trusting Neve.

Talia remembers watching a movie once where two people were tied up together, and they started jumping. They hopped close enough that the one untied the other, and they both went free. She starts wiggling in her chair, bouncing it up and down.

Talia makes more noise so Emerson pays attention to what she's doing.

Emerson tries to do the same thing, but she's not very tall, and her juts and wiggles are unproductive.

Talia thinks about how she grew up and how she's fought too hard to go down like this. Hands tied behind her back, burned to death in the middle of the country.

Her tiny hops are working and she's scooting closer to Emerson now.

Emerson strains her neck to see, but it's a difficult feat, the way they're bound and gagged.

Talia nearly blows a blood vessel straining, but she thinks she can feel the tickle of Emerson's fingers on the base of her hands, which are tied with a rope material. She squeals and nods, flapping her fingers, until Emerson gets the drift. Emerson grunts, and begins using her fingernails to unravel the rope. She quickly unties the knot, and the first thing Talia does is rip the material out of her mouth.

"Oh, God, thank you!"

She unties her ankles next.

Emerson continues to demonstrate a desperate grunt. Her turn.

Talia takes the gag out of Emerson's mouth. "Before I untie the rest of you, tell me why Neve is doing this. You must know."

Talia sways to the side, still dizzy from her assault. She feels a stickiness pooled on her head from where she was hit, but she doesn't dare touch it. The pain radiating from that spot is bad enough without her jabbing at it.

Emerson is heaving like she can't catch her breath, and Talia wonders just how long she's been held prisoner.

"I will tell you, just please untie me and go find my son. Please! I think he's hurt or... worse. I haven't seen or heard from him."

"Answer me first!"

"*Go find him.* This is over for you. Shep will never forgive you for this. The least you can do is retrieve his son, and maybe he won't have you arrested."

Talia would like this woman to take her man's name out of her mouth. "You're so sure of yourself when it comes to Shep, you shouldn't be."

"I don't want him anymore. I don't care about him. I just want Leo."

"That's good because Shep stopped caring about you long before you entered that hospital."

"What do you mean?"

"I mean he had his tongue down my throat at the Christmas party when you were at home, pregnant with your second kid."

"You're lying," she says.

"I'm not. Now tell me what's going on so we can get the hell out of here and find Leo."

Emerson's face turns white as snow. "Neve, well Jenny, is mad about something my family did years ago. She was involved in the blaze that burnt this place down. That's how she got that scar on her face."

It all makes sense now—Neve's lopsided haircut, the over-compensation with the trendy clothes, the way she overreacted when Talia spilled hot coffee on her like Talia had just thrown lava down her blouse.

"And she blames you. Why?"

"I told her to bring the candles to our pre-teen sleepover. *God.* I was just a kid. I made her sleep by the window because I didn't like the draft. Where the candles blew over. She was the closest to the fire when it started. And…"

"And what?"

"And the fire hurt her… face. Disfigured it. She was poor and my mother wouldn't help pay for her surgeries. Her damage wouldn't have been so bad if she had. She would've had an easier recovery. Her father blamed himself for not being able to help out financially and killed himself. I didn't know about any of it."

"*Jesus Christ.* And I thought my mother was bad. Neve's whole reason for getting hired at Brighton was probably to get back at you... But how did she know you'd come here?"

"Maybe she didn't. It looks like she's been planning this for a while though. She transformed the attic into... a prison. She was just probably looking for the right opportunity."

Talia's whole body chills and she snaps out of question mode. "You're right. We need to find Leo and get out of here." She moves toward the stairwell to investigate.

"Wait, untie me!" Emerson wails.

"How did you get out!" Talia whips around to see Neve emerging from a dark corner of the house, holding Leo. He's not moving. Passed out? Or... dead?

"*Leo!*" Emerson screams.

"Just let him go," Talia says.

"He's sedated. If I drop him, he could break his neck. Just like Gus," she clucks.

"What?" Talia asks.

"That bond you think you have with Shep... You don't. I was there. I pushed that greedy bastard from the platform. I watched Shep kneel beside his broken body afterward. He cried like a baby."

"No, that can't be right," Talia says. Shep didn't admit to Talia that he pushed Gus. He only said—"there was nothing I could do." Talia assumed he meant he had no other choice but to shove him. But perhaps he meant there was nothing he could do because—Gus was already dead when he got there. "Why did you push Gus, Neve?"

"Because I wanted Gus's job. And because I was sick of hearing him whine about it. And because I wanted to get closer to you, Talia, which got me closer to Emerson. It wasn't enough to just take Emerson out. It needed to be slow, painful, and gradual the way I experienced my losses. And it has been."

"Oh my god," Emerson groans.

Talia glares back at her, stunned. Neve's ex said that she was part of the dark triad, but he wasn't only referring to Machiavellianism, he meant all three sides—psychopathy and narcissism too. "But... how did you...?" "Remember when you knocked into me and spilled my coffee? Nope. I ran into you. Saw your distracted pretty little head coming from a mile away. Thanks for giving me an early out in the office so I could head to the site and get him all alone. I knew he was going down there. He'd been threatening it all day."

"No..."

"Oh, yes. It all went perfectly. You are the only glitch, Talia. I don't know how you figured out where we were, but you can still have everything you want. Your happily ever after with Shep."

Two women would be better than one to overpower Neve, but she wants to hear Neve out before she unties Emerson. She thought all was lost with Shep and she's curious of Neve's strategy.

"I was going to set this house on fire with Emerson inside. Everyone would believe she did it to herself, with her history, but if you leave with me, we can make it look like Emerson held you hostage when you withheld her visitation. She even hit you over the head."

"Why would it make sense for me to come here?" She shouldn't be asking questions. She should just go with whatever Neve is saying so she can stay alive, but she needs to get this all straight with what she's supposed to say to the police, because she's already in big trouble.

"Because I don't own this house. Emerson does. It's the one place Emerson could take you where no one would find you. She wanted to punish you for standing her up. If she has Shep's car, it means she was at your house first. And she stole it. It all lines up."

"You're horrible—" Emerson starts, but is cut off.

"What about Leo? Is he...?"

"He needs to see a doctor. I think I gave him too much..."

Emerson wails, "*No.*" And Talia can't blame her.

She wants to murder Neve. But Neve is right. If this all works out, she'll get exactly what she wants. Emerson will be gone, just like she intended, and she'll have Shep all to herself. They can start their own family.

The victim. She was kidnapped for them. The ultimate sacrifice.

"Let's go," Talia says before she can change her mind.

Emerson is screaming indecipherable things at their backs as they leave, but Talia has already blocked her out. She made peace with this decision long ago.

Once they're on the porch, Neve sets Leo on a decayed wicker chair and lights the match.

"You're going to burn me alive?" Emerson wails at Neve and Talia through the smashed-in window. "You're monsters. You're going to burn in hell!"

"I guess we'll meet you there then for the three lives your family has taken from me!" Neve screams.

"What's this now? I just counted your dad," Talia says.

Neve stands there, match still lit. "Oh, Talia. She hasn't told you the whole story. My mother is as good as dead in the home we had to put her in after she fell apart; but she left out her worst offense of all. My brother. She had a little help with that one. Her friend, Brooks Stauffer." She flicks the match, and stands there watching the flames start to crackle. "You shouldn't have come here, Talia, but now that you have, I can't let you leave. You've seen too much."

Neve, still holding the fire poker, whacks Talia in the head again.

Talia places her hands up, putting up a fight, but Neve whips out a knife and catches her in the stomach.

Talia falls over, the wind knocked straight out of her. There's a rip of pain, a slash to her insides that spans her left side. It burns so badly, like someone has taken their fingers and pulled out her internal organs. She doubles over and almost vomits.

Neve hovers over Talia as she goes partially down, one knee on the porch. A wet cloth that covers Talia's mouth takes her the rest of the way.

FIFTY-FOUR

EMERSON

I am nearly unconscious when I imagine a man walking through the flames. He's not wearing a fireman uniform, but whatever he has on is fire retardant, because the flames don't seem to touch him.

I'm in Heaven now, I'm sure, and he is an angel.

Why are there flames? Heaven is supposed to have clouds.

"I'm going to get you out of here, darling..." he says.

I recognize his twang, but I can't quite place it.

Or thank him. The smoke has sealed my eyes shut, and the only reason I tried to open them was to see his alien form, because I heard him calling my name. I wasn't able to respond. My lungs don't pump anymore, the tiniest breath escaping when I open my mouth.

He struggles to carry me out of the house, which is consumed in flames—again.

He places some kind of blanket overtop me that I think makes me invincible, because we walked right through the hottest wall I've ever experienced in my life.

Ash touches my body. I'm swimming in fire.

We flee the building as wood collapses all around us. We must've made it just in time.

My eyes shut tighter as the cool air hits them, and I imagine the house has birthed me.

And today is the first day of the rest of my life.

Talia remains on the bottom step. I don't ask the angel to move her. She can burn with the devils.

Emergency vehicles roar up the driveway.

But as they do, I see something terrible.

Neve must be long gone, but a man... The man from my dream is running through the field with my son in his arms. I point at him, but I'm having a hard time speaking.

My angel, who I quickly realize is Kent Bessler, places me on the ground and tries to run after the man, but with his bum knee he doesn't make it far.

Joanna and Detective Ramsey arrive with the ambulances and firetrucks, and I point in the direction of the man—the one from my nightmares. Ramsey takes off running.

Did I imagine him again?

I'm placed in an ambulance. "Please. I need to make sure my son is okay," I manage. They won't let me stay. I have to go to the hospital.

Kent comes to my side.

"Thank you," I croak out. "How did you know I was in there?"

He perks up and takes off his astronaut gear. "I'm glad you're going to be okay, Miss Wilder. I wasn't going to let that house take another one." He's so proud of himself. And he should be. That house needs to burn to the ground.

"I keep a watch on the house, as you know. At first, I thought it was Ernest Whitten, lighting up his torch for the night. And then I realized it was a full-on blaze. And I just guessed... you might be inside. Some of my research takes me to toxic places. I just happened to have this gear with me."

I smile at him. Maybe he's not an old loon after all.

I fight the heaviness of my eyes, because I cannot rest until I know Leo is safe.

Where is my son? And who is the man who took him?

My mind is too heavy for sleep. The weight of all that has happened, searching for answers to all of this and more. And something Neve said dredges up a memory. A big mistake I made long ago that might be the true cause of all of this...

CULVER

Senior Year

"Why won't you tell me what he said about me?" I asked Brooks. He's upset about something one of the kids on his crew team said. Something about me being stuck up, but there's more to it.

"He said your family owes him money," Brooks says. *"Said he's going to make you pay one way or another."*

"What does he mean? Is his family in finance? Did my dad short him or something?"

"No, but I don't think he meant he was going to make you pay in money. He's made some nasty threats, Emerson. So I'm going to teach him a lesson about how I feel about that."

"Brooks, don't do anything. We're almost out of this miserable place. If they catch you, you won't graduate."

"They won't."

"They will throw you out. And Adam is bigger than you."

"They won't catch me. And bigger doesn't mean stronger. Mentally or physically. Sometimes bigger means it's easier to get tangled in the weeds."

Firetrucks. Always the firetrucks follow the drama. Culver had never seen so many firetrucks. Or ambulances. All to cut *down one kid who got stuck on the climbing wall, hung himself and died.*

A kid who went all-state in football.

A kid who had a full scholarship for crew.

A kid who could've walked onto a junior league hockey team if he wanted to.

That kid's name was Adam Conrad.

"Brooks, what did you do?" I asked.

"I admit to nothing." Cheshire cat grin on his face, he really did believe he was making the world a better place.

FIFTY-FIVE

TALIA

The hospital monitor beeps her awake, but there's someone else in the room, and a subtle jangle of something metal. It's hard to focus on anything about Shep's presence, but she can see him fighting with the tight keyring to work her key off.

"I guess I won't be needing that anymore," Talia says.

He glances up, still dressed in his suit and tie from his meeting. "You're a terrible person. I'm only here to tell you that all of your stuff will be boxed up and on the curb when you get out. Don't try to contact me or Leo ever again."

"I was set up, Shep. Neve gave me the name of a private investigator to tail Emerson. I saw him when I almost died on those steps. The cops told me it was the same man who broke into your house and killed your daughter. I didn't know—"

"Stop! You knew enough," he yells. "Maybe not all of it, but enough."

Talia coughs, her side so enveloped in pain she can hardly concentrate. "Is Leo okay?"

Shep stands. He clearly only came in to reclaim his house key. "Please don't say his name. You almost got him killed."

Almost. Such a good word. Her mind is a groggy mess, and

she will feel so much worse about this in the morning. "But... is he...?"

"He's fine. At Children's hospital. I'm going back there now. I'm here to check on Emerson. The cops also had some questions because it appears my girlfriend tried to kill her and they want to know if I was involved."

"It was Neve."

"But you had a chance to save her, and you didn't. You left her in that house to burn."

"That's not true..." She can't remember the truth. It's all a charred mess. "...I thought we were going to the country for a nice weekend. Ask Priya."

"You were supposed to meet Emerson for Leo's visitation. None of this would've happened if you'd only listened to the court order. Nobody would've gotten hurt. Now look what you've done. I hope they arrest you."

She watches him leave.

The silhouette of his back.

She can't help but think how nice it will look, face down in a ditch somewhere—for leaving her.

Maybe she can ask her dad if he can help her again this time.

FIFTY-SIX

EMERSON

When I wake up in the hospital, the first thing I check are my wrists.

They are not bound by handcuffs. I see Joanna standing against the wall.

"Leo?" I manage. My throat feels like it's been coated with hot rocks.

Joanna places a glass of cold water with a straw to my lips. "Drink." She taps the nurse's button. "Leo is okay. He's at Children's hospital. Ramsey arrested the bad guy and Neve is in jail. Talia is in the hospital. I don't know if she'll be charged."

I try to say—*she should be*—but it comes out in sputters. Joanna has such a strange smile on her face. I can't imagine why.

"Did you see the man who was carrying Leo?" she asks.

"Yes, it was... him. Was he real?" I ask. I'm on such fantastic drugs I'm truly not sure what is fact or fiction at the moment.

Joanna sighs, exasperated. "He is. Emerson, you did not imagine the man who was in your house. Or in your apartment in Hartford. They used facial photo recognition software to match the man to a resident of Thompson: Shane Crawford. He's been in and out of jail for years."

"Crawford?" I think of Neve.

"Yes, he's her ex-husband. She kept his name though."

Married?

"Who?" I ask.

"He's Neve's ex. They had a twisted high school romance, got married straightaway. He's the only one who paid attention to her with her deformity, but he was also a town reject. She left him after she went to college. He'd still do anything for her. Including... take intrusive pictures of you on street corners, and break into your house to terrorize you on a night Neve knew Shep wouldn't be home."

"That... can't be."

"You didn't kill Thea when you landed on top of her, Emerson. He did. When he threw you down the stairs. Neve was afraid you'd figure it out when she heard a picture of him was found at Meadowbrook, so she sent him after you again in your apartment to finish the job, but your roommate walked in. Neve admitted to everything once they caught up with Shane and Leo, in exchange for a slightly lighter sentence, but make no mistake, she'll spend her best years behind bars."

"I can't believe it."

"He's been caught. Finally. Not to mention the fact they also confirmed he made a shiv in prison. Just like the one found in that patient's body at Meadowbrook."

I close my eyes and let the truth set me free.

This makes my eyes blow back open. "I don't understand..."

"Someone didn't want you out of that hospital worse than Talia."

"Who?"

"I think you know. When you were close to getting out, Rupert was paid to place that shiv in the patient's room. To target you. He saw your kit and found opportunity."

"Why? He wanted me out of there," I say.

"That... I don't know. But that is what Shane, Neve's ex, told the police. Who knows if it's true."

I close my eyes, unable to process.

When I open them, Joanna is gone and Brooks is there. I'm so angry at him I could spit the fire I just ingested. "You know we can't be friends anymore," I tell him.

"I was protecting you. I killed someone on Cape Cod for you this weekend," he whispers.

I look all around to make sure cameras and speakers aren't watching and listening to us.

"Why would you do that?"

"Because that man was paid to keep you in the system. You solved the case of your daughter's killer, Emerson. Only you knew what that man looked like. And whoever plotted this whole thing out didn't take one thing into account. You're a wonderful artist. No one imagined you'd make a composite sketch of the man who attacked you." Brooks says this with such positivity, I fight every instinct in my body to hate him. "And that nurse turned it over to your therapist before Rupert could stop her."

"What're you saying?"

"I'm saying, your hospital administrator needed extra cash and took what we call in politics, an easy bribe."

"Rupert and his partner have been talking about a stupid second home in Cape Cod forever..." I say. That's why Brooks chose that spot to do him in. He used blood money to buy his vacation home. It sounds like something Brooks would do.

"It doesn't make sense. He wanted me out of there. That hospital thrives on partial-stay patients." My words slur, the alliteration of the "Ps" lost in my lips.

Brooks smiles. "They were going to pin the murder of the new patient coming in on you. Or me. I bought you that kit. Shane, Neve's ex, made him that shiv out the knife, and all Rupert had to do was plant it in a sick patient's room, ready. He didn't even have to get his hands dirty. But you left a day too early. So then Neve had to readjust her plan once you got out."

My skin tingles at the—*too early*—part. Rupert was so eager for me to leave, and then when a spot unexpectedly opened up at that halfway house, he was oddly irate I was shipping out so soon. After a year of trying to get me discharged.

"That's sick."

"I told you someone was trying to get me in trouble." Brooks's voice is dark.

"But then he would've been stuck with me longer." I stare into the ceiling fixture, wondering how people can be so horrendous.

"No, because you would've been transferred to a high security prison for murder of that type. You would've been out of his hair, but you never would've gotten out of the system. They wanted to make you suffer, forever, and they paid Rupert to help them. Shane did the actual murdering, I'm guessing."

Neve. A life behind bars is much worse than anything else. But if I did get out, she wanted to make me pay properly.

"He deserved to get caught in that fishing net," I whisper.

"Indeed. I'll keep my distance from you for some time. I do love you, and hope you'll keep this last little secret."

"I love you too. And... I'll never tell."

He kisses my cheek and leaves. I shut my eyes.

———

When I wake up again, Shep is here. He's crying. "I'm so sorry I didn't believe you."

I can't accept his tears. He tries to hold me, but I push him away. This moment is everything I've ever wanted, but no longer need. "I can't," I tell him.

"I understand. I've been awful. I shouldn't have left you in the hospital like that. I didn't think you were ever getting better."

"For better or worse."

"I broke our vows."

"Twice," I say quickly. And that's what I'll truly never forgive him for. On top of the long list, that one bubbles to the top. "When I was pregnant with Thea, Shep. Really?"

He looks away. "I didn't sleep with her."

"I don't care."

We all have our breaking points. And that is mine.

All I want is my son. And a fresh start.

"And what about all of my money? You took the proceeds from the house and spent it all on your new family and let my house go to tatters."

He has no answers. He only cries.

I have no tears or words left for him.

In my side vision, I see myself making a new door for Shep. I seal him on the other side, lock it, and throw away the key for good.

FIFTY-SEVEN
EMERSON

The next day, I'm more lucid. My voice has returned, the drugs have worn off a bit, which is good because I can think. Bad, because I can feel the pain more. No physical pain can compare to the other traumas I've already experienced.

There's a lightness in knowing I'm not responsible for Thea's death. And a horror in realizing her life was lost as a result of mistakes I overlooked years ago. In time, I'll make peace with it all.

"You have a visitor," the nurse says.

I blink my eyes at the doorway. I can't imagine who it might be. I've already spoken to everyone I know. Then I see him—Kent.

"Hey," I say. I lift my arm with the IV attached and attempt to wave at him. "What a nice surprise. Thank you for rescuing me. You're forever my hero."

He smiles brightly, and I get the sense that no one has ever called him that before and that it means the world to him.

"And you're mine, Ms. Wilder."

"Excuse me?"

"You solved my mystery." He gets a little misty-eyed.

"There were chemicals that wouldn't burn out, so they had to dig a trench. I stayed on the scene, of course. They had to dig pretty deep into the foundation of the porch, and..." his voice quivers. "They found him. They found my Michael."

"I don't understand."

"My stepson. He was buried on your property. In the heart of an old well."

"'Find Michael's... Bones.' That's what the Ouija board was trying to say the night of the fire. You don't think... all this time...?"

"Oh, you know what I think... And yes, I still want to buy your property. It's time for you to get some rest now. You've been due a nap for about twenty years." Kent chuckles.

I drift off when he leaves. I remember the woman from Meadowbrook who said that spirituality is found in the place where you find peace, wherever that might be. Was Michael still seeking his?

And then I remember Halia and the messages conveyed that day. The burned-out face wasn't Claire's. It was Neve's, warning me.

Maybe we really did unlock something otherworldly that day—a boy who'd been gone a very long time, fighting to tell us where to find him, right beneath our feet.

Maybe he's been following me ever since.

I don't know what I believe. Only time will tell.

All I understand is that I did not kill my daughter.

I am not responsible for her death.

And that is all that matters.

I close my eyes... We are finally safe.

A LETTER FROM CARA

Dear reader,

I want to say a huge thank you for choosing to read *The Wife at the Window*. If you did enjoy it, and want to keep up to date with all my latest releases, just sign up at the following link. Your email address will never be shared and you can unsubscribe at any time.

www.bookouture.com/Cara-Reinard

I hope you loved *The Wife at the Window* and if you did I would be very grateful if you could write a review. I'd love to hear what you think, and it makes such a difference helping new readers to discover one of my books for the first time.

I love hearing from my readers – you can get in touch through social media or my website.

Thanks,

Cara Reinard

www.carareinard.com

X x.com/carareinard

instagram.com/carareinard

ACKNOWLEDGMENTS

Thank you so much to my editor, Natalie Edwards, and the entire team at Bookouture for giving *The Wife at the Window* a place on your list. This is a book that sits a little close to home with my own sleep struggles. On that note, I'd like to thank all of my past roommates who lost sleep due to my middle-of-the-night mumblings, and to my husband who still does!

Vanessa Lillie, fellow author and friend, you're a gem for lending me your Rhode Island retreat center to finish this book. Your beautiful home is magic and I don't know if I would've made my deadline without that long weekend—thank you!

I had three readers who were instrumental in giving me notes on this book—Amber Goleb, Lori Jones, and Natalie Schirato. Thank you for taking the time to read this novel and offering suggestions to make it stronger. I value your opinions and friendships so much, and hope I can share more with you in the future.

I'm thankful for the greatest privilege of all—family, friends, and booksellers who support my work. I truly appreciate all of my readers, and a special thank you to JKR for being a wonderful partner and my personal chef as I navigated tight deadlines, and to my children, Jackson and Charlotte, who inspire me every day—this would all be impossible without you. And to my wonderful fluffy Bernese mountain dogs, Lily and Luna, the best writing partners a girl could ask for.

PUBLISHING TEAM

Turning a manuscript into a book requires the efforts of many people. The publishing team at Bookouture would like to acknowledge everyone who contributed to this publication.

Audio
Alba Proko
Sinead O'Connor
Melissa Tran

Commercial
Lauren Morrissette
Hannah Richmond
Imogen Allport

Cover design
The Brewster Project

Data and analysis
Mark Alder
Mohamed Bussuri

Editorial
Natalie Edwards
Sinead O'Connor

Copyeditor
Janette Currie

Proofreader
John Romans

Marketing
Alex Crow
Melanie Price
Occy Carr
Cíara Rosney
Martyna Młynarska

Operations and distribution
Marina Valles
Stephanie Straub

Production
Hannah Snetsinger
Mandy Kullar
Jen Shannon

Publicity
Kim Nash
Noelle Holten
Jess Readett
Sarah Hardy

Rights and contracts
Peta Nightingale
Richard King
Saidah Graham

Made in United States
North Haven, CT
13 August 2024

56023366R00200